SKY CLAD – RADINE

KAREN L. MILSTEIN

Sky Clad – Radine

ISBN – 13: 978-0-9863295-1-7

ISBN – 10: 0986329517

Other Books by Karen L. Milstein:

Fergus and the Princess, A Lasker the Storyteller Tale for young adults

Cover Art © 2014 by Leslie J. Lee

To all people who stand outside at night, look to the stars and wonder...

Thanks to Leslie J. Lee, my cover artist. You are fantastic and I look forward to working

with you in the future. Thanks to my family, for giving me the time and support to write when

I should probably be doing other things.

Table of Contents

Chapter One

King Radine of Taburon strode purposefully through the halls of his castle, his booted feet thumping on the hard stone floor. A tall man at six foot five inches, his long dark honey blond hair flying out behind him, he scowled at anyone who happened to cross his path, his lips tightly pressed into a thin line. His eyes were narrowed, hiding what were normally pupils the golden color of a Taburon sunset. Now they merely sparked and flashed in irritation. That he was trying to hold in his anger was obvious, and as wary eyes followed his path, to whom it was going to be directed became apparent the closer he came to his objective.

Muscles rippled in his thighs under his tight trousers, his chest heaved with every step, straining the fabric of his soft, muslin-like shirt. Around his waist where he'd belted his ceremonial sword, one hand contracted and relaxed on the pommel in time to his steps. His crown had slipped slightly, giving him a rogue appearance that had even the women daring to peek out from the hidey-holes to which they had scurried to avoid his wrath while sighing in unrequited adoration. He had been and still was the darling of the palace, though today as a man most of the female thoughts were rather indecent.

Striding up to a set of heavy wooden doors, he braced his hands on either side of the split and pushed, grunting at the effort, cursing inwardly at the tactics taken by his quarry to further push him over the edge. This little bit of treachery would not deter him. As soon as the doors spread sufficiently, he continued his forward movement until he stopped in front of an ornate chair. The woman occupying it, her head bent to a parchment on her lap, failed to look up.

Radine took a deep breath, letting it hiss out loudly. The woman held up one hand, staying the king while she finished reading. Every moment that passed only saw the king's ire rise until he was sure he was going to explode and do something that he might later regret. His fingers tapped restlessly on the pommel of the sword. Pulling him from court in the middle of a session was one thing, ignoring the summons had been the first inclination that had crossed his mind. Unfortunately, of all the people on his planet that he could ignore, this was the one person he was never allowed to refuse when summoned before her whenever she summoned.

The woman glanced up, calmly rolling the parchment which she then handed off to a servant waiting at her side. The servant executed a sloppy and hurried bow before taking flight, getting out of range of the fireworks sure to follow.

"Radine," the woman began calmly.

"Mother," he replied tightly.

"Radine," she repeated, undeterred. She was a lovely woman of unquestionably ageless years, though had anyone the gall to ask, she would admit to being at least fifty Taburon years of age. Not many knew for sure the exact number, and she wasn't telling. Her posture was that of the queen she had been in her youth and the queen mother she was now, still able to wield power and unafraid to use it if it was in the best interest of the people as well as, unfortunately, her son. He may have been crowned king, and had held that title for going on ten years now, but she still ruled the nest. "Radine," she said for a third time, a hint of exasperation in her voice, "what was wrong with the last candidate I sent you?"

"Other than the fact that she was already engaged and pregnant as well?" he asked acerbically, leaning closer for a heartbeat. Radine straightened, his hand clasping his sword even tighter for just a second until he relaxed, standing with one foot on the platform upon which sat the chair, his arms crossed over his chest. "Not a thing, Mother, she was perfect. When can we have the wedding?" he continued with sarcasm.

Queen Inoa waved his comments away with nonchalance. "You needn't be so sassy with me, young man."

Radine scoffed. He hadn't been a young man for a number of years now. "You've paraded a dozen woman passed my throne in the last month, Mother."

"And you found fault with every one of them."

"They were too tall or short, too skinny or round, too ugly or vain, too shy or obvious, and in every case more interested in the crown than the man wearing it," he retorted, his arms falling to his sides.

"What about Espis? She's got royal blood, she's beautiful, well-educated…"

"Well-acquainted with nearly every man in my guard," he added interrupting.

"Then she's experienced."

"She's delusional. I wouldn't go near her for all of the wealth in the galaxy."

"Then why would you spend four days with her at the winter palace?"

"Curiosity. I'd heard stories about her abilities in bed sport and I wanted to see what all the talk was about."

Her eyebrow arched as she crossed her arms under her breasts. "For four days? I would think you wouldn't more need than a few hours."

"Things came up."

"Your cock came up," she refuted. He was taken aback with her bluntness, but then he had to agree, reluctantly. Espis had been inventive and very motivated to keep him in bed as long as possible. He'd known she was angling for a crown and he'd deftly sidestepped every one of her hints during those four days with grace and aplomb while enjoying her sexual efforts. When it ended he'd dragged himself home, collapsed onto his bed, and slept for a full day, his body exhausted and a certain favorite body part scraped raw from overuse.

He'd also had this discussion with his mother more than once in the last year, the ending always the same. It wasn't like he hadn't been hounded in the past years. At thirty-four, he still had not chosen a woman to become wife and queen. And he heard about it regularly – from his ministers, his advisors, his mother, and even his best friend. He sometimes believed they pestered him on a rotating schedule. But he would find his own wife when the time was right for him, not anyone else, and he would find her where he deemed appropriate, which much to their consternation, had not been, so far, from among the eligible women of Taburon. "Will you not allow me to find my own queen, and wife, on my own?" he pleaded.

"I would, if you showed any signs of doing so. You've been king now for ten years. You need to secure your throne and the only way to do that is by having an heir. A legitimate one," she added with emphasis. "You can't go around spreading your seed haphazardly anymore."

"I am always careful," he ground out. He couldn't believe he was getting into a discussion of his sex life with his mother.

"Yes, well, you are a healthy, virile man, and I know you have certain needs…"

"By the Gods' rods, Mother," he said warningly, his lips thinned again.

She pointed a finger at him. "Don't take that tone with me and watch your language," she scolded. "You think I don't know about your dalliances? And the way you make sure nothing comes of them? I was young once, too. Your father and I had a very active sex life up to the day he died."

He nearly choked. Not just because he'd been told of his parents' sex life – something no child, no matter how old, should have to hear - but because his mother just admitted to having him watched…too well. "You are having me followed?" he asked.

"Discreetly, of course."

His eyes narrowed. "Who?" he demanded.

She raised a delicate eyebrow at the impertinence of his question, ignoring the impertinence of her statement. "I wouldn't tell you if you made me."

"Perhaps some time in the dungeon…" he suggested.

She snorted. "Not even," she promised.

12

"So now I have to look over my shoulder every time I leave the palace?"

"Don't bother. You'll never see my operative."

"You won't even tell me if it's a man or woman?"

"No. And don't think dismissing all of the palace people will help. Number one, my person may not even be a member of the staff and two, I'd only find someone else who'll pledge their loyalty to me and me alone." Rising from the chair, she glided regally to a small table to pour herself a cup of cool wine. "Now, about the next woman I have in mind..."

His relaxed pose fled in a heartbeat. "No," he ground out. "No way, never, not again."

Her shoulders fell slightly as the carafe of wine landed on the table surface with a thump. "Radine, surely there has got to be someone on this planet suitable for your queen."

He started to reply, then held his tongue. She'd said the magic words – on this planet. He knew his people, he knew his planet. Radine knew his mother was right, he needed an heir or two to insure his throne, his rule, and his family lineage. But he also knew that all of the possible candidates had already been found lacking, something about each and every one of them that made him know he could never spend the rest of his life with one of them at his side, on his arm, sharing his throne and most especially in his bed. He wanted a woman that saw him for himself, not his crown and the life of luxury it might bring. Being king was work, grueling, hard work that lasted every day, all day, and sometimes into the night, sometimes for days. The little times he stole for himself were few and far between and even then he had discovered that he couldn't totally let his hair down. Even in the throes of passion, he had his kingdom to consider, the culmination of his 'dalliances' unfulfilling to say the least. Being careful meant never spilling his seed inside a woman and never allowing her to clean it from her body by herself. He always – always – took care.

But Taburons were not limited to their own planet. They had developed space travel generations ago, were known throughout the galaxy as a warrior race that held fairness and compassion high. Taburons traded with other peoples around the galaxy and served time as guardians to peace for all intelligent species, spacefarers or not. They did not suffer fools and hucksters well. They defended their people and planet from anyone who thought to usurp the government and kingdom.

And recently, a planet had come into the galactic fold, not as a space traveling world, but one that had finally conquered many of its problems and was ready to be made aware that there were other life forms beyond their small sphere. In fact, they had, once accepting that they were not alone, reached out to other worlds for help in certain areas, one of which might just solve his problem. He smiled.

Inoa grew leery, seeing his smile. It was never wise to irritate the king, even if he was her son. She could only push him so far before he, like the child he had once been, went off on a tear, doing exactly what she wanted in as wrong a way as possible. She sighed softly. Radine was so much like his father and she missed Tylene so much even after all of these years. Her hope that her son would have found a nice woman to marry and have children and ease her sorrow faded with every passing year that he remained a bachelor and childless.

She took another sip from her cup, her eyes on Radine as he remained thoughtful. Inoa could tell he was plotting something, something she might later regret. Her breath caught. Oh Gods, she prayed, don't let him pick one of the ugly, stupid ones just to spite me. I couldn't stand having ugly, stupid grandchildren.

Radine's smile grew wider and he bowed. "Mother, take care of the kingdom for me for a few days, would you?"

The cup fell to the table with a thunk. "Where are you going?" she asked suspiciously.

"You have your secrets, I have mine," he nearly chortled, turning on his heel.

"Please don't do anything stupid!" she called after him. He ignored her as he left the room. Inoa found her hand was shaking as she reached for her cup again to take a healthy, not quite so calming swig.

Radine only went as far as his own quarters, unstrapping his sword to drop it uncaringly on a chair. "Jaima," he hollered as he began to unbutton his shirt. He shooed away Purnia, his personal servant.

From his left, a side door opened to admit another tall man, equally as well-built as the king, his coloring darker blonde in contrast to his ruler. He executed a perfect bow before helping the king to pull off the shirt, catching it as it started to fall to the floor. "Yes, Your Majesty?" he asked, draping the shirt over the end of the massive bed that took up most of the room. His shoes landed on the floor nearby. Radine's trousers followed, leaving the king totally bare to the other, his buttocks flexing as he bent to pick up the garment, tossing it to rest near the shirt. The crown sailed cleanly across the room to land in the middle of the bed. Jaima pointedly kept his eyes raised, following his ruler as the king strode into his bathing room.

"Ready my ship, we are taking a trip."

"The queen?" the other guessed, lounging against the door jamb. He crossed his arms over his chest. Being best friends with the king as well as commander of the armies and second in command of the king's spaceship gave Jaima certain insights into the king that he shared with no other. They'd shared adventures together as children, and these days as adults. Jaima made sure that the king was always protected, in court, in battle, while training, on a hunting trip, and in the arms of a woman. He knew Radine better than any other man on Taburon, including the queen. And he was well aware of the queen's machinations to get her son married and produce offspring.

"Who else?" the king replied as he gathered toiletries. Piling them into the shower, he turned the water on, shaking his hand of moisture, placing towels nearby while he waited for the water to warm.

"May I ask where we are going?"

"We are going to get me a queen."

"I figured as much. And since you've turned down every woman your mother has thrown at you from Taburon, thank all the Gods, I'm assuming she'll not be from here. So, where from?"

The king stepped under the spray, a bar of soap in hand. The water cascaded down his chest as he ducked under to wet his head, the color of his hair turning from a dark honey to rich caramel. He began to soap himself. "Earth," he replied.

Chapter Two

"No, no, no. Please, baby, don't stop on me," McKenna Primm pleaded, her hands gripping the steering wheel of her car, her foot pumping the gas with futility. She jerked her body forward several times, as if the mere action would help encourage the forward motion of the vehicle. With a cough, wheeze and a couple of metallic clunks, the car stopped, hanging on just long enough for her to steer it to the side of the road and out of the flow of traffic. "Twenty minutes," she groaned, "just twenty more minutes and I would have at least been close enough to home to walk the rest of the way while it was still light out." She heaved a vocal sigh, dropping her head until her forehead rested on the wheel. "Damn," she breathed softly. Why, oh why, couldn't one thing go right for her in a day that had gone wrong from the start?

This was the perfect ending to the perfect day. Any better and she might as well have pulled off at the cemetery she passed every day and buried both herself and her car. Things would have only been worse if her boss had had his way and she'd allowed him to bend her over his desk, flip up her skirt and bury himself inside her. It wasn't as if he hadn't been pestering her for at least six months, but jobs were few and far between these days and at the time she couldn't really afford to lose the one she had.

Times were tough for the most part. There had been peace for the last five years, but only because the world had finally said enough with the shenanigans in the Middle East, banded together and put a stop to it. Hordes of troops from all over the free world - a world that had suffered the idiocy of bombings , threats of terror, and deaths simply because of their political and cultural differences – descended upon the sands and heat, fighting tooth and nail until the terrorists factions were completely depleted of the fanatical individuals and their replacements that ran them. The world had been smart enough to not use nuclear weapons and grateful that they had found the terrorists' hidden arsenals before they could have been used, destroying every last weapon. By the time the last terrorist fell, the people of the region were more than interested in peace and truly policing themselves, laying down their arms - weary of war, weary of poverty, weary of sacrificing their young men for fanatical ideals that the world would not tolerate anymore.

Ten years of world war had brought peace, and its consequences. The Middle East had been bombed all but totally back to the middle ages, technology demolished in order to defeat the terrorists networks that had come to rely on it heavily. Any rebuild of modern advances was carefully controlled now to prevent their resurgence. Control of the oil reserves was divided among the governments of those countries who had provided resources to defeat the terrorists and doled out accordingly.

Ten years of world war had had a heavy cost on the world male population. Forsworn to not stop until the terrorists had been defeated, depleted troops were replenished monthly with able bodied men, no matter their age, until the male population suffered a loss of one-third to one-half of their pre-war numbers.

The direct effect on the female population was both good and bad. With fewer men available, women were beginning to gain power in the boardroom and politics, filling spots left vacant by men who'd gone to war or left unfulfilled because the sons who would have taken the positions had also died in the war. Women were proving to be just as savvy and ruthless as their male counterparts in positions of authority, yet retained the compassion that was so much a part of their inherent makeup. Educational opportunities improved for women as well as they filled positions requiring better knowledge, teaching and attending classes as students. World history at their fingertips, they, as a collective whole, vowed to remember and lead with a softer – though firm – attitude.

The negative effect was women outnumbered men nearly three to one, giving men the upper hand when it came to relationships. Men could pick and choose from a more than abundant pool of women what they wanted for girlfriend, lover, companion, or wife, and if one didn't work out, another was readily available. Laws, both secular and religious, relaxed restrictions concerning fidelity, making it easier for men to divorce with little consequence. Men were given the green light to spread their seed around in an effort to repopulate the male gender. Yet since the best of the men had gone to war, the leftovers were fairly young, too old, too unsuitable for combat and therefore too unappealing, or infirmed, which left women with little choice if they wanted a relationship and children. Because of these new mores, women were becoming more discriminating when making their choices, hindering the efforts to regrow the population. Scientists and governments were conducting studies to determine how negatively this might affect the world population, but it was taking time.

But they'd also found a new solution. Earth discovered it was not alone in the universe. The global conflict had caught the attention of its nearest galactic neighbor who then broadcast throughout the inhabited universe that Earth was ripe for new knowledge and new friends. Spaceships arrived during the seventh year of the conflict, its passengers meeting with world rulers. Treaties were signed, information exchanged, opportunities made to humans that might have not happened until generations in the future. The newcomers also declined to become involved with Earth's conflicts, for who could choose sides when they were strangers? The biggest condition instituted when all was said and done – Earth would discontinue its aggressive space program. The galaxy did not need its inbred tendency to dominate and conquer outside the confines of its own sphere. And to keep the inhabitants of Earth from being attacked by hostile extraterrestrial beings, a galactic police force, made up from those planets with non-hostile intent, kept the peace. Which worked out for the galactic neighborhood in the long run.

So women were offered the chance to go to other worlds to live, explore, take husbands, and a couple thousand had emigrated. Though not enough to relieve the basic problem. Many were frightened by the idea of leaving their home for realms unknown, especially since to date none of the ones who had left had ever returned to relate their experiences. Who knew what had happened to them? Were they happy, or had they been used for nefarious purposes? Did they still live? Who knew what the galaxy held for the human race out there, since the aliens weren't especially forthcoming about their own worlds, even when asked. This veil of secrecy only served to make women wary, and as a whole, unwilling.

McKenna had not been one of the ones fortunate enough to be able to move into a position of authority. Her father and brothers had been lost in the war which led directly to the slow demise of her mother, leaving McKenna on her own at the age of twenty. With no other family and no guidance, she was not able to take advantage of educational opportunities other than basic office work and found herself shuffled off to a male run business upon graduation. Raymond Enterprises was a drug company, acquired and built up on the ghosts of the sons of the competition who'd died in the war. With no one to inherit, his competitors had sold to George Raymond.

Raymond was a man of about fifty five years, stocky in build, a sloppy dresser who poorly wore expensive suits. His weight showed in the moderate jowls that graced his jaw and the slight overhanging stomach at his waist. He was married, but his wife had years ago turned a blind eye to his affairs, knowing she had little opportunity should she divorce him, content as long as he continued to provide for her. All of his legitimate children had died in the war. Rumors had it that he treated the workplace as his own private harem - there were already two illegitimate children who could easily claim relationship to the boss, both, unfortunately, girls. McKenna'd worked for Mr. Raymond for six years now, first as what used to be known as a member of the clerical pool, then gradually moving up to head of the office pool. That's when Mr. Raymond had taken active notice of her.

He'd worked a steady campaign to get closer to her. Raymond stopped by her desk for minor things, standing a little too close, but backing off quickly the minute she showed any signs of discomfort. As time progressed, his visits became more frequent and more intrusive, as well as more obvious. Six months ago, he'd moved her desk closer to his office on a flimsy excuse of needing her closer to be able to get things done faster. It took too much time to walk across the building and down a set of steps, or so he said.

When she heard gossip about her so-called relationship with the boss, and the 'office tramp' name was attached, McKenna had begun to visibly and vocally reject his advances, until it had come down to his visit to her office this afternoon.

Claiming to have a 'newer' version of his office rotation chart, he'd dumped it on her desk and proceeded to invade her space. Leaning close, one hand on the chart as he pointed out its many 'features,' the other hand, which had been on the back of her chair came to rest on the back of her neck, gently squeezing and rubbing. McKenna had pushed her chair to the side until she could go no further and hunched her shoulders - to no avail. Raymond only followed, a scowl on his face that she was being so obstinate. If she needed her job as she claimed, she needed to earn it from him.

But when he leaned in closer to rub his erection against her shoulder, that's when she'd had enough. Her first thoughts had been to run screaming in hysterics from her office. She'd then wanted to open a can of 'wup ass' on him, venting her outrage at his actions and the way he treated all of the women in the workplace. But she kept her dignity, opening the drawer where she kept her small purse, grabbing the two personal items she kept on her desk – a picture of her family and a small plant – and stood. Never mind that one of the wheels of the chair rolled over his foot.

She taken a page from the world history books. Finished with putting up with his unwanted attentions, but unwilling to battle it out with him, she'd quit.

There was no applause, no one to say 'you go girl' as she stomped out of the building. Dropping the picture and plant onto the front passenger's side seat of her old, well-used automobile, she dropped into the driver's seat, shivering violently. The horror of what she had done overwhelmed her. What had she just done? How would she support herself? Where would she get another job? After this fiasco, there was no way Raymond would give her a recommendation. And there was no way she could go back. She had some bit of pride left, though right now it felt as though it had fled thoroughly and completely.

As panic threatened to take over, McKenna took a dozen deep breaths, staring out the front window at the brick of the building where she had spent the majority of her time over the last six years. Her bills were moderate, but she still had rent to pay, food to buy, a car to maintain, and now she had to figure out how she was going to get resumes out on a busted budget. She had little savings to fall back on.

Giving herself a full body shake and a firm word to woman up, she twisted the key in the ignition and started her vehicle. The engine wheezed, a puff of smoke belched from the tailpipe, and her car could be heard for three city blocks as she drove out of town towards home, fifteen miles away.

She had been fighting the whole way to hold in her emotions as she drove. An occasional tear slid down her cheek that she angrily wiped away with the back of her hand. Keeping her eyes forward, she forced herself to concentrate on the road, promising herself to give in to a long crying jag as soon as she closed herself inside her apartment. The silence in the car was broken by a heavy sigh every few minutes that was accompanied by a vigorous shiver, the only signs of her emotional state. She was proud of herself that she was holding it all together so well. Or so it seemed.

Only when the car began to wheeze did she come out of her stupor, looking around frantically for anything to keep the car running just a little further. The vehicle shimmied before wheezing, coughing and finally dying as it coasted to a stop on the side of the road.

All of this was why she now found herself, stalled on the side of the road, gently banging her head on the steering wheel and whispering a chant to herself, "I'm not going to cry, I'm not going to cry," as tears dropped into her lap.

McKenna sat on the road side for a good five minutes, fighting to not totally give in to her misery and slowly losing, repeating her mantra over and over until she realized it was having no effect on the shaking of her body and the spiraling emotions. She was safe enough with the doors locked and windows raised. The temperatures outside were comfortable. When she got herself together and decided to finally to start the long trek the rest of the way home, she would be comfortable in that regard. And she would be safe enough as a woman walking on the roadside by herself. It was just a question of getting herself under control before it became dark and heading out.

The gentle tap on the driver's side window scared her. Her little gasp of surprise, her jerkily sitting back into her seat, her hand rising to her chest did not prepare her for the sight of a gloriously sculpted male stomach that greeted her through the glass. Nor did it give her any warning when the body attached to the stomach bent to allow the most beautiful man she'd ever seen peer at her through the glass, his golden eyes inquisitive and amused. Perfect lips quirked up in a dazzling smile, revealing perfect teeth. His longish, honey blonde hair fell from behind his head to drape over his shoulders, swaying in the slight breeze. He held up a finger and drew circles with it in the air – he wanted her to roll down her window.

She knew better. She should have known better. A woman alone, even on a somewhat well- traveled road could still find herself in a world of trouble and her head was telling her to keep the window up and the doors locked. This was a stranger and her life could be in danger. But there was something mesmerizing about this man she couldn't resist as her hand rose to grab the handle to the window and started cranking. It slowly rolled down, allowing a scent of musk and pure masculine pheromes to drift into the car. His smile grew wider, his eyes more delighted.

"I am Radine from the planet Taburon. Are you in need of assistance?" he asked. Her heart did a little thump in her chest, she felt heat pool in places that had never felt heat before, at least not because of a man. Somewhere inside her a place jumped for joy, a fist pumped, and a voice screamed, "Yes!" All because he was probably the most beautiful man she'd ever seen. All because of the timber of his voice, deep, resonate, and full of promise with just a few words.

What he said finally registered in her muddled, overwrought brain. From Taburon? Another planet? Wanting to help her? Oh. My. God!

Chapter Three

Oh my god! McKenna thought to herself as she stared with amazement at the man. He was simply the most handsome person she had ever seen now that she took a second breath and second look, her eyes shifting from his face to slide down his torso. She wiped her tears away.

His chest was covered in some sort of soft, leathery material, so tight that it showed every curve and indentation of a sculpted body with washboard abs kept hard and muscular through exercise, hard work or both. The material did little to hide the outline of defined pectorals and the slightly smaller than pinkie sized nubs of masculine nipples. A v-shaped opening at the top showed smooth, bronzed skin, as though he spent time in the sun without a shirt. There was an obvious roundness to his shoulders and bulges under the sleeves of his shirt that showed the outlines of firm muscles. This was a man who either vigorously worked out in a gym or just vigorously worked. The shirt disappeared into a pair of dark colored pants made of the same sort of material as the shirt and just as tight across his slim hips. There were pull marks over the crotch. His sex was a healthy bulge at the junction of his legs.

Embarrassed that her eyes were lingering for too long below his 'belt,' McKenna raised them to look at his face, her breath catching. He had no shadow of a beard and appeared freshly shaven, his jaw line defined. His chin was thick, not pointed in the least. Above, he had a pair of full lips, kissable even when pulled back into a smile. He, Radine, had strong cheekbones and a strong forehead. His head was wreathed by long straight hair the color of dark honey, smooth and silky looking. Her fingers itched and tingled to run through it.

But it was Radine's eyes that were the most arresting. Framed by thick lashes any woman would envy the same color as the hair on his head, the color of his pupils was mesmerizing. No one on Earth had eyes that color of gold with the barest of a sparkle in them. She knew – she just knew – that those eyes were commanding. They could flash in anger or twinkle in humor and there would be no mistaking which he was feeling.

Radine was more than amused. Were it not considered rude, he would have laughed out loud at her fascination with him, especially with the way her eyes widened when she saw his crotch. Yes, his trousers had pulled tight, though only after he'd seen the sun glinting through the window of her vehicle on her hair and she'd turned to look at him.

She was a beautiful woman, as beautiful as any woman on his planet, more so probably, and his interest had sparked. As well as other parts of his anatomy.

But it was her eyes that had him mesmerized. A warm brown, the center was interspersed with the darkest of green. This woman's eyes were nothing like those of the woman on his planet. He could easily get lost in her eyes, despite the fact that they were currently filled with fright, anxiety, moisture, and a whole lot of worry. Which made him wonder - what could be so wrong in her life that her eyes held such sadness when they should have reflected the joy of living. It made him want to be the one to bring the happiness back into her eyes.

He'd told Jaima to remain on the ship, despite the other's protests, to keep communications open and to remind the crew when he returned with a female, if he returned, to never call him by title, at least not the royal one and not in Earth speak. Captain would suffice in the presence of the woman and the crew, Radine was okay in private. And if absolutely necessary, they could speak in their own language, though that would have been rude to the extreme. He wanted time for the woman to get to know him as himself, not as the king. Both men were the same, only one had a title that came with a heavy amount of responsibility.

Having seen the woman pulled off to the side of the road from their ship, Radine jumped into his personal shuttle and flew down to offer assistance. Not until she'd seen her did he realize that she was the one he would invite to his planet to become his wife. The decision had hit him that easily, that deeply. The confidently. No use messing around and wasting time when he had a planet to run and people to govern. Even he had his enemies and to be away too long would be to invite those enemies to attempt to take his throne. She was beautiful and from what he could see as she sat in her vehicle seemed to have a pleasant figure that he would enjoy in bed.

"I am Radine from the planet Taburon," he said as the window to her side lowered. "Are you in need of assistance?" The scent of flowers drifted out of the car, her perfume reminding him of the fields of *freema* blossoms in summer.

"Oh my god," she whispered, giving voice to her thoughts. She pulled on the door handle, forcing Radine to step back as the door swung outward. "You're one of them, aren't you? Someone from another planet?" She stepped out of the car, keeping the door between herself and Radine – just in case. "An alien." Oh, Lordy, he was tall, probably six foot six to her five foot five. Were she to look directly at him, she would have gotten a great view of his hard chest.

"The term alien is just a matter of perspective," he replied, "but yes, I am from another planet. My world is called Taburon."

"Taburon," she repeated, trying the word out. "I've never heard of it."

"This is a first visit by any of my people to your planet." He glanced over her shoulders to the car. "You are having difficulties with your vehicle?" Leaning to the side he tried to get a better look at the woman as he pretended an interest in the car. When the sun hit her hair, it burst into shades of reds, browns and gold. Long and curly, it draped her head and cascaded over her shoulders, resting softly along her back and just at the tops of what appeared to be generous breasts. Breasts that would fill his hands if her ever got them on her. The pulse at her throat beat fiercely, her cheeks were slightly flushed and her lips were pinkish bordering on red. And while she was beautiful the outfit she wore, a non-descript dress, the color, a gods-awful green, made her skin look sallow. He would make sure she never wore that color again when she became his wife.

She followed his gaze. "It died. It's old and I haven't been able to afford keeping it repaired properly, just enough to keep it running one more day. I guess it decided it had had enough."

"It would please me to take you to your destination."

McKenna's head tilted slightly. "Why?"

Radine was taken aback. "Why what?"

"Why would you take me home? Shouldn't you be meeting with scientists or the government officials, working on some treaty or something? I mean, I know we've welcomed you folks from other worlds for a while now but…"

33

"The Kardians made a treaty with your governments when they first arrived eight of your years ago that applies to all galactic peoples who would visit you. So there is no need for me to speak with your government save to ask permission to obtain orbit, which I received." His forehead creased in a frown. "I do not know why I should meet with these scientists."

"Maybe they might wish to know about your planet and people."

"It is not in my plans to remain long enough to speak with your scientists about my planet. I have but a day or two, then I must return home." He offered her an arm. "So, may I take you to your home?"

Chapter Four

McKenna stepped from behind the car door to give Radine a long hard perusal, one hand on the door, just in case. She knew she should be wary of taking up an offer from a stranger, and an alien to boot, but there was something about Radine that pulled at her, a feeling that he was an honorable man even if alien. There wasn't a predatory look in his eyes - unless one considered the lust he allowed to show predatory - nor one of masculine superiority, as was seen in many human men since they held all of the power when it came to relationships with women. If there was something about a woman that a man didn't like, there were always other women waiting for him from which to pick and choose.

Yet there was something about Radine that made him appear to be in charge. A sense of confidence exuded from his stance, it fairly glowed in his eyes. He was a man who cared for himself as evidenced by his body, hard and sculpted, his hair well-kept and shining in the sunlight. The cloth of his shirt and trousers was fresh, new looking and well-tended, not faded or patched, the stitching so fine that there wasn't a single sign of thread, indicating fine craftsmanship.

Not to say that a man of position or wealth couldn't be untrustworthy or unscrupulous. She only had to look at her ex-boss, Mr. Raymond, to see the truth in that.

But Radine had a feature that Raymond did not – his eyes were warm instead of cold. The gold fairly sparked and fired, heat flashing from their depths that was irresistible. That was enough for her to believe in his sincerity. Whatever his intentions, McKenna thoroughly believed she would be safe with this man for whatever reason he deemed to want to be with her.

McKenna offered him a smile. "Of course you can take me home," she replied pleasantly. Following his glance as he turned his head, she noticed for the first time the vehicle that was parked well off the road and behind her own. Almost car like, but bullet shaped, it glimmered in the late afternoon sunshine, the outside silvery in color except for the window that stretched across the front. Two small wings projected from each side and the vehicle rested on three wheels. McKenna breathed out a short breath. "Is that a car?" she asked.

"My shuttle."

Her glance slid to the sky, her eyes narrowed. "You have a spaceship?" she whispered with awe.

His amusement showed in his voice. "Yes, but you cannot see it from here. It would require a strong viewing scope to see my ship. The shuttle is used to travel between a planet's surface and the ship."

Her hand rose to her chest. There was wonder in her voice. "I've always loved to fly," she murmured, "though I don't have much chance these days. I haven't been in an airplane in years."

Radine held his hand out again in invitation. "Then let me give you a chance to fly again."

McKenna looked to his hand, the shuttle, back to his hand again and up to his face. He smiled and it was beautiful, reaching from one side of his cheeks to the other, his eyes lighting up, soft crinkles appearing at the outside corners of his eyes. She reached out to place her hand in his, her left foot stepping in his direction before she pulled up. "Wait," she said anxiously, turning back to her vehicle. Bending, she reached into the interior, grabbing at her purse, keys, the picture, and the plant.

Radine nearly choked at the sight of her backside as she rummaged through the dead vehicle. She had the most rounded arse, split evenly down the middle. They jiggled and flexed, two rounded spheres he itched to get his hands on, to smooth over the edges and explore them, up, down on the outside and inside along the split between them, even the small flower he knew existed there that could give so much pleasure when handled the right way. Her right leg lifted slightly as she reached further into the car, the slight breeze blowing the skirt up to reveal the back of her thigh. She wore no coverings on her legs. The skin appeared soft and flawless, a light pink that matched the color of the throat of a *tuaxa* flower. She had defined muscles from the top of her leg, through her knee and down to the delicate ankle and tapered feet.

While her back was still turned, Radine covered his crotch with a hand and took several deep breaths, promising his cock that there would be time for him later. By the time she straightened, her hands filled, he had brought himself under some semblance of control – at least enough that he wouldn't embarrass himself in front of the woman he intended to bring home before he even got her onto his shuttle. She preceded him to the shuttle, giving him a chance to watch her walk, telling his treacherous body to keep things in check. But oh, how her back globes flexed and relaxed with every step and he would never tire of watching her walk. Giving his head a shake, dispelling his naughty thoughts, he followed on her heels.

Touching the side of the shuttle with a hand, doors lifted on each side. Two seats were revealed facing a multicolored, complicated control panel where several lights blinked steadily. There was a small storage space behind the seats, not large enough for a person, but she easily stored her belongings behind the passenger side. "I hope you do not have a fear of enclosed spaces," Radine said with a meaningful look. His finger hovered over a yellow light.

She shook her head vigorously. She was about to fly in an alien craft with a stranger who looked like a god who had fallen from the heavens. Her heart was beating wildly, her voice was frozen in her throat.

Radine's chuckle was deep and soothing. He had no fear. Punching the yellow button, the doors dropped down and sealed with a hiss. Following a series of steps, touching a pad of his finger to buttons in the correct order, McKenna felt the vehicle begin to vibrate as the engines powered up and her stomach dropped to her knees as the craft rose. Once they had risen to several meters in the sky, he faced her. "I assume since your vehicle was pointed in this direction, that we are going to the small city ahead."

McKenna swallowed, finding her voice. "Yea," she stammered, cleared her throat and tried again. "Yes, Newton, where I live." The shuttle began a forward movement, controlled it seemed by the mere touch of his fingers in the right places on the control panel.

"Why could you not afford to keep your vehicle running? On Taburon, if a citizen needs to repair his vehicle and cannot afford it, the government will provide the repairs for him." He glanced once out the window. "Of course, we do not have as many powered vehicles as your people, but rely more on *crufas* to travel within short distances."

"What's a *crufa*?"

"Do you not have animals to ride here on Earth?"

"Yes, but for pleasure, not as a means of transportation. Even the most remote places have cars or trucks now to get themselves around." She sighed. "As for myself, I didn't have a lot of money for big things like major car repairs. I fixed what I could just enough to keep it running. And prayed." Her shoulders sagged. "Of course, now that I have lost my job, I can't even afford that. I don't know how I'm going to get around to interview for a new position."

Radine kept his tongue. He had a new position for her, in fact several came to mind as soon as she'd mentioned it, but he wasn't quite ready to make the offer yet. He willed his cock to control. He wanted to see her home and there were still questions to be answered. He had no right to jeopardize the treaty for others if he was going to make a mistake by having her go with him. He wanted her, his body was quite clear about it. Much more so than it had ever been with any other woman with whom he'd shared nadryl. But would she be willing to come with him?

"You must tell me where your home is. We will be there soon."

"Oh," she whispered with disappointment. "Okay." She faced out the front window, her brow furrowed, her eyes sheltered.

"Is something wrong?" he asked with concern. "Have I offended?"

Her hands gripped the edges of the seat. "No, Radine. I thought it would take longer."

His lips parted in a smile. "I see. Perhaps I might take you on a longer flight before I have to leave."

"I would love that, thank you."

"Give me directions."

Though she'd never approached her apartment building from the sky before, she managed to get them to the right place where he set the shuttle down on the rooftop, killing the engines. He would have parked on the street, but he didn't want to garner too much attention, and the roof would assure that his shuttle would still be there when he decided to leave. McKenna had told him that while her apartment was still in fairly good shape, the neighborhood was a bit iffy.

Taking Radine through the rooftop door and down the stairs, McKenna took him to her fourth floor apartment, unlocking the door and letting him enter first. She closed and locked the door behind herself. "This is my home," she introduced. Apprehension filled her. She'd never thought of what her home might look like to someone from another planet. Would it appear cozy, the way she believed, or rather poor and decrepit? Anxiety made her hold her breath as he looked around.

Chapter Five

Radine stood in the middle of her living room and turned circles, taking it all in. Her furniture was eclectic, a mishmash of different pieces of mismatched colors, but comfortable in appearance. A couch was bookended by two tables, a lamp on each one. To the right, behind the couch and in the front of the building overlooking the street was a large window, covered by light drapes of an off-white. The afternoon sun was filtered by the material, bright enough to not require turning on the lamps yet.

To the left down a small hallway was a kitchen, big enough for one to move around comfortably but with limited counter space and cabinets. Further down the hallway, at its end was a door, another on the right side half way down. On a wall opposite the kitchen before the hallway she had a bookcase filled to overflowing with books, some orderly, some laying wedged into whatever space she could fine for them. There was little else in the way of decoration, but the entire place smelled of cleanliness with a hint of the fragrance of flowers. The same smell, he recognized, as that she wore.

McKenna set her picture and plant on the closest table, dropping her purse on the couch. "I'm sorry it's so plain."

"Are you comfortable here?" he asked without judgment.

She glanced around once, her eyes warming. "Yes. It's my home."

"Then do not apologize. The most humble of men can live in a hovel while the most arrogant may reside in a castle. The home does not make the man."

She blushed prettily. "It's just you seem so…" she tried to say before waving her hand dismissively, turning to face the kitchen. "May I get you something to drink?"

Radine moved until he stood in front of her, a finger tucked under her chin to raise her face. "I am so what?" he asked.

She flinched, not really wanting to finish what she was going to say and embarrass herself, or him. Staring in to his eyes, they narrowed, commanding she tell him but held no contempt or ridicule. McKenna shrugged. "You look like someone who lives better than I, your clothes are obviously better quality, and you said you have a ship. That can't come cheaply."

He chuckled again, a pleasing sound, his hand gently caressing. "I have the ear of the king," he explained.

"You have a king?"

"He is a pleasant, generous man, but lonely. He seeks a bride before his mother can parade every single Taburon woman before him, both the young and old." No censure, but a kind of resignation tinged his voice.

"Is that why you're here? To look for a woman for him?"

"In a way. He wished to know what this Earth has to offer before making a decision."

"Well, I'm sure there are plenty of woman here who would like to be chosen for a queen. We have many beautiful women he can look at. Ones suitable for a king."

"Yes, I am sure," Radine agreed tonelessly, his voice tinged with disappointment. Any woman who considered herself candidate material would most likely be vain and selfish. This one did not consider herself candidate material. He would disabuse her of that thought soon enough.

"Let me get you something to drink," McKenna reoffered, backing away from the handsome Taburon. He was on a mission for his king to find a woman to be a queen. She most likely had to be tall, like they, or close to it, and of course, beautiful. No man wanted a plain woman for a queen. A queen needed to be intelligent, well mannered, know how to converse with all kinds of people, and in Radine's king's case, intergalactically as well. McKenna was certain that within the government there would be a woman to fulfill the requirements for a king, someone trained to handle protocol and royalty with great aplomb. Someone perfect as a go-between for two planets.

Since she had no chance to compete, and was quite frankly still puzzled why Radine was spending so much time with her when he should be otherwise occupied, she steeled her wayward heart and thoughts. Though it would be easier now to just relax and enjoy what little time they had, exchanging pleasant conversation, since she didn't have anything to prove. She would provide the man with something to refresh himself and reluctantly send him on his way.

In her kitchen, she took two glasses from a cabinet to set on a counter, opening the refrigerator with the other hand. "I have iced tea, soda, and some beer. I wouldn't try the beer, it's been there for a while now and might have gone stale, but the tea I made yesterday."

Radine crowded her in her kitchen, his mood sombered. "I know what tea is, but what is iced tea?"

"It's the same as hot tea, only chilled." She started to pour when he nodded yes.

Radine sipped from the glass, giving it a look of approval after the first taste. "We don't have anything quite like this on Taburon. It is good, thank you."

She poured a glass for herself, returned the container to the refrigerator and grabbed her drink. "We can sit in the living room for a while," she indicated.

Radine settled on one end of the couch as McKenna took the other. "I have realized you have not told me your name, yet I sit here in your home."

"It's McKenna," she answered, "McKenna Primm. My friends call me Mac."

"May I be among those so privileged?" She nodded. After all, it was only for a little while, then he'd be gone. "Though I prefer McKenna, it is much more harmonious. So, McKenna, tell me about yourself. Have you no mate? A man who would not approve of my being here with you?"

McKenna sputtered, wiping her chin with her hand as she coughed twice. "No," she finally managed, "I'm not married. How about you?"

"No, I have no wife. I am always busy in service to the kingdom and have had little time to look."

"What do you do for your planet?"

He looked thoughtful a moment. "I command the armies and have a significant hand in the government. As I said, I am kept busy. What will you do, now that you have no employment?"

"I don't know. This place isn't much, but it still costs rent. I might give it a couple of days, take a break, and then start looking again."

"I am sorry you lost your job."

"I didn't lose it, I quit it. My boss was a prick and kept hitting on me. Today, he was too blatant about it, so I quit."

"I do not understand these terms you use, prick and hitting on. What are they?"

"Do you know what it means to call someone an asshole?" He nodded once. "That was my boss, a prick. He kept making sexual overtures to me, subtle at first, but today he all but came out and said he expected me to sleep with him. He rubbed himself against me. I had enough, so I quit."

"Then you were right in calling him a prick. A man should not force himself on a woman if she is not interested."

"Well, things have changed since the war. We woman outnumber the men and while it has given us opportunities we might not have had as easily, it gives the men pick of the litter, so to speak. Plus I refused my boss's attentions. He's not bound to give me a glowing recommendation."

"Do you not have you family to turn to?"

Her glance drifted to the picture she had placed on the table. "My family has gone. My father and brothers were lost in the war, my mother died of a broken heart soon after."

"I am sorry for your loss, McKenna," he said softly, reaching out to touch her cheek gently. His simple gesture of sympathy swayed her. She started to lean into his touch, but drew herself back at the last moment, remembering that he was here for a reason that did not include her. She sighed so softly she did not think he heard, but he frowned at the forlorn sound.

As the light faded, she turned on the lamp closest to her before standing abruptly, ignoring his words. She'd gotten over her loss a long time ago. Just because this gorgeous man expressed sympathy with more meaning than anyone had ever given before, she couldn't let it affect her beyond mere words. "It's unfortunate, especially for my tush, that whenever I have a downturn in luck I have a terrible upturn in hunger. I don't suppose you've ever tried pizza?"

Radine hated that she pushed off his expression of sympathy. She was alone in the world, had been abused by a man with authority over her which forced her to leave her employment and she dismissed his offer of compassion and comfort. He would never abuse her, always be there for her when she wanted, always available to give her comfort if she had a downturn in luck. He would love her with everything he held sacred for as long as he lived. She had no one to love her. Radine knew he would make her happy.

But first things first. "I have not tried this pizza," he replied. "And your tush is fine."

She reached for a device next to the couch, picking up a piece of it to hold by her ear, stopping for a second as his words penetrated. Her face flushed and her breasts lifted with a deep breath as she absorbed the compliment for a heartbeat. Her lips curled in a smile as she started to dial, then looked at him. "Do you eat meat?" she asked. "I can order vegetarian, but a meat lover's pizza is so much better. Also, how hungry are you? A large may not be enough for a man of your size."

"What is a pizza?"

"It's a circle of bread, about this big," she explained, tucking the small part of the phone into her neck, making a circle with her hands, "and it has on it cheese, vegetables, different meats, tomato sauce, or any combination of those things. It's very popular with nearly everyone on the planet and not a bad choice for your first taste of our food." She grinned. "I could have sardines put on it."

His eyes sparkled with amusement even as he frowned. "You say that as a joke."

"Yes. I wouldn't do that to you."

"Then ask for a large for me and whatever you wish for yourself. I am afraid I cannot pay you."

"No problem. They don't cost that much. I can manage." She punched at several buttons on the device then spoke into the piece she held to her ear. Ending her conversation, she put the ear piece back. "It's the year twenty-seventy, and it'll still take nearly an hour to get here," she complained mildly.

"No matter," Radine dismissed as easily as she had earlier. "We may talk for that time, and you may show me your home."

"It's nothing fancy," she dismissed.

"But I am interested," he insisted. "Please, McKenna, show me."

"This is…" Radine said later, "different, but delicious." He'd held the slice delicately in his long hands, peering at it as a scientist might some unusual specimen before he took another tentative bite. His mouth chewed and his lips curved into a smile. They were seated again on the couch, plates of pizza slices before them as well as replenished glasses of ice tea. Night had fallen outside and McKenna had turned on more lamps and lights to give the apartment a soft, yellowish glow.

Once Radine had gotten her to talk, he found her intelligent and he loved listening to her voice. The books on her shelf varied in subject, her tastes in reading materials were as eclectic as her furniture, proving that she tried to better herself without formal education and did not neglect her mind. She also liked what she called romance stories, explaining that they were stories about the relationship between a man and a woman, or multiples as the case may be. He paged through a few of them, surprised at the graphic language of some of them. And while some of the words were not familiar, he could discern their meaning by the content. It appeared humans and Taburons were sexually compatible, a question he had not dared to ask. At least not yet.

Before the pizza arrived, while she had disappeared into a bathroom to 'freshen up,' Radine called his ship to let Jaima know that he had found his intended, he was safe, and not to worry. He hoped to return in the morning. Jaima wished him luck. Radine promised to bring him a slice of the pizza, should any be left, leaving Jaima shaking his head in puzzlement as he headed for the bridge to research the strange food.

McKenna grinned around her own slice, biting off a chunk, stretching out the cheese until it broke. A string of it hung down her chin. She giggled and Radine fought the urge to lick the cheese with his tongue, nearly choking on his own mouthful, watching her tongue scrape along her chin to catch the offending string and pull it into her mouth. Had he given in to the urge it would have led to kissing her, which would have led to touching her, which would have led to… He filled his mouth with pizza instead.

"Do you know how to make this?" he asked around a mouthful, forgetting all manners. "It would be quite a treat on Taburon."

"I can try. It's the dough – the bread – that makes it. Everything else is just icing."

"Icing?"

"Sorry. Flavor. I'm sure it won't taste exactly the same on your planet, unless you have the exact same ingredients. Most of it is a matter of personal tastes."

"We have cheese that does not stretch, but tastes much like this. Our *pobla* is much like this tomato, and the meat is easily enough obtained. You would have to show the palace cooks how to make it and cook it."

McKenna swallowed with a gulp. "What?" she asked stunned.

Radine set his slice down and wiped his mouth with the paper towel she called a napkin. "I did not tell you everything about my visit to your planet," he confessed. "Not only is the king interested in finding a wife, but I am as well. I am glad to have spent this time with you, since I want you to return to Taburon with me, as my wife."

McKenna's slice dropped onto her plate with a thud. Her eyes were wide with disbelief. "You're joking!" she accused with a wavering voice.

"No, McKenna, I am not," he replied calmly.

"But your women, surely there's someone there who's worthy of you, that you don't have to go to another planet to find a wife."

"There are many women who would take me for their husband, but like the king, I am not interested in vapid, power hungry and vain women. My mother would have me wed, and she does her Gods' be-damned best to show me every available woman in the kingdom, but I am a man full grown and will make my own choice." He dropped the towel on the table. "I found myself attracted to you from the start. After the hours we have been together, I am sure that I want you. I can give you a good life, McKenna, whatever you want will be yours, and I hope I would make you happy."

"But you said you are always busy, too busy to look for a wife. You want me to go with you to a strange planet and then leave me alone while you do what you do?"

"I would let others handle some of my responsibilities. I would not abandon you, McKenna."

"What about children? I've always wanted some. Could we have children, are we compatible?"

He smiled, leaning towards her, his voice lowering, seductive. "If I understood the writings in your books, we can share sex the same as any man and woman. Whether or not you conceive, I do not know. I know seeing you, watching you, speaking with you, has made my cock hard and I desire to bed you. I can show you such pleasure as to make you scream my name when you peak." He reached over to caress her cheek, lingering against the smooth warm skin. "If there are no children, then that is what it will be. I will care for you the rest of my life."

"What about love?" she dared to ask. She wouldn't be a convenient repository for his lusts.

"It will come, sooner I would hope than later. We are well matched, you and I, and you would do me proud to be on my arm."

McKenna stared at him a moment before she stood, moving to the window to stare at the curtains and the night beyond. Go to another planet, be a wife? Had her life suddenly taken a turn for the better? Or worse? Radine had said this was their first visit to Earth. No one knew anything about alien planets since not a single woman who'd left had returned in the last eight years to talk about what awaited people beyond their galaxy. Were they happy? Alive? These aliens seemed friendly, but anyone could put on a gentle face, then turn evil once in private and back on their own world. What choice did the Earth women have, stuck on an alien world with no way to get home if things went badly? And since the Earth was restricted from exploring beyond their own galaxy, there was no way to send ships to other worlds to see how the Earth women were faring.

McKenna had trusted Radine enough to allow him to bring her home, to stay with her for a few hours, to share a meal. Could she trust him to follow through on his proposition, to protect her and care for her, to come to love her? She'd not had anyone to love, or love her for her entire adult life. There had been one young man a few years ago before she'd begun work, but he had wanted what he could get and moved on before she'd realized what had happened. That's the way it was in their world – plenty of oats to sow and more than enough fields in which to plow them.

And if Radine wanted children and they could not have them, would he eventually grow to resent her for something that wasn't her fault? What would happen to her then? Tossed aside for one of his own women, as distasteful as he made them sound, but able to reproduce and give him children. She'd grow old, alone, away from all she knew, unless he promised to return her. Would he accept that as a condition?

More importantly, could she go, give herself to this man, body and soul, for it would be her soul if she went with him. He was fun to be with, he showed he cared by his actions, by bringing her home, offering to pay for his food. She liked the way he smelled, like a warm summer day when fields were in full bloom, a hint of musk mixed in. And there was no doubt she was attracted to him. His body turned her on like no one had ever before. Her body responded to his without thinking. The way he moved, with grace and strength at the same time, in tune with his body. His masculine body would cover her fully should he try to hold her, and she had always thought herself a little on the larger side. He made her feel like a pixie just standing next to him. And the erection he sported between his legs was full of promise, one that peaked her feminine side, one she was willing to consider, was not against wanting to see it and touch and feel it inside her body. She too felt a physical attraction to him, maybe even the beginnings of affection.

Could it turn to love, would it turn to love considering all of the changes she was facing if she took him up on his offer?

Radine came to a stop behind her, taking her shoulders in his hands, warm and heavy, yet gentle as he squeezed. He pressed gently against her, protective, yet his desire unmistakable. "McKenna?" He watched her face reflected in the glass of the window.

"I don't know what to say, Radine. It's so unbelievable, fantastic in reality. A big change you're asking for in so little time. Could you stay a few days longer, give me a chance to get to know you more?"

"I am sorry, little one, I cannot. My duties are pressing, I must return home soon."

"Would you return me, back to Earth, if things don't work out on Taburon?"

"We have not gotten to my planet and you are asking about returning here?"

"Radine, if you decided we weren't right for each other, what am I supposed to do? I'd be a stranger on a strange planet, I wouldn't fit in or belong. I would want to come home."

"We are right for each other. I know this," he argued against the hesitant look on her face. He sighed. "If it came to it, yes, I would make sure you are brought back here." He squeezed her shoulders. "But you must give me something in return." He could feel her tense, uncertain about just exactly he might want in return for his promise. One night in her bed, perhaps? While that might have suited him fine, he knew she wouldn't have agreed, and might have turned him down outright had he made the suggestion. He softened his voice and gently rubbed where he held her. "I would ask that you promise to give Taburon, and me, a chance. Do not go into this with your mind made up that you are not going to be happy, that I will discard you. I will not, you have my word."

"May I still have some time to think about it before I give you my answer?"

"Until the morning, that is all I can afford before I must return to my ship."

She nodded, twisting in his hands to face him. "You'll have an answer by the morning. If you don't mind, it's been a long day and I'm tired. I'll get you some pillows and blankets, you can have the sofa."

"I would like two things first. One matters not, but I wish to know. Are you a virgin?"

Her face reddened bright pink, a delightful color that swept down her chest. He smiled with reassurance. She blushed so prettily. With a deep breath of courage, she shook her head. "No." Well, that definitely left her out of the running, if the king was looking for a virgin. But a soldier could get by with a woman with experience, even if it was limited.

"Then I also want this," he warned her before he touched his lips to hers.

Oh. My. God! Being swept off your feet didn't even come close to the rush his kiss gave her. He molded his lips to hers, pressing lightly until she responded, lifting up on her toes to arch into him, her breasts pressed tight against his chest. His mouth was firm, sliding across hers, his tongue darting out to taste her lips, encouraging her to open. He wanted to explore her mouth, her taste, to let her come inside his mouth to feel him. She whimpered, her lips opening wide. He didn't hesitate, sweeping his tongue inside to plunder her warmth.

She was sweet even through the spices of the pizza, the cavern of her mouth soft, warm, and wet. Sucking her tongue, he danced his tongue with hers, mimicking the ancient dance between man and woman, one he would hopefully be soon engaging with this woman.

Radine's hands slid down her back, coming to rest on the upper curve of her arse, pulling her tight against his own body, letting her feel the fullness and strength of his cock between their bodies, his legs spreading apart slightly to let her better feel how much he wanted her. With his hands slipping further down, he grabbed the flesh of each full globe and squeezed, lifting her until she fit perfectly in the cradle of his hips, rocking her into his swollen member, the head of his cock tight against the vee of her legs. She moaned into his mouth as he plundered it.

McKenna was on fire, her heart was about to beat right out of her chest. Her breasts felt heavy, her nipples were hard points that abrased against her dress. She could feel moisture begin to gather between her legs and when he lifted her, setting her against his swollen cock where she could feel the tip pressed into her, she melted. Her body ached to have him, naked, around her, over her, inside her, doing things to her she had only dreamed about. Her blood pulsed, her breath caught, she melted into him like ice on a hot day. Her panties were getting wet, the warmth pooling in the material until it could no longer be contained and spread, leaking out the sides to coat her thighs.

Radine licked her lips, following the line of her jaw to the spot under her ear, nipping the delicate flesh there and pulling lightly. He lifted her higher, bracing his legs further apart for support. He was breathing harshly, coming up for air only after he'd thoroughly explored her throat and the other side of her face with his lips and mouth. Radine paid special attention to the soft spot where her jaw and ear met, biting her gently, then soothing with a lick. His cock lengthened even further, more than he'd ever been before, hardening until he thought it would turn to actual stone, or burst, whichever relieved the pressure building in the shaft. He could feel himself weeping from the tip, fluid soaking into the placket of his trousers and cooling against his skin. McKenna threw her arms around his neck, giving him the chance to grab her thighs, lifting them to wrap around his hips, her pussy resting against his cock. He vowed to himself that he would take her like this one day, sinking into her fully and pumping until they both were spent. With her head thrown back, he accepted the invitation to nibble down her throat, heading towards her breasts.

As she pressed herself tighter against him, he let his hands slide around her thighs, feeling the part of the soft delicate skin he'd caught a glimpse of earlier. Mindless, she didn't protest when his fingers slipped even further along the inside of her thighs until he could feel the heat of her pussy, then the moisture of her juices that wetted the material covering her sweet spot. Radine lightly rubbed against the material, pressing it into her pussy, the lips swollen, her clit bulging. She squeaked softly when he touched her, lifting, her body tightening and he withdrew, not wanting to scare her off by moving too fast. He moved his hands to grab her thighs, squeezing.

Her moan pulled him out of the haze in which they were wrapped. Pulling back, he took a deep breath, letting her slide down gently, her arms unlocking as her feet touched the floor. Radine still held her, his arms enclosing her, holding her tight against his own body, his erection full next to her belly. Her head rested against his chest where she could hear his heart thumping in his breast. "I knew it would be good between us," he murmured, the sound a deep rumble against her ear. "If that is what happens with just a kiss…" he added, bending to show her once more how he could devastate her as he swept her into a kiss.

A moment later, Radine released her, pushing her back by the shoulders. His eyes were closed and he took deep breaths, his head hung

60

down slightly until he got himself under some semblance of control. "I will lose control if I continue," he explained to her confused look. He rubbed a thumb across her lips, swollen from his kisses, wet and red. "You should flee before I do something I will regret," he advised. "Go, get your pillows and blankets and leave me to my misery." He pushed her further from him. "You look beautiful, your lips kiss swollen. I can feel the heat of your arousal from your body. I hope you enjoyed that as much as I."

"I won't be able to get to sleep too soon," she confessed softly. "You're a dangerous man, Radine, and you don't play fair."

He grabbed her hand before she could flee and pressed it flat against his clothed cock. 'Oh my God,' she thought, 'he is hard and thick and so very big. So very tempting.' Many hours would pass before he would shrink to a comfortable level. "You are not alone, McKenna Primm. I have never been this hard for a woman before, and I know this will take a long time to settle. Go, now, while I still retain some sanity about you."

Chapter Six

Radine would have sworn the Earth had stopped rotating during the night, the hours dragged until he could stand it no more and he slid from the couch, groaning as strained muscles protested from the rigor into which they had set from the uncomfortable piece of furniture.

McKenna had rushed to her room to grab bedding for him, dumped it on the couch then disappeared as though *stelar* hounds were on her heels. The door to her room did not slam though, but closed with a definitive click. Radine reached for the placket of his trousers to relieve the pressure, opening it so his cock could find freedom from its confines. Wrapping his hand around his cock, he gently stroked it, the member sensitive, his breath drawing in in a hiss. Looking around, he remembered the kitchen and strode there, cock in hand. Unless he found some relief, there would be no sleep for him. So he stood by the sink and worked his shaft, scrubbing up and down, pulling his testicles free with his other hand to fondle and roll the heavy sacs. Not as good as having her play with him, no way close to actually being able to sink into her balls deep, but the pictures he generated in his head were sufficient to bring him to completion as he emptied himself into the sink. Once the last drop of seed fell from the end of his cock, he ran the water to wash it down, wetted a towel to gently wipe himself, then went back to the living room, his cock hanging loose, turning out the lights as he left the room.

He spread a blanket on the seat of the couch and sat. Lifting one foot, he pulled off his boot, then the other, dropping both to the floor. Standing, he finished opening his trousers, shoving them down his legs and off his feet. Taburons as a people did not wear underclothing, and Radine was no exception. He grabbed his shirt, opened it at the neck, yanking it over his head in one move. Naked now, he stretched out as much as possible on the couch, tossing a blanket over his still heated body.

Hours later, Radine knew it was no good. The couch was way too short for him. He could choose to put a crick in his neck or hang his feet off the end of the couch. He honestly tried, but between the aftermath of kissing her, his reaction to the kiss, and the length of his body, he would never get any rest. In the morning he hoped to be returning to the ship with a wife, a woman he could closet himself with in his quarters and share nadryl the entire return trip. Jaima was competent enough to fly the vessel without him. He only had to come out long enough to get the ship started on its return voyage and then to show her Taburon from the sky before they landed.

Then the real trouble would begin, as soon as she found out he was the king for whom he was searching. He did not wish to deceive her to cause her harm, but he wanted a woman who wanted Radine, not King Radine, but would then accept him once he revealed the truth. McKenna was already scared about coming to Taburon, he didn't need to magnify that any more. Perhaps once he got her beneath him, hopefully to get her pregnant on the trip home, she would have little choice. She proved earlier that sex between them would be amazing, that he affected her strongly. He was not above using a little deceit and forcing biology to achieve his goals.

Rising, padding naked and barefoot, he first visited the kitchen. That iced tea was addicting. He would have to have the palace keep it on hand. Drinking directly from the container, he drained it and put it in the sink for washing. With the night vision inherent to his people, he did not need to turn on any lights as he walked down the hallway, stopping outside the bedroom door.

She was sleeping on her stomach, her arms flung out to the sides, her face turned to the side, the blankets up to her shoulder blades. Her breaths came in short puffs, her sleep disturbed by some dream, but not a serious one. He hoped she dreamed of him. By the bed on the floor lay her dress and panties. He picked up the flimsy silky garment, holding it up to his nose, taking a deep sniff. The scent of her feminine moisture was strong, a heady odor that proved she had been as aroused as he from the kiss. His cock hardened and lengthened, rising from the nest of hair at his groin to point directly at the object of his wanting. 'You'll get your chance,' he thought, 'just be patient.' Radine let the panties fall to the floor. She wouldn't need them on Taburon, let them lay.

Perching a hip on the mattress, he placed a hand on her shoulder. "McKenna," he called softly.

She woke instantly, lifting herself by her elbows to stare blearily at the shadowed figure at her bedside. Startled, she gasped loudly. Her brain was sleep fogged and she didn't remember for a moment the huge hunk of gorgeous manhood that she had given her sofa.

He placed a hand on her shoulder. "It is me," he said calmly. "Do not fear. I wish to ask a favor of you."

McKenna snapped on the bedside lamp, a dim light that only kept dark shadows at bay. "What?" Her breasts dangled underneath her, her nipples buried in the mattress. Radine was forced to take a deep calming breath before he could continue.

"I am going to kill myself on that couch before the night is through. May I share your bed?"

"You can have it," she said, starting to rise, keeping the sheet tucked over her breasts and under her arms.

"No, you do not have to give it up for me, you have done so much already. I would just simply share until the morning sun rises." He shot a glance downward. Her eyes followed his, then widened as even in the dimmed light she could make out his cock, thick, heavy and erect, standing up from his lap. He gave her a sheepish grin. "I promise I'll behave, and so will he."

"I have your word as a soldier?"

"You have it."

She scooted further to one side. "All right then. No hanky panky," she warned.

"No..?" he asked in confusion, giving his head a shake once then rising to go the other side of the bed. She swore she was going to go blind, watching him walk, his muscular body better than she imagined. He was buff all over, from his shoulders to his shins, front and back, his chest as sculpted as his shirt had hinted, his ass even better. He was hard perfection, including the large cock that swung as he walked, topping a set of extra-large egg sized balls. He was big all over, everywhere.

Lifting the blankets, he dropped onto the mattress, making it dip deeply, forcing her to grab onto something before she rolled into him. She was almost saddened to see him cover himself. One arm he tucked behind his head, the other rested on his hip, making ready to go to sleep as he kept his promise to behave. So much for him taking unfair advantage and ravishing her against her will. McKenna snorted, reaching out to turn off the light, settling back herself. While she appreciated that he was going to be a gentleman, there was a part of her that honestly wanted him to roll over, grab her and have his way with her, whatever way he wanted.

Earlier, McKenna had masturbated fast and furiously once she'd reached her room, not bothering to remove her panties, just shoving them down her legs as one hand slid between the swollen folds of her pussy while the other plucked at her breasts and nipples. She'd turned her face into a pillow to muffle her cry as she'd come hard. Exhausted, she'd collapsed onto the mattress, panting until her breathing slowed. With heavy limbs, she peeled her dress off and finished taking off her panties, leaving both on the floor. McKenna only had enough strength to pull the blankets up before dropping into sleep.

But now, how was she supposed to sleep with Adonis right next to her? Adonis and his staff of happy times. All of the times she listened in on the other woman in the office talk about their lovers, comparing techniques and equipment, none of it compared to the weapon Radine sported and wouldn't she have loved to be the one bragging? She wondered if it was because of his overall size, or were all the men on his planet similarly well endowed? McKenna wondered how she was going to fit all of that inside her if she went with him. She didn't care. If he used his cock the way he kissed, she'd die happy even as he split her open the first time.

McKenna huffed, thumping her head against her pillow, flipping the blankets unnecessarily. She shuffled under the blankets.

Radine rolled and pinned her with an arm over her waist. Her breath hitched. Was he going to fulfill all of her wanton wishes? "If you wish me to keep my promise, cease," he warned, his breath against her ear. McKenna instantly stilled, becoming a board. Radine sighed. "Relax," he ordered. "This is just as bad as the moving." Dragging her across the mattress, he pulled her next to him, draping a leg over one of hers, insinuating it between her thighs. McKenna could feel him, like a thick rod, poking into her hip. "Sleep."

She nearly vibrated with anxiety. "Are you kidding me?" she squeaked into the darkness.

"No. Sleep." McKenna huffed again, Radine tightened his hold in warning. He sighed. "Have you never slept with a man?"

"I told you I wasn't a virgin."

"That is not what I asked, McKenna. Have you never slept with a man, through the night, cuddling up to him, letting him hold you, absorbing his warmth and touch as you slept?"

Her head shook slightly. "No," she admitted. The few times she'd shared her body, the sex had been okay followed by a few minutes of coming down from that high, which she'd never thought all that high, and then he would rise, dress, thank her for a good time in a non-committal voice and leave. To never reappear. She'd always wondered what she'd done wrong, or what was wrong with her that she became unacceptable after that first time. Had she not done something he'd wanted, or had she done something he didn't want? Did she come off as too needy? Were her hips too big, her breasts not large enough? Did she say something he didn't like? Was it that she appeared that naïve, that she was easily taken advantage of, a prey to the sexual predator many men had become with the readily available number of women, an easy pussy in which to expend their lusts without conscience? Only after her few encounters did she come to terms with life and love as it was today. It didn't take much to convince her to put love and caring on the back burner, concentrating on just getting by day to day. Someday, she kept telling herself, someday.

Maybe, just maybe, that someday had finally come.

"Try this," he suggested. With his mouth close to her ear, so close that his voice was barely above a whisper, he spoke. "Close your eyes," he instructed and waited until she complied, lifting his head to check. Her eyelids fluttered down. "Think of the best place you want to be, picture it in your mind. Where is it? A flowered meadow, warm with sunshine? In front of a fire on a cold winter's day, curled within your favorite blanket? In a soft, warm bed, the covers wrapping around you like a lover? With a lover? Where are you?" She opened her mouth the tell him. "No, don't tell me, but be there. Feel it, pull it around you until there is nothing else but that. Now take a deep breath and hold it a second, let it out slowly and feel the tension go with it. Let it flow from your fingers and toes. Feel it leave like waves of light." Her chest expanded as she breathed deep while the whole time he'd been speaking one hand gently smoothed up and then down her arm. He could feel her body relax. "Now take another deep breath, even deeper than that last one, and let it out slowly. Stay in that wonderful place you have found." She did and found herself relaxing even more, her body starting to sink into the mattress. "Once again," he said, "deep breath, out slowly." She did and finally, her body completely sank into the bed and relaxed against his body, her legs releasing their tension and her hands unclasping. "Good girl," he whispered, placing a gentle kiss on her ear as he took his own deep breath and rested back. Continuing to breathe deep, she forced herself to relax, tuning into the warmth and security his body provided until she felt herself drift off. Radine, smiling, followed close behind.

Chapter Seven

McKenna woke at her usual time in the morning, remembering a few heartbeats later that she had no reason to rise to go to work, not having a job to go to. As her mind began to function, she felt her face warm when she realized she was not alone in bed. And just exactly how not alone she was.

Radine was tight against her, his front to her back, skin to skin, the heat of his body melting into her. His face was buried in her hair, his soft huffs of breaths sounding in her ear, tickling her hair with each puff. The arm he had draped over her waist now cupped one of her breasts, curled around it possessively, her nipple dead center in his large palm.

But it was his cock that had her flaming. Nestled in the split between the globes of her ass, were she to tilt her hips just so and swivel a little this way, he could enter her pussy with little effort. Even in his sleep, he was still a large man, he would fill her, stretching her inside like she'd never been stretched before. She had to accept that she wanted him, wanted to make love with him, spend her life with him even if all it meant was mind-blowing sex every day for the rest of her life. Waking next to him felt so right, so perfect, and she wasn't being selfish for wanting it. He had assured her that on Taburon, once wed, there was no bed hopping. Taburons mated for life.

His breathing was steady and even. Radine slept deep yet. As much as she wanted to remain nestled next to him, she needed to get her head together and get away from the temptation of his body. Slowly lifting his arm, she slid out from beneath it and scooted from the bed, pulling the blankets back into place. For a moment, she stood at the bedside staring down at the sleeping man. He was so gorgeous, his face relaxed in sleep, long golden eyelashes resting on his cheeks. His lips were slightly parted, his nostrils flared as he took each breath. McKenna felt so damned lucky that her car had broken down yesterday. She knew she was falling in love with him.

Finding clothes in her closet in the dark, she pulled on a pair of sweats and an overlarge shirt. First thing in the morning, McKenna needed coffee as much as she needed to breathe. Barefoot, she went to the kitchen, flipping on the light. Taking the instant from the cupboard, she filled a cup with water, put it in the microwave and heated it. Mixing the coffee grains, she added sweetener, then carried the cup to the living room.

His clothes were dropped on the floor, scattered around the couch. Putting her cup on one of the tables, she bent to pick up his shirt, running her fingers over the soft material. Holding it to her nose, she inhaled deeply. His scent permeated the garment, masculine and clean, heady. McKenna folded the shirt. Grabbing the trousers, she folded them as well, placing them on top of the shirt. Looking around, she could not find any underwear. The man dressed commando, a pleasant surprise. He'd be available for her whenever she wanted, no fumbling with layers of clothing. Folding the blankets, she set them aside as well before taking a seat on the sofa. She had to start thinking about what she was going to take with her to another planet, what was important enough that she had to have it with her.

McKenna jumped at the knock at her apartment door. She wasn't expecting anyone, especially at this time of the morning. "Who is it?" she called softly through the door.

"Open up, McKenna," Mr. Raymond demanded.

McKenna laid her head against the wooden door. Her good mood of a few moments ago fled faster than a race car. She had no desire to see or speak with her ex-boss. If he wanted to withhold her last paycheck, that was fine. There was no way he was going to lure her back into his clutches. She glanced over her shoulder. Hopefully, she could get rid of the man or if not, Radine would wake and maybe provide a buffer – if she let him in.

"What do you want?"

"I want to talk to you. Open up or I'll make such a fuss it'll draw your neighbors out."

She sighed heavily. She'd had such wonderful dreams last night, dreaming of days with Radine, exploring his world, nights of passionate loving. Right before she'd awakened, there had been two children in the dream, a boy the spitting image of his father and a little girl he would dote on shamelessly. Now Raymond showed up threatening to spoil her happiness. He pounded on the door.

McKenna twisted the lock. "I'll give you a minute, then you have to leave. I don't work for you anymore." She opened the door, hanging onto the frame, blocking him from entering. Raymond didn't care, shoving past her, ignoring that she tripped and nearly fell and only remained standing by grabbing for the door as he came to a halt in her living room.

He gave the room a dismissive glance. Her place was pitiful, ramshackle, a sorry excuse for a place to live. "I know you don't work for me. I have a different proposition for you."

Hanging onto the still open door, she waited for him to proceed. She hoped he'd get the hint and leave, that he wasn't too dense to understand. Instead Raymond pointed at the entryway. "You sure you want to let everyone know your business?"

McKenna sighed again, pushing the door shut, but not locking it. "You have one minute," she reminded him, facing the older man, crossing her arms over her stomach. She hoped he didn't notice that she wasn't wearing a bra. She didn't need his unabashed leering.

"I'll get right to the point. I want you. I think I made that clear yesterday. If you don't want to work for me fine. I'll pay you twice what you were making, set you up in a nicer place, get you new clothes. You just have to be there for me when I want you, to fuck you. And you don't have to do a single thing that's work, not even cook." His smile was predatory, confident, smarmy.

She stared at him dumbfounded. He'd just suggested she become his mistress – no, his whore – and he expected her to fall to her knees in gratitude? Did she come off as that needy? Or stupid? Her hands dropped as though suddenly weighted down. Disbelief crossed her face. "Are you kidding me?" she screeched. "You want me to be your whore? Wasn't I clear enough yesterday? I don't want anything to do with you, in any way, shape or form. No, not ever, never!" she finished. She swiveled on her heel and made to grab for the door.

Raymond was fast. Invading her space, he reached out suddenly and grabbed her by her hair, pulling her flush with his body, tugging until she cried out. His mouth smashed down onto hers in a brutal kiss. One hand groped across her shirt to find and mash her breast, squeezing painfully. Her efforts to push him away were futile, he keeping her off balance as he leaned over her pressing into her with his hips, forcing the head of his cock to grind against her body. If she hadn't been so frightened, she would have laughed – he was nothing compared to the man who'd just spent the night in her bed.

It was all she could do to not lose her footing and she knew if she ended up on the floor, he'd be on top of her in a heartbeat. Her lips were wet with spit when he lifted his head. "What are you going to do, little bitch? You think you'll get another job? I'll make sure you're living on the street in a box before that'll happen. You'll come crawling to me, begging to take you back. And you won't like the terms then," he promised viciously, spittle spraying from his mouth as he grabbed her other breast and squeezed until she whimpered.

Grabbing the hem of her shirt, he lifted it until her breasts were exposed, his eyes going directly to them to drool over them. "Nice tits," he spat, reaching out to painfully pinch the closest nipple, "and all mine. Just like your cunt. You'll spread your legs for me any time I want, you'll let me shove my cock inside you, in your cunt, in your ass, even your mouth, wherever I want to cum, and you'll take it and love it 'cause you need it, you whore. You women are all whores, needing a stiff cock in your holes." He pinched her nipple again, twisting it viciously, taking his anger out for her rejection on her sensitive nub. McKenna cried out as his nails dug into her flesh.

"You will unhand her, now!" came from behind the two of them, the voice full of threat

and menacing.

Raymond spun, dragging McKenna with him, her screech of pain loud in the room. She reached up to grab at her hair, but he'd tangled his hand in the soft strands. "Who the fucking hell are you?" Raymond demanded before he noticed exactly how naked the other man was. While he should have been intimidated by Radine's size, nearly a foot taller and at least fifty pounds heavier, and sporting a resting cock that would make any man jealous and every woman as wet as a pool, he had McKenna and was sure he could control the muscle man by controlling her.

Nor could McKenna hide her reaction to seeing full-frontal Radine in light that was better than a forty watt bulb. He was pure sex wrapped in a warrior package, vibrating with furied muscle. There wasn't a hair on his body except for what graced his head and covered the top of his sex to cushion his cock during intercourse. The chest that fronted his body was pure sculpted masculinity right out of a Greek statue. A lean waist dropped to trim hips and even tighter thighs that rippled with corded muscle. Below the knees, he had hard calves, strong ankles, and long, long feet. His balls were clean, large, pendulous sacs that swung heavily as he stalked his prey. Ridiculously, she knew she was in for a treat when they finally consummated their relationship. But for now, she had to get free of the bastard that held her by her hair, ripping strands of it free from her scalp.

"It matters not who I am," Radine answered calmly, a deadly tone in his voice. "You are hurting my McKenna. Let her go before you regret that you ever laid a hand on her."

Instead, his eyes darkening, Raymond shook the girl like a terrier did a rat. McKenna's eyes teared at the pain he was inflicting on her, sure he'd pulled a swath of hair loose. "Who is this prick? You sleeping with him? After you turned me down, bitch?" He gave her another vicious shake. She bit her lip to keep from crying out, a bead of blood blossoming on her lip.

Radine advanced slowly, deliberately, his hands clenching and unclenching, his body tightening in preparation for a fight. He wouldn't go easy on this man – he was abusing his McKenna, and from what he'd heard in the hallway before coming into the living room, this was the prick she had told him about last night. This Raymond appeared out of shape, using his weight to intimidate his woman, to control her through a tight hold on her hair. Even from where he stood, he could smell the sweat on the other's body, an unpleasant odor that emanated from people who didn't take proper care of their body.

"I will count to three. If you have not released her by then, I will not be responsible for the consequences."

"Bring it on, asshole," Raymond invited, reaching with a free hand behind his body to drag a knife from his waistband, previously hidden from sight. McKenna whimpered at seeing the knife. Would he cut her first, or stab Radine? Raymond waved the knife forward and back, twisting it so the blade gleamed in the muted sunlight from the window. He kept his eyes on Radine and they suddenly switched from absolute viciousness to mild horror as they narrowed, he finally recognizing the differences between them. "What the fuck are you?" he asked, at last taking note of the color of Radine's eyes and the fire that seemed to crackle in them.

"I am from Taburon. One."

"An alien?" Raymond asked shrilly. "A fucking alien? You fucked a fucking alien? " He shook her again, hard. McKenna was crying openly. He pressed the knife against her throat, scaring Radine, afraid that he meant to cut her throat. "Fucking whore bitch," Raymond snarled.

But he couldn't back down, wouldn't back down from protecting his McKenna. "Two."

"If I'd known you'd do animals, I would have taken you sooner and made you available to a whole bunch of horse hung men. Damn, McKenna, you would have brought in a pretty penny whoring for me." He gave her a vicious shake with her hair. She screamed with pain.

"Three," Radine said then sprang. He feinted to one direction then changed mid-stride, head butting the other man, both men tumbling to the floor, McKenna finally released from the hair rending pull, dropping like a rock and scooting out of the way as much as possible.

"Get off me, you bastard," Raymond said, his breath coming in gasps as the men rolled around the floor. A table tipped over, the lamp smashing to the floor. There were thumps and grunts, Radine punching at Raymond wherever he found an opening, trying to avoid the slashing from the knife, the two men dancing around each other. Raymond made it obvious that he would gladly cut off Radine's cock if given the chance, aiming his jabs low. Splitting apart, they both stood, facing each other, bent at the waist, sizing their opponent. Radine feinted to the right and Raymond lunged in that direction, but recovered fast enough that Radine could not avoid the sharp knife, feeling it slice along his bicep. Blood spilled out, dripping down his arm. Radine ignored it, it wasn't the first injury he'd ever gotten from a fight. McKenna cried out in alarm, reaching towards him. "Radine, be careful!" she cried.

Raymond laughed. "Got her good did you? Was she a good fuck? I hope so, since she's going to be your last. Don't worry, I'll make sure she doesn't miss a big cock between her legs." Raymond lunged, but Radine was ready for it.

Bending his body to the side, Raymond's knife missing cutting him at the waist, Radine grabbed the man in a headlock, squeezing until Raymond began to realize he was in real trouble, dropping the knife to claw at the tall man's arms, trying to pry them loose. His face began to turn red. It was soon darkening blue and purple as his air was cut off, his cheeks and eyes bulging in fear.

"Shall I kill him for you?" Radine asked McKenna. "I need only snap his neck."

McKenna stood on shaking legs, her face wet from tears, her body visibly quaking. She pushed her hair away from her face, shaking her head. "No. He's not worth it."

Radine squeezed a little harder, totally cutting off Raymond's air until he passed out. Letting the body fall to the floor, he stepped over it to go to his woman, wrapping her in his arms, giving her his warmth. "It's all right now," he soothed, "you're safe."

McKenna held onto him for a moment, sniffling, fighting the urge to break down completely in front of this man. She'd been so frightened, not just for herself but for Radine after Raymond had pulled out the knife. If he had killed the Taburon, she didn't know how she would have coped, she was falling so fast and hard for the big man. And then to be left at the mercy of her ex-boss, helpless as he did god only knew what to her, her body, letting anyone at her to satisfy his warped desires. Yet Radine had prevailed. She should have had faith in him, a large, muscled man who claimed to be a warrior, proving himself against a knife wielding madman while not only unarmed but naked to boot. And then to have no concern for himself and instead offer her comfort, calming her shaking body with a gentle embrace. He was so warm and strong, her hero in flesh and blood. Blood…he'd been hurt. She pushed away from him to grab his arm, studying his wound. "You might need stitches," she decided.

"Just wrap something around it to catch the blood. It can be repaired on the ship." He went to where his clothes were piled on a table and shook out his trousers. Sliding one leg into the garment, he looked up at her as he bent to shove his other foot into the second leg. "You are coming with me?" he asked, pulling the garment up over his hips.

"Yes, I am."

He took her by the shoulders, his trousers unfastened, holding her gently, comforting. "I am pleased, McKenna. You will not be sorry." Brushing a kiss across her lips, he gave her a rueful smile. "Get me something for my arm. I do not wish to bloody my shirt. It is one of my favorites." He smiled again.

She returned his smile with a wary one of her own, but nodded sharply before going to the bathroom. He'd pulled on his boots by the time she'd returned, the handle of the knife protruding from the top of his right boot, his face scrunched in pain. The wound was beginning to smart, shocked nerve endings screaming in protest at their violent abuse.

Dropping to her knees in front of him, she gently bathed some of the blood from the wound and his arm before slapping a large gauze square over it. Wrapping a towel around his arm, she tied it tightly, but not so tight as to cut off the circulation. "Thank you, little one. It is starting to hurt."

"I'm sorry you had to fight that man. I never should have let him inside."

"He was, as you said, a prick. I heard what he said, all of it, and he should be in prison. He is not fit to be called a man. A real man does not need to treat his woman as he wished to treat you." He grinned mischievously. "He probably has a small cock."

She giggled softly, holding her hand up, her thumb and first finger only an inch apart. "He does. I felt it when he pressed against me. Thank you, for that, and for saving me."

Radine reached out to finger-comb through her scalp. "Are you hurt?"

"I think he pulled a few hairs loose, but I'm fine."

"Such beautiful hair, it does not deserve to be treated so poorly." He kissed her again. "I enjoyed sleeping where I could smell your hair, feel it on my face." His look was downright lascivious. "I would have made love to you when I woke, had you been next to me."

She gave him the same look in return. "And I would have let you."

Gathering her close, Radine enfolded her in his embrace, reveling in the feel of her in his arms for a few moments. "Ah, little one, we need to go before the prick awakens. Though the thought of having him watch the way a real man loves his woman is worth giving it a moment."

"Don't even think about it, Radine," she warned. "I never want to see that man again, and he doesn't need to see me naked, ever."

"Very well, little one. Go get what you think you need for the trip. I will make sure you have Taburon clothes when we arrive, so don't bring much. I am sure that females are the same throughout the galaxy, bringing much more than they need, but please pack light. We will leave as soon as you are ready."

She stood, starting to turn to head to her bedroom, but faced him again, bending down to kiss him, a hand caressing his jaw. "I won't be long," she promised.

He waited until he was alone before connecting with the ship "Jaima."

"I am here, Your Majesty."

"We are leaving soon to return to the ship. Make sure our course home is plotted and confirmed, we'll break orbit as soon as we're on board. Have Sistan stand by as well."

"Is there a problem?"

"I was attacked, my arm has been sliced."

"I knew I shouldn't have let you go by yourself..." Jaima began to rant.

"Enough," Radine commanded. "Just have him stand by. Once we've left Earth orbit, you have control of the ship. I want to stay with my bride. Oh and Jaima."

"Yes, Your Majesty?"

"She still doesn't know about my being the king, so drop it. I'll tell her in my own time."

He could hear the chuckle in his friend's voice. "Of course, Your Majesty." Communications were cut before Radine could reply. The king smiled to himself. He'd get even, and soon. And he'd enjoy it, too.

When McKenna returned, she'd changed her clothes, wearing a pair of comfortable jeans and satin blouse. She carried a small bag, mostly toiletries, setting it on the floor by the door. Raymond was starting to come to as she moved to her bookcase, quickly scanning the titles. She pulled two thick volumes from the collection, grabbed her picture, the plant from yesterday and her purse. With an expectant look, she faced Radine, who'd risen when she'd come back to the room. "I'm ready," she announced.

He quirked an eyebrow. "That's all you're taking?" he asked in disbelief. His mother never traveled without at least four trunks, even when she'd be gone just a few days.

McKenna nodded. "Just a few toiletries and two changes of clothes, the picture of my family, my plant, a book on human anatomy,

85

which your people might need, and a dictionary. Of course, my purse. Did I forget something?" she asked expectantly.

He grabbed the small case and books. "No, I don't suppose you did. The prick is waking.

Let's go."

Chapter Eight

"Are you all right?" he asked as they approached his ship.

"Nervous," she admitted, her hand over her stomach. "I've never been on a space ship. I'm going to a new world, a new home, with a man I'm going to marry. That's a lot to process."

"If you have any questions, simply ask. I will do all I can to make the transition as easy for you as possible."

"Thank you, I know you will." She looked out the shuttle window, the vastness of stars stretched out before them, a small silver speck hanging in the void that he had pointed out as being the ship. It grew larger as they approached.

"Taburons have been traveling in space for several generations now. It is safe."

"But your planet isn't in Earth's solar system. How will we get there in so short a time?"

"Have you ever heard of wormholes?"

"No."

"Eons ago, a race that no one can name nor can they remember traveled through the universe by creating tunnels, or wormholes, to decrease the amount of time needed to travel from one galaxy to another. They still exist and once found, can be utilized by other space travelers for the same purpose. The first non-Earth people to visit your planet used one, and shared the coordinates with those of us who share in the goals of peaceful relations with people of other worlds. Your people, in the future, when they have matured and developed space travel will also use them. By making precise calculations, we can control our destination. It will take us two of your days to reach Taburon after using this corridor. Without it, our children's children children would be old and feeble before they would arrive. I for one prefer my home on Taburon to living the rest of my life in space."

"How old are you?" she asked.

"I am thirty four of your Earth years of age. A Taburon year is slightly longer." He grinned. "Fair's fair. How old are you?"

"Twenty-eight."

He took one of her hands in his. "We will have a long life together," he promised. He stared into her eyes for a moment, reluctantly dragging himself away before drowning in their depths. "Look," he indicated.

Facing forward, she felt her breath catch in her chest. The ship was beautiful, sleek and powerful looking as it hung in space. Not saucer shaped, instead it was shaped like a long cylinder, dolphin appearing, as though it was meant to cleave through the emptiness of space as a dolphin did through water. There were lighted portholes along the side they could see and a single large viewing port cut across in front. There were engine nacelles at the back of the ship. Lights blinked steadily around the vessel.

As they neared, a portion of the hull opened large enough for the shuttle to enter, closing behind them as Radine set the shuttle down on the floor of the bay. McKenna could hear a hissing noise as the gravity and atmosphere was restored in the bay and Radine cut the engines, turning the shuttle off completely. "Ready?" he asked, noticing the contingent of men that entered the bay and began to line up outside the shuttle, welcoming their king back on board. He easily picked out Jaima and the physician when they entered, strolling between the two lines of men.

McKenna took a deep breath, her hand at her chest, reminding him of the first time he'd seen her in her car. She nodded, her confidence restored by his smile and the squeeze he gave her hand. Punching at the yellow button, the shuttle doors opened.

"Leave your things, they will be brought to you. Come meet Jaima, my second in command and best friend." He climbed out, hurrying around to take her hand, wrapping an arm around her waist to guide her. He could feel her quivering with anxiety, but she took another deep breath, forcing herself to calm. "Good," he complimented. She would face the unknown with bravery.

Jaima bowed. "Welcome back, *Sthula*," he greeted. The man with him also bowed as the contingent of men straightened sharply. They all wore swords belted to their sides.

"Thank you, Jaima. This is McKenna Primm, my wife to be."

Jaima bowed to her as well. "Welcome aboard the *Veleda*, my lady. I thank you for deciding to take my friend and brother for a husband. If you ever want to hear about his bad bachelor days, please feel free to ask." Were Radine not standing next to her, had she not met him yesterday, she would have considered the man he called Jaima an absolutely gorgeous man. He also had long dark honey blonde hair, as did the third man – perhaps it was a species trait – and he stood slightly taller than Radine. The uniform he wore could not hide the sculpted muscles beneath, his chest thick, as were his thighs and arms. There was a sparkle in his eyes as he perused McKenna, an amusement she didn't understand just yet, a silent sort of communication between the two men that only they understood. If Radine considered him his friend and brother, then she was willing to give him the benefit of the doubt and accept him as a friend as well. And it had been a long time since she'd had a brother.

McKenna giggled softly, feeling Radine tense at his friend's outrageous offer. "Thank you, Jaima, I shall keep that in mind."

A bit of possessiveness took over Radine as he leaned close to her ear. "If I ever catch him telling tales, I shall certainly beat him senseless." She tossed him a shocked glance, then looked to Jaima. The second man was smiling broadly, alleviating her fears that Radine would actually do what he promised. Radine addressed the other man. "Sistan, I need you to look at my wound."

"Of course, *Sthula*. I have prepared Medical for you."

"Jaima, McKenna brought some things with her, if you would put them in my quarters while I go with Sistan."

"It shall be done, *Sthula*."

"Make ready to head home, my friend. I will take your report when I am through in Medical and after I have settled McKenna."

Jaima bowed again. "As you wish, sir." McKenna didn't miss the warning look Radine sent to his friend as they followed the physician. Jaima bowed to her, his smile leaving as he began to tend to matters though his eyes never left off following the young woman.

Sistan had him remove his shirt then sit on a chair as he began unwrapping the towel. Radine hissed when the physician pulled the gauze from the wound, dried blood having glued it to the injury. "How did this happen?" he asked as he worked.

"My *Sthulae* was being accosted by a prick. When I stepped in, we got into a fight and he sliced me." Radine pulled the knife from his boot to pass to the physician, its blade still blooded.

Sistan perused the instrument for a moment, then set it aside. He would examine the blade later, test it for germs. "You allowed yourself to be sliced so easily?" he asked with disbelief. The king was a seasoned and well-trained warrior.

"I was careless and for one moment, he was faster than I."

The physician turned to gather material from a tray he'd placed near. "And what, may I ask, is a prick? Is it some kind of animal?"

"*Tritio,*" Radine mumbled with disgust.

The physician shot him a glance, then went back to his equipment. *Tritio* was the word they used for someone who deserved nothing more than hanging - just because. Soaking a piece of material with a green liquid, he began to clean the wound.

"Gods' rods!" Radine shouted, his entire body tensing. He came close to jumping up from the chair. "What is that stuff?"

"You should know. Never good to tangle with a knife, never know what they've been used for, besides stabbing people."

"*Whemin?*"

"What else would you use on a wound if you wish to prevent infection?" He continued to clean the wound. "Now sit still." Radine followed his instructions, but grumbled the entire time, never passing up a chance to complain. "Take note, my lady, your man is no better than an infant when it comes to getting hurt."

She laughed softly. "Aren't they all?" she asked, smiling at him indulgently.

"Sadist," Radine replied. He hissed louder when the physician probed the injury, making sure there was no internal damage that needed more intensive care.

Satisfied the wound was clean enough, Sistan grabbed a metal instrument. Pointing it at the wound, he pushed a small button on the side. A blue light shot out of the end, covering the open gash on his arm. Slowly, the wound began to close, the edges pulling together, until the entire thing was sealed. With the light off, a long incision remained, closed, reddened, but sealed. McKenna watched in wonder. There was nothing like it on Earth. How many lives might have been saved if their medical community had a device that sealed wounds.

Sistan wrapped the injury with white material. "Keep that clean and dry. Give your arm a rest, don't do anything strenuous with it for at least a week. How is the pain?"

"I can manage it."

"If you can't let me know immediately. I shall send a report to your physician at home so he might keep an eye on the injury."

"Thank you, Sistan."

"I want to see it again tomorrow."

"I'll make sure to stop by," he promised.

Sistan bowed. "As you wish, Sthula Radine."

Radine escorted her out, his arm around her waist again, leading her through the corridors. Each Taburon they passed stopped and bowed in Radine's direction until he'd passed by.

"Why do they do that?" McKenna asked.

"I am their captain. It is a show of respect."

"How long have you been the captain?"

"Since this ship was built, well over ten years. It was made for me." They turned down corridor after corridor, climbing into an elevator to plummet down until she became hopelessly lost. Once the doors opened, they walked through the corridors again for several minutes.

"How big is this vessel?"

"It is the largest in the fleet. Big enough to hold one thousand soldiers and all of their arms, or one thousand, five hundred non-fighting personnel, such as now. In times of peace, like now, we mostly use it for transporting goods from our planet to other planets, or for shipping necessities to Taburon."

"So you spend a lot of time in space?"

"Not really. Jaima is quite capable in flying this ship, and there are others as well. I only come on important trips, like the one I just completed."

"You were supposed to find a bride for the king," she remembered.

"I think he'll be satisfied with what I discovered," Radine assured coming to a halt in front of a cabin. "These are my quarters," he explained. "It is one of the best protected places on the ship." The door slid to the side and he invited her to precede him, waiting in the doorway for her response.

His quarters were huge, as large as the workroom she'd spent most of her working life in before getting her own office. They entered into a sitting area, couches and chairs spread around in a conversational circle, a table between them. There was a statue of some sort in one corner, a large plant in another. Paintings were hung on the walls, scenery most likely of Taburon. She would study them another time. To the left of the seating area was a long table, six chairs surrounding it, a conference center.

To the right she spied the sleeping area. A large bed took up most of the area, king-sized, plush with pillows and thick blankets, raised on a platform that he would easily be able to climb into, but she would need a step stool or short ladder. Six humans could easily fit on it, but she could see how he might take up the entire bed if he wanted. Tables graced either side of the bed, each holding a lamp. In each corner by the lamps were potted plants, six feet tall at least with large elephant ear like leaves. Facing the bed was a dresser of sorts, a tall piece of furniture that had drawers. Over it was a mirror. Beyond the dresser a door lead into an expansive bath, polished stone on the floor and walls. The shower was bigger than her entire bathroom had been in her apartment. At the foot of the bed waited her small bag, the books piled on top. Her small plant looked lost on top of the dresser and someone had thoughtfully placed the picture of her family next to the plant so she could see it from the bed.

Radine covered her shoulders with his hands. "Does it meet with your approval?"

"It's beautiful," she breathed softly. "Your entire ship is beautiful."

There was delight in his expression as he folded her in an embrace, her body melding into his, his reaction easily predictable. Nuzzling her hair, he took a deep sniff. Whatever the scent, he loved it, reminding him of being in the middle of the gardens at the palace when the flowers were in full bloom, sweet, spicy, heady. His hands wandered along her back, up and down her spine, slipping below her hips to pull at her buttocks, lifting her until she stood on tip toe.

McKenna did her own nuzzling, her face buried in his chest, his scent erotic. Like a warm rain or a Turkish bazaar, he filled her senses with a rich aroma of sex and command all at once. If he used some sort of cologne, wow. If he didn't, well…He was off the charts and needed to be packaged and sold. His nipples had tightened into hard buds, his muscles flexed as he smoothed his hands along her spine before bunching to lift her by her rounded gluteal flesh.

His mouth found hers, plundering her in a kiss that demanded she give him everything she had and more, promising he would give all back to her. With his tongue he enticed her to open her lips to let him in, their tongues tangling. He could taste the remnants of the coffee she had had before Raymond had appeared, the remainder of the cup forgotten in the ensuing fight and flight. His head tilted from one side to the other as he explored, breathing in deeply the scent of her arousal as she fell under the spell of his kiss. One of her legs lifted, seeking to wrap itself around his thigh, opening her legs to permit him to rest his swollen cock against her aching, needy pussy. Gathering handfuls of plump flesh, he brought her higher against his body, tilting his hips until she lay in the cradle of his groin.

"McKenna," he murmured against her mouth "I must go." He breathed deeply, slamming his mouth to hers. "I have to see Jaima about his report." His mouth said one thing, but his body made a lie out of every word. He wasn't releasing her one iota.

"Stay," she whispered. "I can't take you leaving me like this again." She finger combed his hair, locking her hands behind his neck, pressing her lips like a lamprey to his.

"Gods' rods, woman," he groaned. "Jaima can wait. I am the captain." Lifting her bodily, he gave her a little toss towards the bed.

Chapter Nine

She landed with a soft thwump and squeal, laughter bubbling up as he stood at the foot end of the massive bed, peeling his trousers from his body, toeing his shoes off first. His turgid cock was thick and heavily veined, lifting straight out from his groin, pointing him in the direction he wanted to go, needed to go, having no choice in the desire to go straight to her. Never taking his eyes from her, they turned dark gold and glittered with passion, sparks nearly shooting out of them as he crawled onto the bed and stalked her.

Stretching out above her, he resumed the attack on her mouth, balancing on his uninjured arm as the other crept under her shirt, pulling the garment free from her jeans. Radine's hips nestled against the junction of her legs, forcing her to part her thighs to accommodate his large body. He left off from her mouth long enough to jerk the shirt, unbuttoned, over her head and off her arms, dropping it to the floor.

There was wonder in his gaze at her bra. Tracing the outlines of the restraint with a finger, he smoothed along the tops of her breasts, into the hollow between them. Her skin was soft and warm, perfect, dark pink and flushed with passion. "What is this thing?" he asked.

"A bra. It holds my breasts so they don't jiggle too much."

"Your breasts are firm and beautiful. Too beautiful to hide behind this bra. And a man likes to see his woman's breasts jiggle, her nipples hard and pointed, knowing they are hard for him and free for him to touch any time." He perused the garment. "How does it come off?"

She giggled and arched her back, reaching behind to unhook her bra. Once it was loose, Radine pulled it free, holding it up to study for a moment. He frowned before discarding it to the floor as well. "No more bra," he ordered. He would see to it that the offending garment was tossed in with the garbage and jettisoned into space.

He couldn't take his eyes from her breasts now that he had them bared to him. "These are beautiful, so round. Your nipples are perfect berries, red and swollen." Her nipples perked up at his words, hardening into stiff points. "So responsive, that they harden without my having touched them. But not hard enough, I think, not yet."

That was her only warning as Radine's mouth descended to her left breast, taking the nipple with his teeth. With his tongue, he flipped the hard nub to even harder proportions, pulling it with his teeth until they pulled off of the hard nub. Thoroughly wetted, his lips enclosed the entire areola, sucking like a child starved until she arched her back, lifting her breasts higher, begging for more. He released her nipple with a popping sound, staring down at the flesh, a satisfied gleam in his eyes. Flattening his tongue, he swiped it across the tip of her breast then blew softly.

Turning his attention to her other breast, he repeated the entire process until both nipples were hard and achy, straining towards him. "Beautiful, sweet," he murmured, placing a kiss on each one. He lifted his gaze to her face, her eyes hazed in passion. "No more bra," he repeated. McKenna nodded.

Radine kissed and licked his way down her body, nibbling her skin until he reached her belly button where he delved inside, swirling his tongue around, thrusting in mimicry of the sex act. His hands caressed her body as he moved over her, plumping her breasts, squeezing the tightened nipples before flowing over her stomach and around her waist.

McKenna was in heaven. Her previous lovers had never spent as much time stimulating her body as Radine did, giving her quick pecks for kisses, tweaking her nipples once or twice, swirling their fingers around her pussy to make sure she was wet enough to thrust into her. They had been 'wham, bam, see ya later,' leaving her wanting and unfulfilled. After her second experience in much the same manner, she'd given up on trying find a sexual partner who gave as much as he took, vowing celibacy. Until Radine.

Now, he lit her on fire, her body hummed, her blood didn't flow but instead raced through her. The sensation of his mouth on her breasts, tugging tightly on her nipples, went straight to her pussy, her channel flooding. Her legs scissored open then closed. Each time they parted it allowed him to sink further against her and she wanted so much to have him do something, anything, more. Even the barrier of her jeans couldn't prevent the tingles that zipped through her pussy. She wanted them off.

But he was in control, his body pinning hers to the bed as he wandered around it, kissing, licking, tasting, wetting her skin with his tongue then blowing on the wet spots to take her from hot to cold in seconds yet setting her on fire. He growled as he came to her jeans, fumbling with the button and zipper, neither opening fast enough to suit him.

Grabbing the edges of the opened split, he ripped the garment in one rending tug, lifting his body up far enough to shove the pants down her legs, pushing them off with one of his feet. Left in her panties, he studied them for a moment. Taburon women did not cover their pussies with such material, but the satin and lace intrigued him.

The garment did very little to hide her pussy, nor the wet spot in the center of the part that covered her between her legs. It covered her mons, puffing slightly because of the mat of hair below, cupping lovingly along the sides where her thighs met the lips of her genitals. He could smell her arousal, the core of her body oozing out, hot and a little salty, like the ocean on a warm day. Swiping his finger along the wet spot, he pushed it against her flesh, rubbing circles over her clit, the material harsh on her sensitive nub. McKenna groaned, lifting her hips slightly in offering, pleading.

Slipping his finger under the leg band, he pulled the material away from her pussy, revealing it to his gaze for the first time. While not shaved bald, McKenna did keep the hair trimmed neatly, an inch wide swath that arrowed to the heart of her sex. Radine pet her gently, the hair a novelty, something he would have taken care of when they got home. For now, he found the rough curls fascinating as he parted them with his hands to reveal the rest of her treasures.

Her outer lips were pink, the inner ones pinkish purple, both swollen with desire, covered in moisture. Her clit pulsed, peeking out from its hiding place at the top of her slit. With two fingers of one hand he parted the lips more. The other fingers pulled the hood higher, exposing her clit more. That thumb gently touched the nub, flicking over it. He grinning as it throbbed and grew harder, longer. Wetting it with her juice, he continued to torment the little organ, her hips jerking up and down.

He glanced up along her body to watch her as he played. Her face was flushed, her eyes filled with lust and need. She kept lifting her breasts towards the ceiling, seeking, wanting, needing…They shuddered with every breath. Her lips were parted. "Radine," she breathed, "please, I need…"

"What do you need, little one?" he asked.

Her head lifted. Her eyes were dark with passion, her lips swollen from her biting at them. Her chest rose and fell in panting breaths, her breasts jiggling with each breath. "You," she demanded hoarsely, "I need you."

His return grin was devilish. "Soon, little one, soon. Once I have done playing, making you so wet, so needy, so thoughtless with want, I will give you what you want." And with that, he closed his mouth over her clit.

McKenna creamed and keened at the same time. His lips sucked at her, his tongue flitted over the hard nob of her clit, soothing then with long, luxurious licks that went from the very bottom of her slit to the very top. Radine curled the tip of his tongue to gather her moisture, smacking his lips as though it were a delectable treat. "Delicious," he murmured. "I could spend all day here and never be satisfied." He licked again, long and slow, swirling around her clit, holding it with his lips, nipping tenderly, then again soothing until she was mindless, her hips thrusting faster.

Radine pinned her legs with his arms, still holding her open to his torment, stilling her so he could enjoy at his leisure. Finding the opening to her body, his speared into it with his tongue, over and over.

Still not satisfied that she was ready for him, and curious himself as to how well she would take him, he inserted one finger into her pussy, slow, slower, slowest, deep until he could go no further.

"Tight, McKenna, you are so tight. You will hold my cock like a warmed glove. So wonderful." Radine added a second finger, pumping her with even strokes, entering a third finger into the mix after a moment.

McKenna sighed as he drove into her with three fingers, then squealed when he spread those fingers, stretching her, pulling out to add his fourth finger. "Oh, god, Radine," she hissed, "so full. Please, I want you in me. Fuck me, please."

"What is this word, fuck?" he asked, slamming his fingers into her pussy, twisting his hand. "That human used it at your home. What does it mean?"

McKenna needed a moment to gather her wits, trying to ignore what he was doing to her body, her voice rasping and harsh. "Sex," she ground out. "Your cock inside me and pumping until we come."

"I do not like that word," he growled. "It is crude and distasteful. On Taburon we make love or share *nadryl*. We do not fuck."

"Then *nadryl* me, and quickly," she demanded, "before I lose my mind. I'm so close, I need to come soon or I'll explode."

Radine chuckled, leaning back. "Very well, then." He swiped across his mouth, cleaning the moisture that had gathered on his chin. Rising to his haunches, he grabbed her by the hips. "Turn over," he ordered. "On your hands and knees, your hips in the air." He helped her to twist around, pushing down at her shoulders, raising her hips with a hand between her legs and lifting her by the crotch. With a single tug on either side of the panties, he tore them apart, discarding the pieces to the floor. "Spread your legs, wide, McKenna. I am a large man, penetration will be easier if I come at you this way." McKenna opened her legs, he forced her to spread them further until she felt the tendons in her thighs burn with the tension.

Grabbing the twin halves of her ass, he spread the cheeks wide, gazing at her charms. She nearly dripped with moisture, her pussy lips swollen and glistening. The rosebud of her anus winked at him once and he found himself looking forward to the time when he might penetrate her there, knowing she would be painfully but deliciously tight around his cock.

Bending slightly, he faced his goal and sniffed deeply. She was so aroused that the smell of her sex was strong. With his tongue, he licked from her clit to her anus, the juice in which she was covered sweet to his taste. Someday soon he would take time to bring her to orgasm just by licking her on her pussy, but he would take his time doing it. For what fun would it be if she came too quickly, but begged as he brought her close to her peak multiple times before driving her over?

Moving up behind her, placing his knees between her thighs, his grabbed his cock by the root and swirled the bulbous head around her pussy, wetting it with her abundant moisture. He leaned back slightly, scooting forward more, separating her legs even further, took aim and penetrated the entrance to her body with the heavy knob of his cock, her flesh parting easily. She closed around him so tightly he feared she would nip off the head of his cock. McKenna screeched, grabbing a fistful of the bed covers and pulling them to her mouth to muffle her cries.

Using his legs as a lever, Radine rose, parting her folds more, sinking more of himself inside her. "Gods' rods, you are tight," he ground from between his clenched teeth. She had him in a vise like grip, her sheath hot and wet. Falling back onto his haunches, he pulled out slightly, then rose again, more of his cock going into her. After several repetitions, penetrating deeper before pulling out slightly, he finally seated himself fully inside her, relishing how she tightened on him, quivering. He waited for several heartbeats, letting her adjust to his size.

Radine grabbed her by the hips. Flexing his buttocks, he started to piston her, slowly until she adjusted, increasing the pace when she began to shove back at him, wanting more. Her sensitized nipples scraped across the rougher material of the bedspread, abrasive and making them more sensitive. With a strong, furious pace, he thrust into her, laying over her back, one hand searching through her folds until he found her clit. Pinching the nub, he held it tightly, cutting off the blood supply. His other hand found a nipple and grabbed it, pinching it tightly, dragging it towards the mattress to stretch it until she felt he was going to pull it off, but the pain went straight to her pussy. His hips moved powerfully, drawing his cock out to the tip, then slamming back in deeply to kiss her cervix.

After a moment, he released her clit and nipple. The flow of blood back into the buds was painful in a pleasurable way and McKenna screamed as she fell over the edge into her first and greatest orgasm ever. Her sheath fluttered, the muscles spasming on his cock. With a yell, Radine buried the head of his cock tight against her womb and exploded in her, pumping shot after shot of cum against her cervix. Hot fluid bathed the mouth of her womb as he emptied himself, thrusting forward with every pulse, punctuating each thrust with a grunt.

Emptied, he rested over her back for a moment, then rose, his softening cock pulling out of her. His hands smoothed up her sides, taking her by the waist as he dropped to his side next to her. He settled McKenna beside him, her back to his chest. They were both still panting. Cupping a breast, he placed a kiss at the back of her neck.

"Are you all right?" he asked. His hand tightened on her breast and he was pleased by the shudder that ran through her.

"You can nadryl me anytime," she managed between pants.

Radine chuckled softly, his breath tickling the back of her neck. "I shall do my best," he promised.

His chuckle turned to a husky laugh when her stomach rumbled loudly. McKenna flushed. With a final squeezed to her captured breast, he rose, standing by the side of the bed as she rolled to face him. "I must speak with Jaima," he said. "I will have an attendant bring you some food shortly. I cannot give you pizza, but you will enjoy Taburon food." Bending, he picked up his trousers. "Feel free to use the shower," he offered. "By tomorrow, I shall have new clothes made for you. Until then, I like the way you look right now, naked, satiated, open, and waiting." He placed his hands on the mattress to lean towards her. Bussing her lips, he grinned against her mouth. "I do not wish to leave you, you look so inviting, but I must attend to my duties. Stay here, rest. I won't be long." He opened one of the drawers in the bureau, pulled out a clean shirt and trousers and sauntered into the bathroom. By the time he'd finished showering, she'd fallen into an exhausted sleep, sprawled over the bed in wanton appeal. Taking a blanket from his closet, he draped it over her body. Shaking his head, telling his cock to bide its time, he left for the bridge.

Chapter Ten

The bridge was its usual well-run self when he entered. Jaima, sitting in the captain's chair, rose as soon as Radine stepped up behind the seat. Radine dropped into it with a heartfelt sigh, his friend taking a position next to his captain and king.

"Are you all right?" Jaima asked. His smirk showed that he knew what had kept the other occupied up to now.

An aide immediately placed a cup of cold liquid at his king's side. Radine took a hefty gulp before answering. "I am pleased to be going home, and with a bride that I find most delightful."

"I assume she has satisfied you then?"

"More than enough, my friend. My lonely nights are over, my bed will be quite well used."

"Then I am happy for you, Your Majesty."

Radine's gaze was plotting, studying his friend. "Maybe once I have settled with my queen, you can return to this Earth and find a woman for yourself."

Jaima bowed. "No offense, Your Majesty, but I have no interest in shackling myself down with a woman."

"You would be content to spend the rest of your life with the pleasure skalas?"

"As long as I have coin to pay…"

Radine laughed, smacking Jaima on the shoulder. "We'll see, my friend, we'll see." The king faced forward. "Where are we?"

"We shall enter the corridor in three minutes, Your Majesty. It is estimated our journey will take six hours to complete. Then we are two days from Taburon."

"Good, good. I shall hear the rest of your report in a moment, but I need food taken to McKenna. She has not eaten since rising this morning. Make sure there is enough for two. I have not eaten either. Do we still have some of my mother's dresses on board?"

"I believe so."

"Have a steward take an armful of them to McKenna to choose from. He can adjust them if they need. Remind them to knock before entering our quarters. McKenna was asleep when I left."

"I shall see that it is done," Jaima promised.

"And Jaima, do not forget, she does not know yet."

The other bowed. "I shall remember, sir." Jaima went to a station behind the captain's chair as Radine turned his full attention to the instruments and crew before him. He would stay on the bridge until they entered the wormhole and were stable within it, then head back to spend more time with McKenna. Now that he'd had a taste of her, he wanted more. He was like a man who'd go to long without a meal and was starving. How he could have felt such an emotional attachment for this woman so soon he didn't understand, but she filled a hole in him he'd not known was there until he'd met her.

All of the women before McKenna, he now realized, were but passing indulgences, a way to fulfill a need, take care of certain tensions, pass a pleasant night. But McKenna…McKenna was days of loving, days of conversation. Days of walking through the palace gardens hand in hand. Days of watching children grow. And nights of gentle caresses, soft touches, deep kisses and even deeper thrusts into a warm, wet, and tight body with a hard cock until both reached the ultimate pinnacle of pleasure. She was forever, until the day they parted through death and even then joining in whatever afterlife might exist for their souls beyond there. He would protect her and love her and give her everything she wanted within his power.

And she would give back to him the love he'd been wanting, easing the loneliness, being there when he felt at his best, and worst. She would give him children – he hoped – a legacy for the future, a continuance of his family and his rule, the simplicity of childhood that he'd never really had a chance to experience since he'd been the only child and groomed for the throne that he would someday inherit. He would learn to play again, children's games, not the adult ones he indulged in now. And he would teach his children everything it meant to be a Taburon, a warrior or a lady, to someday be a ruler, a kind and compassionate person who the people would love as they did him.

Yes, life was good now, and was promising to become better every day, the closer they came to home and he got to wedding the woman he'd found and discovered to be his perfect mate. He took another sip of his drink as he rested back into his command chair, stretching his legs out in front of him. Yes, life was good.

Chapter Eleven

Radine held McKenna close to his side as the ship approached Taburon. She was shivering, but not violently, more in excitement, her anxiety controlled by his nearness. Her eyes were wide with wonder.

Taburon was a blue and golden planet, sporting hints of green through the breaks in the golden yellow clouds that covered about a third of its surface this day. She could see several continents separated by turquoise oceans. One side of the planet was in darkness but lights from cities sparkled into the night. The ship made for the day side of the planet where a space port hovered miles above the planet's surface. Radine had explained that the ship could not land on the surface, but they would dock at the port and take a shuttle down to the city where he had his home.

The docks were huge. Several ships were harnessed already to the sides of the space station, but Radine's ship bypassed all of them to come to a halt in front the largest station. From the bridge they could hear the clang of metal as the ship connected with the station, locking mechanisms falling into place to hold it tightly.

As one, the crew on the bridge bowed to their captain and king, a blush rising furiously up his throat. McKenna's quizzical look said it all as he returned an embarrassed expression her way.

"McKenna, there is one more thing I need to confess," he said, repentance in his voice.

They had spent the past two plus days in close companionship. Radine had taken her all through the ship, his pride in his vessel obvious as he showed her around. She greeted each of the crew with smiles, asking about their jobs on the ship, listening with interest. Radine could not have been more happy. Her genuine interest meant that she would be interested in his people and planet, which would lend to her being a great queen.

He told her about Taburon. The planet was believed to be twice as old as Earth, the people inhabiting it at least half again as old as humans. Like humans, they began as wandering groups of nomads who followed their food sources until they learned how to cultivate and grow crops. Settlements became villages, then towns, then cities which grew around the trade of foodstuffs and other goods. And as with all species, as they became more intelligent and curious and figured out ways to improve their lives, their technology grew with them until it had reached the point where they lived comfortably among themselves, ruled by a single king who oversaw the entire planet.

Their technology had been as advanced as present day Earth until several hundred years ago. It was then that a mineral called vireck had been found and discovered that when its atoms were excited with an electrical charge, it emitted a powerful source of energy that could be harvested and stored. And its life as an energy source was long lived, nearly twenty Taburon years. Even the smallest of rocks could provide enough energy for a moderately sized home. Taburon was rich in vireck. The Taburons had been mining it for over a hundred years and still had not done more than scrape the surface of the amount of deposits available.

This made the mineral extremely valuable, for both the Taburons and outworlders, once it was leaked to the galaxy. An almost unending source of energy that could power space ships for longer voyages was highly desired. It was clean and stable and required a minimum amount of mineral to provide that energy. Yet the Taburons controlled the selling of vireck stringently, guarding the mines with an almost obsessive need, for the mineral had a secondary property that come to light quite unexpectedly.

Once the atoms had run out of energy and stopped being agitated, the molecules settled into a crystal pattern that changed the structure of the mineral and turned it into a deep, sapphire blue gem-like stone suitable for jewelry. Which made the Taburons even more guarded about their vireck, and as rich as Croesus. The people prospered as their planet prospered.

There were several continents on Taburon, each inhabited. The seat of government was the city of Duguid, on the continent of Desgin, where the king had his palace. He ruled through vassals placed around the planet, men of royal blood who had sworn an oath to uphold the king's laws and govern with compassion accordingly. The king was a fair man but could and would exercise his full authority, even harshly, when necessary, which was rare. He believed that if you cared for your people, they would care for you in return. The wealth was distributed evenly and everyone was cared for, no matter their status in society. Children were educated, the old cared for, the sick treated. In return the people agreed that they would hold dear the planet they lived on and forsake most things that might have caused it harm. Some had even gone so far as to completely forsake any modern advancements, relying instead on natural sources of energy – wind, water, fire, sun and wood.

The present king's family had ruled for ten generations, winning the right after a particularly vicious battle in which they drove off a group of people who believed that all technology was evil and to be abhorred. They would have taken the planet back to times when all there was was living from day to day and depending upon the weather and animal migrations to survive. The planet had long passed that time period and was unwilling to go back. And the king intended to make sure they never regressed ever again. The opposition was relocated to another planet, given tools to make a successful start and left alone.

When not directing her lessons on Taburon history, Radine focused on other matters. He helped her to pick out several of the dresses that had been brought to her that first day, delighting in sneaking in gropes while the steward had him help in making adjustments. The steward had gotten his measurements and left, shaking his head as his king and queen to be collapsed into a fit of laughter. He'd never seen the king so happy.

They'd had their evening meals with Jaima. McKenna liked the second in command. He was also an extremely handsome man, nearly as tall as Radine with eyes only slightly lighter in color than his superior officer's. It was obvious they had a long time relationship, for Jaima took Radine's teasing as well as dished it out, but always with the deepest respect. She enjoyed hearing about Radine as a lad, the trouble they both got into and the punishments they suffered for their misadventures. Dinner was a pleasant affair, with lots of laughter.

But at night, that time was reserved only for them. His quarters were well used, on every surface, in every possible position, ending on the bed amongst tangled sheets and blankets. The loving was fast and furious, gentle and sweet, but always ended with them thoroughly satisfied, falling asleep in each other's embrace, sometimes waking to resume their lovemaking. They learned each other's body, every inch, crease, and blemish until it was a map in their brains they knew well.

Her first try at a blow job had created more frustration than anything, her lack of knowledge and experience obvious. Radine, despite his unfinished state, had held her, assuring her that with time she would become more proficient. Then he'd turned her ass up and plunged into her ruthlessly until they'd both fallen from exhaustion.

He, on the other hand, was an expert in the 'oral arts,' as he called them, diving with glee into her pussy to bring her to glorious orgasm after glorious orgasm until she cried mercy. She had no more to give. Only then would he plunge his cock into her to drag one more orgasm from her, emptying himself into her body at the same time, satiated beyond satiation. When he did appear in the corridors, with or without her, the knowing looks Radine received from the crew were both embarrassing and pleasing. They were happy for him and accepted McKenna readily, which boded well for when they finally landed and he presented her to his people.

Now though, he caressed along her cheek, standing close enough to smell the scent of the soap she shared with him in his shower, a not unpleasant scent, but a masculine one. He would have his mother help her pick out one for her and her alone. "I told you that I was on a search for a bride for the king?"

"I know. You said he would be pleased with what you discovered."

"Know that he is, very pleased, McKenna, for you are the bride I have chosen."

"What?" she said in disbelief. McKenna couldn't believe her ears. He'd lied to her after telling her that she was to be his wife? Been sleeping with her this whole trip, and it was for another man? Was he testing her, to see if she would be able to satisfy his king, to report what worked to bring her to orgasm? Was he some kind of sex master, teaching her what the king would like, preparing her to more readily take the cock of a man the same size as himself? She had read that in ancient time rulers sometimes kept such men to instruct their concubines in the erotic arts so they could be easily satisfied without having to work too hard at it. How could he do this to her? When she had fallen in love with him so far, so fast and so deep. "What?" she repeated, so stunned she could not form words. Her eyes began to tear, she would have to go home, she couldn't stay on this planet where men were so devious. She'd been used - again. Maybe someday she would learn to never trust a man again, they were all alike, the galaxy over. Out to get what they could, then move on to the next gullible woman in line. And she would certainly make it her goal in life to warn other women to run the other way if a tall, gorgeously handsome alien approached.

McKenna ironically hoped his report was favorable, and that the king could then find more time to spend searching, since she wasn't going to be staying except for as long as it took to get back to Earth. She wished she had some way to part Radine of his cock, just retribution for a man who could use a woman so thoughtlessly, so manipulatively, and then pass her over to another man.

Not having a weapon, she used the next best thing. Pulling her leg back as she hitched up the front of her dress, she kneed him in the family jewels. Jaima had already been on the move, reading the intent in her eyes, knowing Radine had gone the wrong way in telling her the biggest secret of all that he'd still kept, but had not been fast enough to stop her. Radine's face paled deathly white, his eyes darkened to a deep gold before they squeezed tightly shut and he clutched himself between his legs as his legs buckled, sinking to the deck, his breath a rattling wheeze. McKenna moved to step around him. She had the few things she'd brought with her to gather.

All hell broke out on the bridge as crewmen rushed to Radine's side, reaching out to take him by the arms. "Your Majesty!" Jaima cried out, forgetting. "Gods' rods that is a damnable thing to do!" He looked around at the surrounding crew, indicating for someone, anyone to send for the physician. Two crewmen blocked her way from leaving the bridge.

McKenna didn't get far when Jaima's words penetrated her fury. She stopped and turned. "Majesty?" she murmured in horror. She felt the blood drain from her own face as the realization settled over her.

"You may have just unmanned *King* Radine of Taburon," Jaima said hotly. He grabbed the king under his arms and with the help of another crewman, the two of them transferred him to the captain's chair where he sat, hunched over in misery, hands still between his legs, his face still pale, his breathing haggard.

"Why didn't he say so?" she asked. "All this time and he never said a word."

A glass of water was handed to Jaima which he passed to the king. Radine first waved it away, but Jaima persisted until the royal took the glass and sipped, his hand shaking. "Because he has spent his entire adult life being chased by women who wanted him because he is the king. His mother has spent the last year parading every eligible woman on the planet before him in order to get him to choose a queen. He wanted a woman to love him for him, not his title."

"Oh my god," she whispered, her horror increasing. She'd kneed the king in his genitals, possibly harming him permanently. He would surely send her back now. What man wanted a woman who retaliated in the worst possible way when angered? Her feet were rooted to the deck when she really wanted to go to him and comfort him, apologize for her mistake and her misunderstanding. Two guards flanked her, ready to haul her to the ship's brig once ordered. She would understand if he didn't want to see her ever again, as long as he could someday, somehow, forgive her. She hoped they didn't have a dungeon on their planet.

With a wheeze, he croaked out her name. "McKenna."

"Radine," she started, moving near to kneel humbly at his feet, her head bowed. "Your Majesty, I'm so sorry. I have no excuse for what I did. I just assumed you were going to turn me over to some stranger.

We spent all of that time together and you never told me. I thought *you* were going to be my husband."

He grinned sheepishly, his face still contorted in pain. "I am. You are going to be my wife, McKenna," he rasped. "Just remind me to never get you angry at me in the future. Your aim is dead on." He flushed as he realized they were still on the bridge. "I'll never live this down," he mumbled.

"Everyone here will swear to silence, Your Majesty," Jaima assured him. Sistan entered the bridge and took over. After a quick exam he had two crewmen help the king, still bent over, stumble to Medical where he could ease the man's injury. McKenna followed sheepishly – hopefully.

Of course, that was the time his mother decided to call him. Sitting in a chair, his trousers shucked and a cooling cloth held to his still throbbing manhood and balls, Sistan gave him a painkiller that eased the pulsing ache before he answered her call, keeping the viewing device well above his belt line. At least his color had returned and he could speak coherently without wincing in pain every few seconds. "Mother," he greeted. McKenna waited outside the exam room where she'd been relegated while Radine was being treated.

"Radine, where have you been?" she demanded with exasperation. She was not too pleased that he had left, been gone for days and not even told her where he had gone to. She could run a kingdom, yet she couldn't control her son. He may be an adult and the king, but she still worried about him.

"I went to find a queen."

It took her a heartbeat to process his words. "What?" she questioned calmly. "You what?"

"I went to Earth to find a queen."

Inoa held her peace for a moment. "And?" she finally demanded, her voice rather sedate in the face of his news.

"You will meet her shortly, Mother. There has been a slight delay in our transporting down."

"What is wrong that you can't come down now?"

"Not important," he lied, "ship's business that I have neglected for the last few weeks."

"Have you married this woman yet?"

"You know it won't be official until the sky clad ceremony, but I consider her my wife."

"You've slept with her already?"

"Mother!"

"Well, if she becomes pregnant, you're stuck with her now aren't you?"

"Then I certainly hope she is pregnant, because I don't plan on letting her go for the next sixty or seventy years or more."

The queen looked resigned. "You're that sure?"

His eyes rolled. "I am. Especially after today, I certainly am." Sistan returned to the room, a device in his hands. "I have to go, Mother, pressing business. We'll see you as soon as possible. I'll let you know." He cut the communication before she could say anything.

Sistan passed the device to him. "Place this over your genitals, Your Majesty. It will hold everything up and prevent chafing until you feel better." Radine took the device and studied it. It was a cup that would hold his cock and balls against his body, not allowing the rougher material of his trousers to rub against the now overly sensitive area. "Do not lift anything heavy, and curtail your practice with the troops. You might wish to soak in a warm bath when you get home. Are the painkillers helping?"

"Things have become tolerable. It only hurts when I breathe now," he answered wryly.

Sistan smiled. "Your queen certainly knows how to show her displeasure. I hope you have learned your lesson."

"Never piss her off, but if I do, get my cock and balls well protected first."

"If you wish children I would consider that sage advice."

125

"There has been no permanent damage has there? I can still have children?"

"There should be no problem with you having sexual intercourse. Of course the first time, if before you're thoroughly healed, might hurt. I would wait a day or two. As for children, that is up to the Gods, if you are in their favor. You might wish to have your queen examined by the physicians below. They may be able to determine if you are genetically compatible." He shoved his hands in his pockets. "Or you can simply keep having fun trying." He patted the king on the shoulder. "Give it time, Your Majesty. Things will work out as they are supposed to." He made to leave. "Will you need assistance getting dressed?"

Radine shook his head. He'd been embarrassed enough for one day.

McKenna's face flamed red when he rejoined her, she would forever carry the shame of having injured him in the most basic of ways. Hesitant, unsure of his reaction, she reached out to him, sighing in relief when he pulled her against his body in a full body hug. "Radine, I am so sorry," she repeated, her fingers smoothing against the fabric of his shirt.

He smiled as he pushed her back to look down to her face. "You will nurse me back to health," he commanded, "and when I am better, you will feel my wrath at your actions."

For a second she feared what he might do, but the mischievous look in his eyes promised there would be no tortuous punishment, unless the time he spent tormenting her body to orgasm after orgasm counted. "Are you in pain?"

"No, Sistan's medicines work quite well. But he suggested I soak for a while when I get home." He led her out of Medical and towards the shuttle hangar. "Of course, I may have to postpone that bath for a while. I've been gone for nearly a week, I'm sure there are a million things waiting for me to attend to. And I must take you to see my mother, now that she knows I have brought you home." As they walked through the corridors of the ship, she now totally understood the genuflecting going on as they passed crewmen. "We also have to plan for a wedding and coronation. It's not every day a king takes a wife and makes her a queen."

She stopped suddenly. Radine nearly tripped over his feet by her abruptness, a frown on his face as he turned to see what had stopped her. "McKenna?"

"Queen?" she asked in a whisper.

That mischievous look was back along with one of contemplation. "Well, you could settle for consort, but that puts you below me. Which would still mean my advisors, and mother, will continue to insist that I take a wife and make her queen. I could also label you my slave, but then my ministers might demand to sample your charms." He grinned at the horrified look she shot him. "Believe me that will never happen. I would rather have an equal in my kingdom and my bed."

"But, queen?" she repeated. "Why…" she asked. "How…" she stammered. "I don't know anything about being a queen."

His laugh was hearty, full throated as he gathered her close. "Little one, you will learn. My mother will be more than pleased to teach you. And I'll tell you a secret – she had no experience at it before she married my father. She turned out very well." He kissed her nose, then pressed his lips against hers. "I love you, McKenna," he murmured to her so only she could hear it. It was the first time he had said the magic words to her and she felt herself suffuse with warmth. "I will always love you."

"I'm glad, Radine, because I fell in love with you the day you stepped between me and my ex-boss to defend me. You really are my hero."

Chapter Twelve

They landed at the dock and boarded a shuttle that held more than two passengers, several of the crew joining them as they headed for the planet surface. As they drew nearer, she could see the buildings of the city, modern in material but ancient in design. From above, the palace rose from the center of the city, a gleaming structure of white and crystal, towered on three sides and with extensive gardens surrounding it. The city fanned out from there in all directions, a mix of homes and shops lining paved roads, hundreds of people walking amongst the buildings, going about their business. There were several squares where the people could meet and at one of them, some sort of gathering was going on, she knew not what exactly since they passed over it so fast.

At the edge of one of the gardens around the palace was a large landing pad. The shuttle touched down here and powered down, the hatch sliding open to discharge the passengers.

Grabbing her hand, Radine tugged McKenna from the vehicle, giving the waiting attendants a passing nod as he dragged her towards the grand portico leading into the palace. Several of the attendants followed swiftly on his heels, ready to serve their king anything he might want or fulfill any order he might give.

He led her through the palace faster than she could take it all in – the highly polished floors, the ornate wall hangings, the people who bowed deeply as their king passed, he barely acknowledging them with a singular goal in mind. He wanted to get the first meeting with his mother done and over with so he could steep in a warm bath. The device was helping, but he still felt a pulsing throb between his legs. And he wasn't above tormenting McKenna, taking advantage of her feelings of guilt to have her cater to him until he decided she'd been punished enough. He figured it would involve a great deal of groveling and waiting on him as well as her hands on his body until he went out of his mind. But what a sweet way to go.

So he dragged her through the palace to the large doors he'd pushed open in exasperation only days ago, though this time they were opened as the king approached by the two guards on either side. The queen sat in the same chair she'd been in before, her eyes forward, anxiously awaiting her son's arrival, her crown on her head. She was the regal woman who had raised him, who had stood by his father for thirty six years, sharing his rule, defending his kingdom and making the previous king's life all he had asked for.

Inoa smoothed her skirt over her legs, unusually anxious. She had tried, she had to admit, to get him married, and after thinking more about it, perhaps her attempts to get Radine to find a queen and wife had been a subtle way to force him into doing exactly what he had done. Inoa could be devious when needed, even after the fact. She'd not been happy at first when he'd taken off, but upon learning that he'd gone in search of a queen, while she'd waited for him to arrive, her worry and displeasure had turned to pleasure, then anxiety to meet this woman that would bear her grandchildren and share her son's bed.

Radine stopped several feet in front of his mother and bowed, the Earth woman held by the hand, her dark eyes wide. McKenna's own anxiety poured from her in waves. "Mother." Remembering, McKenna bowed from the waist as well.

Inoa gave her son a perusal reserved for a parent concerned for their child. He had taken off without word and she'd been worried for his safety while he'd been away. She didn't miss the bandage on his arm, nor the unusual size of the bulge at his crotch. Radine took after his father, but not that much.

"What happened to your arm?" she asked.

The king shrugged. He'd forgotten about the wound, its importance taking a back seat to more pressing matters. "A scuffle with someone not worth thinking about anymore. It is but a flesh wound." Radine pulled the woman forward more. "Mother, this is McKenna Primm, from Earth, my wife and queen to be."

131

Inoa's glance was all encompassing, looking the girl up one end and down, her eyes widening once as she recognized the dress as one of her own, but altered. She had to admit the girl was quite pretty, exotic, with dark eyes, fair skin, and a pouty mouth. Had she been a Taburon, her build would have been the envy of many of the women on the planet, long legs, nipped in waist, more than adequate bust. Her auburn hair fell in soft waves around her shoulders. She was well shorter than most Taburon women, but Radine seemed taken by her, his expression filled with affectionate emotion.

McKenna bowed. "Your Majesty, it is an honor to meet you." She had a pleasant voice, rich in timbre. Inoa wondered if she ever did any singing.

The queen rose from her chair to move to a chaise couch. "Come here," she indicated, patting the seat next to her. McKenna looked up at Radine for guidance. He nodded slightly, giving her a slight push as he headed towards a chair for himself. "You may leave us, Radine," the queen ordered, bringing him up short. "Have Catio bring in refreshment for us on your way out." Radine flushed at being so summarily dismissed, but he bowed before turning on his heel.

"I shall inform Catio," he offered. "Send someone to fetch me when you are through." If he was lucky, his mother wouldn't frighten the woman too much, nor tell too many tall tales about her son. The doors closed behind him with a resounding thump. The king was not pleased.

"You are from Earth?"

"Yes, Your Majesty."

"How did you and my son meet?"

"He helped me when my car died on the side of the road. He offered to take me home."

"Radine could never tolerate not lending aid to a woman in need. Did he injure his arm on Earth?"

"Yes. My boss had been harassing me at work and I'd quit the day we met. When he showed up at my home the next morning and started to abuse me, Radine stepped in to save me. My ex-boss had a knife and Radine was injured."

"I see." To the right of where they were seated, a set of doors opened and two servants entered, each carrying a tray. Placing the trays on a nearby table, they arranged the food and drink to their satisfaction before bowing to the queen.

"Shall I pour, Your Majesty?" one asked.

"Thank you but no, Catio. You may leave." Another bow and the two men returned through the door they'd entered. Inoa poured from the teapot, filling a cup. She passed it to McKenna, who sniffed at the contents first. It was the same type of beverage she had had on the ship, scenting a mix of cherries and cinnamon. Inoa filled a second cup, spooning in a whitish brown powder from a container. "I prefer my *palma* sweeter," she explained. "Please help yourself to the pastries," she invited.

McKenna looked over the sweet treats, picked out one and a napkin, spreading the towel over her lap. "Did he kill this man, the one who was abusing you?" Inoa asked.

McKenna choked on her tea, setting the cup onto the saucer carefully. "No, Your Majesty. There was no need for him to. We left him unconscious in my apartment."

Inoa nodded, pleased that Radine did nothing to jeopardize their place in galactic society. Her head tilted slightly. "I can see why my son was taken with you. You're quite beautiful."

McKenna flushed deep pink. "Thank you, Your Majesty."

"How old are you?" the queen asked.

"Twenty six, Your Majesty."

"Have you been married? Had children?"

"No."

"Are you a virgin? I would assume you are not, or knowing my son, at least not anymore."

McKenna choked. Her blush deepened, her face reddening, the color traveling down her chest. "I don't know how to answer that," she responded.

"My son is a very virile man. He has not denied himself the pleasure of a woman even though he is king. And if he is anything like his father, he is quite…enthusiastic."

"I would think that sort of information should be between Radine and me, Your Majesty, with all due respect."

Inoa's glance was penetrating. "I can see my son has deep affection for you."

"He has told me he loves me."

"And you love him?"

"Would I have left my home, my world, to come to a strange place if I didn't?"

"Unless a woman grows up under her intended's roof, don't most women leave their home, family, and all they know when they wed?" The queen chose a pastry and bit into it delicately. "Did your family approve of you leaving Earth?"

"I have no family, not anymore."

"What happened to them?"

"My father and brothers died in our last war. My mother withered away from a broken heart a year after that."

Inoa's look was sympathetic. "I am sorry for you. How old were you then?"

"Twenty."

"There was no one to take you in?"

"The state took charge of finishing my education, then provided me with a skill that I could use to support myself."

"And what sort of skill did they give you?"

"I was a clerk for a company, then I was promoted to taking charge of all of the clerks in the company."

"And this man that accosted you?"

"My boss. You see, on Earth, there are more women than men, so while women have found themselves gaining more opportunities to be in charge and control things in business and the government, men, especially those who were too old to fight, still have the advantage. They can pick and choose whatever woman they want for whatever reason and then move on when they tire of the first one. My boss thought he could pressure me into giving him sexual favors because he knew I needed the job. I found him repulsive and turned him down, then finally quit."

"He should have been jailed for his actions. Radine would never allow that in this kingdom and would take action should he ever hear of it."

"He did a fine job as it was. He was ready to kill Mr. Raymond, but I asked him not to."

"You should have allowed him to rid your planet of this *tritio*," the queen said vehemently. With her hand at her throat, she took a few deep breaths. "No matter now, you are safe here from such men." She plucked up another sweet. "I really must stop eating these things," she mused as she chewed. "Too many of them make too much of me."

McKenna smiled. "'A moment on the lips is forever on the hips,'" she quoted softly.

Inoa chuckled lightly. "Indeed, my dear, indeed." She licked her fingers noisily like a child. "So tell me more about yourself. What do you like?"

"I love to read. I always get, or rather got books from the library, to spend the evenings reading. Didn't matter what, just as long as I had something to read. I did bring a book on human anatomy for your scientists or physicians to see, as well as a dictionary. Radine said I am the first human to come to your planet."

"That was very thoughtful of you. I am sure they will appreciate it. You shall find our libraries quite extensive, and you may use any of the books you find there. It will be to your advantage to learn what you can about Taburon, if you are to be queen."

"I'll be honest, that scares me."

"Being queen?" McKenna nodded vigorously. "Oh my dear, you'll find it easy enough if you follow Radine's lead until you feel comfortable with the title." She leaned closer dropping her voice to a

137

loud whisper. "Mostly, you need to learn who you can insult and who you cannot," she confided, "and the best way to do it so they don't know that you have."

McKenna giggled, then sobered. "Radine said you've been trying to get him married for a while now."

"He's old enough to have produced more than one child by now, yet he's dragged his heels over the last years. He needs to secure his kingdom for the future of the people, otherwise there will be civil war as the throne is fought over." She scrunched her face in distaste. "Nothing good ever comes of war." McKenna saddened, knowing first-hand the results of war. Realizing her gaffe, Inoa gently laid a hand on McKenna's arm. "I'm so sorry, my dear. That was thoughtless of me."

McKenna shook it off. "It was a long time ago, Your Majesty. I miss them, but it doesn't hurt as much anymore. Especially now that there's Radine."

"Oh, that boy will be devoted to you for the rest of your life, have no fear about that."

McKenna remembered their last night together, his hard body and strong cock, thrusting into her time and time again until she felt she would explode. No, what he did to her wasn't anything a boy should know about, let alone do. She couldn't help the blush the rose in her cheeks. "It's hard to think of him as a boy, Your Majesty."

Inoa laughed, guessing the younger woman's thoughts by the way she blushed. "That good, eh?"

McKenna's head lifted. There was sass in her eyes. "I'll never tell," she promised. Together the two women gave in to a fit of giggles.

"You look lovely in that dress," Inoa said. "I'm glad I left it on Radine's ship."

As her glance fell to the dress she wore, McKenna felt embarrassed, then grateful. "It's a beautiful dress," she observed. "I didn't bring much with me in the way of clothes when we left Earth."

"I shall have my dressmaker visit with you. As queen, you will be expected look the part. You will also need an appropriate dress for the wedding and coronation, though not for the sky clad ceremony."

"What is that?"

"In the old times, for someone in Radine's position, his choice of wife needed to be approved by the Gods. In the sky clad ceremony, you will beseech their divine sign that they find you both compatible. The ceremony is tradition. It's like a wedding, but usually takes place before the marriage vows are made. After those, you will be crowned queen."

McKenna swallowed deeply. "What if there's no approval?" she dared to ask in a small voice.

A thoughtful look crossed Inoa's face. "It has never happened that I recall. I'm not sure what the procedure is from there. I shall have to look in the history to see if there is any mention." She caught McKenna's consternation. "Don't worry, my dear, I'm sure Radine and you will meet with the approval of the Gods."

"Doesn't Radine have any brothers or sisters? He never mentioned it."

"Unfortunately, Tylene, Radine's father, and I did not have any other children. I hesitate to think about the others who could lay claim to the throne if he were to abdicate or, Gods' forbid, be killed. He is a good man, and a great king. The people will do just about anything for him, he is well loved and appreciated. In all things he has put the people first. Now he'll have someone to think about for himself and about him, finally." She smiled. "If I sound a little overbearing, there are few people willing to stand up to Radine for his own good. I'm one, Jaima is the other. Do not let him overwhelm you, McKenna."

"He won't, Your Majesty."

"Please, call me Inoa." She tilted her head as she shot McKenna a wondering look. "Perhaps someday, you could change that to mother."

A mischievous glint appeared in McKenna's eyes. "I would be honored, Your Majesty."

Inoa laughed, signaling with a hand. Immediately a servant appeared at her side. "Send for the king. Her Highness Princess

McKenna needs to be shown where she'll be staying." The servant bowed with a soft 'yes, your majesty' and fled.

"Her Highness Princess McKenna?" McKenna queried.

"You are the intended bride of the king. You are to be shown appropriate respect. I will make sure you have a servant to attend you…" McKenna started to shake her head. "Don't argue, you will need someone to help you learn what you need to know. She will help you dress and do your hair for you. Believe me, when you start attending state functions, you'll be glad to have the help. By the way, I envy you that hair color, it's gorgeous. You are going to make so many women jealous."

McKenna sat back in shock. "Really? I'm head over heels about Radine's eyes. They're so beautiful and expressive."

"They're from his father. He had the same eyes." Inoa's eyes saddened for a heartbeat. McKenna did not know how much just seeing her son sometimes made her heart bleed for missing her Tylene. Maybe it was why she kept such a close guard on Radine, unwilling to even contemplate losing him as well. As long as Radine lived, she had a tie to her husband and common memories she could share.

Inoa shook herself visibly. "I hope you'll like your rooms. Please let me know if you find them lacking. As soon as Radine told me he had brought a woman back, I had them cleaned and set to order. If there is anything you want or need for them, please do not hesitate to let your servant, myself, or Radine know. I'll send for the seamstress for tomorrow. Unless Radine has other plans?"

"I don't know what his plans are right now. He did say he needed to catch up with affairs here."

"Things do tend to pile up when he's out of the palace," Inoa agreed. "Ah, here he is," she announced as the door opened to admit the king. Radine smiled at McKenna, his crown askew on his head as though he'd put it on in a hurry.

"Did you have a pleasant conversation?" he asked. "Dare I ask if I should duck or wear protection?" McKenna exchanged a conspiratorial look with the queen before sliding her glance at the man she loved. She smiled. "Gods' rods," he groaned. Who knew what kind of mischief his mother was up to. And enlisted his wife to be into as well. Snatching her hand, he pulled her up. Waving good bye over his shoulder to his mother, he led McKenna away, Inoa's laughter following.

Chapter Thirteen

Luckily for McKenna, or Radine depending upon one's viewpoint, her rooms were right next to his, the palace hundreds of years old and built at a time when the royal couples usually did not sleep together except to procreate. With a connecting door, it allowed visitation between the couple, or at times when the king was unwed, a discreet way to spend a night with his current paramour. Radine gave her ten minutes to look over what had been provided for her – the large airy space more than she had ever had and would ever need. There was a huge sitting area with half a dozen comfortable couches to lounge around. Plants filled every corner, some blooming profusely, filling the air with their perfumed scent. The bedroom had a king sized four poster bed against one wall, the drapes from the posts filmy and drifting on the breeze that flowed through the room from the large walk-through windows. A dressing table waited to the left of the bed, a large carved wardrobe graced the right wall. Next to the wardrobe was the entrance to the baths. McKenna could smell flowery scents lingering in the air.

"Satisfactory?" Radine asked.

"I couldn't imagine anything more grand," she said breathlessly.

"Then come."

He dragged her to his rooms, dismissing his servant Purnia as he entered, not stopping until he'd tugged her into his bathroom. There the tub was filled already, steam rising above the water. Puzzled, she watched as he began to disrobe, stretching his shirt over his head. "Sistan suggested I soak in a warm bath." He unfastened the placket of his trousers, letting it hang open. His hands at her throat, he unlaced the fastening to her dress, the bodice falling free to reveal her breasts. Her nipples tightened at the lust in his gaze.

From behind her, he loosened her skirt, the garment falling to her feet to leave her naked. With reverence he touched her nipples, circling the tiny points with just a fingertip. Bending at the waist, he closed his lips around one nipple and sucked, hard. McKenna arched her back, grabbing onto his shoulders to keep herself steady as he assaulted her breasts with his experienced mouth.

One hand slipped down her body to delve between her legs, finding her soaked and swollen. Her clit poked from its protective hood and he found it without hesitation, flipping his finger over the swelling bud. Her legs shook, her thighs opening more to allow him further access to her pussy. Two fingers penetrated her, sliding in and out, her pussy weeping heavily.

Radine straightened. "Perfect," he decided examining her flushed face and skin. She was aroused enough that if he bent her over and slipped his cock inside, she would come almost immediately. But he had a bit of pay back to exact before he gave into her lush curves and tempting charms.

Her confused expression told him all he needed to know. He had been so close to giving her an orgasm, a welcome to his planet that she would never forget, when he stopped and pulled away just as she teetered on the edge. Radine stepped back. "Finish undressing me," he ordered, spreading his hands out to his sides and separating his legs slightly.

"Radine?" she queried.

His look was imperious, his stance unyielding, his eyes sparking. Though his voice was hoarse with lust when he spoke. "Your king has given you a command. It is best that you follow it."

A spark of defiance flitted through her eyes for a heartbeat, then a mischievous devil took over and she sank to her knees before him. Two could play at this game, if that's what he was wanting. Splitting open the placket of his trousers, she found the device he had to use to cup his genitals. Keeping it held in place, she pulled the material away from his body one side at a time, reaching around to yank at it across his hips, making sure her nails scrapped across the flesh of his arse, a grin crossing her face as he hissed softly. Once it had cleared his firm, rounded buttocks, it was easy to let it pool around his knees. Lifting the device, his cock dropped free, already hardened, pointing straight at her. His balls swung down. She put the device on the floor.

With one hand on his thigh, she covered his cock with the other, petting him gently. He didn't show any effects from her kick, there was no bruising or swelling…well, other than what she expected. Wrapping her hand around his cock, she squeezed gently, keeping her eyes on his face to gauge his expression. He groaned but did not stop her as she slid her hand up and down his shaft. Rising to her knees, she took the head of his cock into her mouth, her lips stretching, sucking lightly, again watching his face, not wanting to hurt him. She licked the smooth, bulbous head then the underside, teasing the ridge there. Her tongue made wet forays along his length, up the top and down the bottom to circle around the crown of the head before taking it inside and suckling. Pointing the tip of her tongue, she flicked it in the slit that wept heavily, the taste of his fluids heady.

But it was when she clutched her hand around his balls to tease and taunt him there that he loudly hissed and hunched over, obviously in pain. She released him from her mouth, gently lifting his balls to look underneath. There she found bruises. Her heart lurched. "Radine, I'm so sorry. I didn't know." She let his balls gently fall back onto his thigh.

"Well, now you do," he said after taking a deep breath. "Finish undressing me," he mumbled, though he drew a finger down her cheek.

With his trousers hanging at his knees, she first unhooked his boots and pulled them off, then finished drawing his pants down his legs. He stepped free of the garment, reaching to take her hand, making her stand.

Together, they entered the bath, Radine sinking to his chest in the water. "That feels wonderful," he breathed as the warmth soaked into him. Slicked by the oils in the water, she slithered against his body, pressing into his side. "It took all I had to not squirm on the throne and give myself away. Do you know how hard it is to listen to a boring recitation of import export reports when the only thing you can think about is your balls?" He grinned ruefully. "Not easy, I can assure you. All I wanted to do was strip out of my trousers and let things hang free, if you get my meaning. We're a progressive society, but not that progressive."

"Radine, I'm…"

"Don't say it again," he warned, covering her lips with a finger. "I should have been more upfront with you, maybe not from the beginning, but once I was ready to confess all, maybe it would have been better to come right out and say it." He slid an arm around her shoulders and tucked her under his arm. "You know you've also denied yourself don't you? There is no way I'll be able to share *nadryl* with my cock with you until I'm healed, or at least until it doesn't hurt as much."

147

"I deserve no less."

"Oh, you deserve more," he corrected. "In a while you can wash me. We'll save the punishment for later." He ignored her exasperation reaction. "I'll think of other ways you can repay me," he promised. Spreading his legs, Radine settled McKenna against his lap, pinning her legs with his own. Sliding his hands under her arms, he cupped her breasts. "So what did you and my mother talk about?"

"A lot of things, how we met, how you were injured by my ex-boss. She asked me about myself."

Cupping his hand, he poured water over her breasts. Gathering her hair, he draped it over a shoulder, leaning forward to nibble at the curve of her neck. "She didn't tell you any embarrassing stories about me?"

"All she said was you were a very virile man, but I knew that already. I think I'll have plenty of time to hear the stories you won't want me to know." As he continued to pour water over her breasts, she ran her hands along his legs. His hairless condition extended down there as well and she was jealous. She hated having to shave her legs every two days to keep them stubble free.

"You think so, do you?"

McKenna decided to rat out his mother. "She said you didn't deny yourself women. Makes me wonder how many women you've had over the years."

"I am but a man, McKenna."

"And a king. I bet you could've had any woman you wanted."

"I was always careful, little one, never sharing nadryl with a woman when she could get pregnant, pulling out before coming inside a woman. I never allowed her to clean herself by herself, but always did it myself or stayed and watched while she did."

She shuddered. "That's disgusting."

"No, it's making sure that there would be no woman claiming to have had my bastard child who would then challenge my legitimate children for the throne. If I had left my seed on a woman's belly, she could have put it inside her and become pregnant. A king's hold on his throne can be very tenuous. If he is not careful, it can drift away like a *tuaxa* flower on a strong wind. I learned from my father, and my hold on my title is concrete."

"You didn't answer my question."

"How many women have I had?" He felt her nod against his shoulder. "It matters not, because there will be no other for the future. You are *Sthulae*, you will always be *Sthulae*."

She twisted to face him. "What does that mean? I heard people in the ship call you something similar."

"*Sthulae* means queen. *Sthula* is king."

"So they were calling you king and I didn't know it," she accused, poking him in the ribs.

He grabbed her hands. "I had asked they not use the word king in front of you."

"Jaima said you've been pursued for your title."

"Since I became old enough to take a wife, even, in some cases, old enough to have sex. I was way too young to take a wife then. Even before then, people tried binding me into an arranged marriage for when I came of age. My parents didn't want to tie me down, thank the Gods."

"Do you think we'll be able to have children?" she asked softly. "Your mother wants grandchildren, she said that you need an heir to secure the throne. What if we don't, or can't, have any?"

"McKenna, I would die before I would abandon you for as simple a reason as not being able to have children. And there are a few to whom I would entrust the throne if I do not have a child to inherit. What my mother wants is second to what makes us happy." He drew in a deep breath as his hands slipped down to delve between her thighs. Separating her folds, he unerringly found her clit and circled it gently, teasingly. "What my mother needs is a lover. She has been alone too long and a man in her bed would keep her too busy to meddle with the lover in mine."

McKenna giggled. "Perhaps you should give her a taste of her own medicine and steer a couple of eligible men her way."

His hands stilled as he contemplated her suggestion, then he grinned with devilment. "I know several men from the guard who would be more than willing to take on my mother. I shall have to start whispering in certain ears to get it started." He played with her clit again, pressing on the little organ hard enough to make her squirm slightly.

Her hips rose and she took a deep breath so she could concentrate on the conversation and not what he was doing to her clit, which had poked its head out to beg for more. "Just assign them to her to guard her the next time she needs them. Send them all. She'll be surrounded by lustful men."

Radine laughed. "Especially if I put out the suggestion that she might be amenable to their attentions. Of course, if it goes wrong, there will be hell to pay. I may have to move fast to spare those men a trip to the dungeon or worse."

She turned just her head to face him. "Scared of your mother?"

"You have no idea," he admitted and pinched her. She flinched at the slight pain, but her body warmed and she felt her pussy swell and flood. His hands sought out her nipples.

She relaxed back into him though her back was bent to thrust her breasts forward. "I like her. I think I'm going to enjoy having a mother again."

"She is a fierce woman when it comes to those she loves, McKenna. If you think she's bad about me, you should see her with

Jaima. He's not the king and she runs right over him." Plucking at her nipples, he pinched them until they had tightened into hard points. "How would you feel about putting rings here?" he asked.

"Only after you put a few in yours," she challenged.

She could hear the disappointment in his voice. "Well, maybe something that doesn't pierce. You would look so pretty, with jewels hanging from your nipples, or maybe bells that ring softly as you walk."

"And let everyone know I have bells on my nipples? I don't think so, no, thank you."

His hands slipped between her legs. "What about here?"

McKenna rolled her eyes, but gave the idea a moment's thought. Bells between her legs? Would the sound be audible? Or would people, being able to hear it but not seeing where the bells are placed, be confused about from where they were actually hearing them? She was intrigued, but she would have to think about it more before agreeing to it. "I shall think about it," she conceded.

Pinching her clit, he chuckled. "Maybe just here, a little ring, gold of course. You'd forever be aroused, ready for me at any time."

She felt her body soften and swell. "I'm always ready for you, my king."

152

Radine plucked at the curls covering her mound. "This will have to go, of course. No woman on Taburon has hair on her pussy. The next time we share nadryl, you will be bald here."

"I can do that," she readily agreed.

"Good. Your servant will be able to provide the cream to remove the hair. Just ask her." Radine shoved his fingers into her pussy, swirling them around until he touched the entire inside of her folds, delving as deep as he could possible go from this position, then pulled them free and made her face him, planting a grueling kiss on her lips before standing. He had plans that did not include remaining in the chilling water of a bath. She couldn't help the shiver that ran through her as she watched the water sluice down his body, dripping from his nipples, the six pack of his abdomen, and the marvel that was his cock.

"The water chills. You may wash me now." His voice was so imperious, but she knew it was just another ploy of his to punish her for the injury she'd caused. She would find a way to get even, to both their mutual pleasure. In the meantime, McKenna laughed, reaching for the soap and a cloth.

So intent was his gaze on her as she soaped his leg, first tapping on it for him to raise his foot from the water that neither he nor she saw the woman that lounged in the doorway to the bath.

She was tall, at least six foot four, and model gorgeous with long legs, trim ankles, narrow hips and waist. Though unlike most models, she had melon sized breasts that were firm and stood high on her chest, the nipples tightly perked and light rose in color. Between her thighs, a hairless deep cleft of flesh split her sex, the petals of her lips thick and pouty, swollen, glistening from obvious arousal. Long, pristine golden-white hair fell down her back to reach the tops of the curves of her buttocks. Her lips were full, pulled into a moue of displeasure. Her golden eyes sparked with interest, fervent on Radine, slipping only for a heartbeat to the woman at his feet, dismissed before returning back to the king. A sheer sheath covered her body but didn't hide it, the rest of her clothes a trail behind her.

She twirled a lock of hair around a finger, her head tilted as she watched the byplay of the king and the little alien whore who dared to touch his body, washing him, paying undue and obscene attention to his cock. "Make him good and hard for me, *skala*," she drawled, "I have plans for that cock."

Chapter Fourteen

Radine's head shot up to the woman as McKenna screeched, sinking into the water to hide her nudity. Scowling, the king grabbed one of the towels by the side of the tub and passed it to McKenna before taking a second for himself. The woman sauntered closer as he wrapped the towel around his hips.

"Espis," he growled, sloshing through the water to the edge of the tub. He climbed out. He'd had little intention of actually sharing *nadryl* with McKenna, but having her touch his body, rubbing the soft cloth over him, soapy and slick, was working to change his mind, no matter the consequences, the price was worth it. He'd chased Purnia out to have privacy, yet here was this woman interrupting him and his love.

And for it to be Espis. He'd spent those three days with her purely out of curiosity, the rumors unavoidable among the guards in the service to the palace, a group with whom he spent a lot of time on the training field. He knew she was a slut, he accepted that when he'd issued the invitation to join him, but he'd wanted to see for himself just how much of a slut she was.

She'd proven true to the rumors, taking him every way possible until he'd had to beg off for a half day to recuperate. She'd also wanted things from him that he would never have been able to give her. She liked her sex rough, very rough, and that was not something he could do. It had not been, never had been and never would be a part of his nature. A little bit of mastering – maybe some corporeal punishment - yes, he could do that. But the things she'd asked for went beyond the pale. He'd given her the rest of the weekend, then gotten free of her as soon as possible. Or so he thought.

Espis pouted. "Ah, Radine, you don't need to cover that magnificent cock. It's not like I haven't seen it before." Her hand ran possessively over him through the towel, cupping his sex and squeezing tightly. He batted her hand away, his body tense with anger.

Radine was livid. "How did you get into my private chambers?" he asked, stepping away from her.

"It was so easy. I let a *salor* lose in the corridor outside your chambers and waited until someone screamed. The guards went to investigate and I just slipped in." She again sidled up to him, bumping his side with her hip. Her hand caressed across his chest. Her voice lowered seductively. "I'm disappointed you didn't call me when you got back."

Radine moved away from her, reaching back for McKenna's hand to help her from the tub.

Espis's eyes narrowed. "I guess you can have your *skala* join us. I've never shared *nadryl* with a female, though she looks fragile. Where did you find her? Obviously an inferior people, and she still has hair on her pussy. Disgusting, like an animal." Espis fingered a strand of McKenna's hair before taking the hank of it in hand and pulling, tilting her head back. It wasn't a hard tug, but it was enough to cause McKenna to cry out. As a *skala*, the whore had no say in how she was treated by someone superior to her. "Where is she from? Not Taburon."

"Get out!" Radine ordered, pulling McKenna's hair free from Espis's grip and then shielding McKenna with his body. "You are never to enter my chambers, or my palace ever again. Leave before I have you thrown out and banished from the city." He stepped around the woman, still guarding McKenna physically as they headed for his bedroom. He placed her next to the bed, stooping to reassure her, anger notching up higher at the distress and confusion in her expression. He rounded on Espis with anger flashing in his eyes.

Espis pouted further. "I didn't mean to make you angry, Radine. I just missed you and thought I'd surprise you, welcome you home."

"It's 'your majesty' to you, Espis, and I never gave you any reason to believe we had more than a passing few days of pleasure. Get out!" he repeated. In order to emphasize his point, he started to gather the clothes she'd strewn across the floor, balling them up and tossing them at her. His look was furious as he waited for her to take the hint. Finally, he strode to the door and pulled it open. The two guards turned, snapping to attention.

Espis huffed, tossing a contemptuous look at McKenna, who huddled by the bed, frightened. Her perfect afternoon had turned into a nightmare. Espis was angered, McKenna could read the fury in the Taburon woman's eyes plain as day. Her desire to continue cementing her place with the king, and the crown, usurped by an insignificant *skala*. She would have gotten him into bed and not let him out until she was sure she was pregnant. And her parents would have made enough of a public fuss that a wedding would have been assured and she would have been crowned queen. "Then enjoy your little *skala*," she spat, "but this isn't over. You're mine, and I will have what is mine." Head held high, she stomped from the room, ignoring the looks the guards tossed after her.

Radine turned his attention and anger to the two men. "You are to never, ever, for any reason, leave these doors," he ordered, his anger radiating off him in waves. "Your duty is to guard the king, and you have been derelict in your duty. I will be speaking with your commander in the morning regarding a fitting punishment."

"Yes, Your Majesty," they responded together. Radine slammed the door shut with a thud.

His anger faded in a heartbeat seeing McKenna. She was still scared, shivering from the chill in the room against her moist body, gripping the bedpost until her knuckles had turned white. "McKenna," he crooned, "little one." Radine enclosed her in a full body embrace, lending her his warmth until she stopped shaking. Grabbing the quilt from the bed, he wrapped it around both of them.

McKenna's voice quivered. "Who was that woman?"

"She is not important."

"She said you belonged to her. What is a *skala*?"

She could feel his chest rise as he took a deep breath, following him as he swung around to perch on the edge of the bed, pulling her to stand between his legs. "We spent a few days at the winter palace and did not deny ourselves all of the *nadryl* we wanted. We were exhausted at the end of it. That was six months ago. I never made her any promises. Whatever she thinks, it is all in her own mind."

"You didn't tell me what a *skala* is," she reminded him after a moment.

His second sigh was resigned. "Whore," he replied.

"She thought I was your whore? Why didn't you tell her the truth?"

"I am sorry, McKenna, I was taken by surprise. I will make sure she is told as soon as possible."

"You're going to see her again?"

"No, I will send Jaima. He will make it clear that there is nothing between her and me. You are going to be my wife and queen."

McKenna shook her head. "We're not done with her," she predicted.

"She will be banned from the palace, no one will permit her to come inside. I promise you that." He bent slightly so he could read the feeling in her eyes. Cupping her face, he kissed her, gently, lovingly, his kiss as full of promise as it was regret that she'd had to endure the vehemence of a former sex partner. Gathering her closer, he let her absorb the warmth and confidence of his body. "I wish I could share *nadryl* with you. But I can make you come."

McKenna pushed away from him slightly to stare into his eyes. He had banked his anger, but it still glittered in his gaze. She knew he wanted to soothe her, but the incident, and insult, was still too fresh, humming through her too much like sizzling energy to allow her to feel anything more than a cloying heaviness. Her head shook twice. "No, I don't think I could handle that right now. I'm just tired, and hungry."

Standing, he swiveled, lifting her onto the bed. "Then rest here, my McKenna. I will send for food for us, then you may sleep here where I can keep watch over you." Numbed, she nodded, anything he wanted short of sex was fine with her.

Chapter Fifteen

Radine lounged on his throne, listening to more interminable reports. The drone of his ministers was often enough to make him want to flee in desperation. Only he knew he would have to go through the entire process upon returning. He wanted to be out with his men training, at least as much as Pologa, his physician, would allow. He felt the need to slash at things, to test his mettle against those of the palace guards and soldiers. To work out his frustration at not being able to ease the need in his groin, to relieve the heaviness in his cock, to empty himself in McKenna's warm body. To show her how much he loved her with that physical connection all men used to express their love.

He sat on a cushion, the bruising from McKenna's well placed kick having expanded to the underside of his buttocks and tops of the back of his thighs. His physician had suggested the added padding, which had been added during the night and covered to look like nothing had been placed on the throne. He'd also been forbidden from riding a *crufa*. He was not content.

Except when he finally finished with the day's business and could go back to McKenna, soak in her quiet presence, share a meal and curl up next to her in bed for the night. She was a solid sounding board for the events of his day, her advice when he asked was level and practical.

His mother was teaching her about the history of Taburon and the royal family, slipping in lessons on etiquette and protocol for royal functions. McKenna had met with the seamstress and new dresses were being made for her. She'd done a small amount of redecorating on her rooms and met her servant, Annatt. The woman was amicable, young, enthusiastic, and delighted to have been chosen to aid the queen to be. She assured McKenna that all of her friends were green with envy that she had gotten the position.

Radine sighed softly, lifting his butt from the seat high enough to adjust himself, realigning the pressure on his buttocks before lowering down gingerly. Scanning the crowd in the throne room, his mood lightened upon seeing Jaima enter, the officer taking a spot towards the rear of the room, leaning against the wall, his arms crossed over his chest. He would wait.

"Minister Casta, if you'll put your report in writing, I'll be able to look it over in more detail," he told the man who had never learned to speak in any way other than a monotone. Ten years of listening to the man and his voice grated as much now as it had when Radine had first become king.

"Of course, your majesty," the minister replied with a scowl. The king always asked for the same thing, yet Casta refused to comply before he made his monthly report, to making and handing a copy to the king for him to follow. He bowed and with a huff, turned on his heel to leave.

Radine looked out over the rest of the people waiting for an audience with the king. "Gentlemen, ladies, if you will excuse me, please." Radine rose as the group bowed. Going down the few steps that led to the throne, he walked across the floor to meet with Jaima, trying hard to keep his walk as normal as possible. There was no need to alarm or set the tongues of the ministers and others wagging. The other bowed. "Come with me," Radine commanded, settling his hand on the other's shoulder.

There was a private meeting room not far from the throne room. Radine steered Jaima here and sat in a chair with a sigh. He dropped his crown on the top of the table.

"Still in pain?" Jaima asked.

"Only when I have to sit for interminable hour after hour listening to boring reports and droning sycophants."

"Can't be all that bad."

"I'll let you sit in my place one day and see how you like it."

Jaima held his hands up defensively. "No, thanks, you're the king. I leave it all in your capable hands."

"What do you have to report?"

"There's no sign of Espis in the city, Radine. No one recalls her leaving, and no one seems to know where she is either."

"Spread out then, send a troop on the route she's most likely to take to go home. Then send a second one on the next likely route. I want her found, and now I want her brought to me. She scared McKenna, and insulted her. I won't have her continue to think she has a claim on me."

"How is McKenna?"

"Quiet. She's continuing her lessons, but there doesn't seem to be as much life in her as before. She's lost her enthusiasm and her smile. And since we haven't been able to share *nadryl*, and she turns me down to give her pleasure, I am worried. I sleep with her in my arms every night. Yet I feel like I'm sleeping next to a stranger."

"You've only known her six days, Radine."

"And up to three days ago, I felt as though I'd known her all of my life."

"You're still planning the wedding and coronation?"

"Yes. I'm not going to let Espis take that away from me or McKenna."

"And the sky clad ceremony?"

"We leave in seven days."

"Have you told McKenna about it?"

"I'm afraid I can only handle one kick to the balls per lifetime," Radine replied wryly. "Do you think the armorer can make me a metal device to wear when I have to deliver unpleasant news to McKenna?" Jaima's face scrunched up in sympathy, then he grinned, going through the possibilities in his mind.

"Maybe tying her down before hand? Could prove interesting after, having her at your mercy for anything you might want to do."

"Yes, but eventually I'd have to release her and then run faster than she can."

"Not unless you wear her out first," Jaima suggested.

"She would remember, believe me."

"Perhaps you need to shore up your battle skills. It's been a while since you joined the men in the training field."

"And it will be a bit longer, I'm afraid, at this point. Pologa would have a fit if I aggravate my injury."

Jaima chuckled. "Remember when you dislocated your shoulder? When he tied you to the bed because you wouldn't stay off a *crufa*?" Of course, Radine had been seven at the time, full of bravado and princely snottiness. Pologa had been more stubborn, with the parents' approval.

Radine shared the laugh then sobered. "I'm worried that Espis can't be found. Could she have gone to ground?"

"It's possible. There are any number of places someone can hole up in the city."

"Can you check them out for me? I want this finished as soon as possible."

"I have a few people sleazy enough to get in and take a look."

An eyebrow of surprise rose. "You, sleazy? Really, Jaima, who are you spending time with these days?"

The other bowed formally. "I do what I can to serve my king. I will need some extra coin to pay."

"I'll have it drawn from the treasury. Give me an hour."

"She is a vicious woman. I remember telling you to not get involved with her."

"She was very convincing."

"You let your cock do the convincing," Jaima corrected. "Your only interest was in getting her into your bed, especially after hearing the rumors about her proficiency in *nadryl*."

There was a wistful tone to Radine's voice. "She did things most men only dream about."

"If you wish to keep your balls, you will never say a word to McKenna about that."

Radine's look was rueful. "You do not have to keep reminding me."

"No, the extra cushion on your throne is doing that, I'm sure."

"You caught that?"

"I've seen your father and you sit on that chair for the last thirty years. Of course I noticed. Your head is higher against the carvings."

Gods' rods, Radine thought. That had never occurred to him, something so simple, yet he'd never noticed. He would have to remember that the little things could make the difference, and bring a person down. "In the future I would like for you to point out anything like that."

Jaima nodded assent. "Of course."

"Will you join McKenna and me for dinner? Maybe a different face will lift her spirits."

"I'd be honored. And with the chores you've given me, I'll try to not be late."

Chapter Sixteen

McKenna sat on the opposite side of the carriage from Radine, watching out the window as they traveled along the road through town. He had hoped their first excursion out of the palace since arriving on Taburon would lighten her mood and pull her out of whatever had her somber. There had still been no clue as to the whereabouts of Espis, something that had Radine more and more worried every day. Wherever she was hiding, she was doing it well.

Radine wore one of his royal outfits. White trousers hugged his calves and thighs, a gold stripe down the outside from waist to ankles. Black boots covered his feet to his knees. His shirt was white as well, long sleeved with a high neck, also trimmed in gold at the cuffs and neck. There were gold braided epaulettes on his shoulders. At his waist he had a belt that held a laser weapon on one side and a sword on the other. He'd tied his hair back with a gold ribbon. One of his lesser crowns perched on top of his head.

McKenna wore one of her new dresses, deep blue in color, form fitting, hugging all of her curves to show her off at the best advantage. Radine had picked it out for her and after shooing all of the servants from her chambers, helped her into it, sneaking in a grope or two. He also wanted his woman to look her best, to compliment him, to let everyone know she was his. She had smiled while attempting to bat his hand away, one of the few times she'd smiled in the last few days.

On her feet she wore matching shoes, a soft leather dyed to the same deep blue. Her hair had been dressed into dozens of curls that framed her face and graced her shoulders, ribbons interwoven in the tresses. Annatt had spent two hours fussing about to style it for her.

He watched her as she watched the passing scenery. Two more days had passed and he was feeling up to being able to share *nadryl* with her, but only if she was willing to participate fully. And that wouldn't happen until he could get her back to the delightful, playful person she had been before Espis. How he regretted that episode, and the guards had been severely disciplined for their dereliction. He had heard that Espis had boarded a carriage and made her driver drive like the Hounds of Bernar were after them. She had disappeared after that, to Radine's dismay.

"McKenna," he called softly. "Please little one, won't you talk to me about what is bothering you?" He swung his body around to sit next to her, crowding her on the seat, his sword rattling. Taking her chin in hand, he made her face him. "Please, I hurt for you, but I do not know why. I miss you."

"You sleep with me every night."

"Your body, but your emotions are somewhere else. Was what happened with Espis so terrible that you're having second thoughts about us?"

Her hand gripping the edge of the window tightened until her flesh turned white. She'd been not only frightened by the intrusion, but shaken in her belief that she was right for the king of this planet. How could an Earth woman, so different from the rest of his people, ever hope to be accepted by his people? McKenna was learning about Taburon, but only someone born and raised on the planet could ever truly understand the intricacies of how these people lived.

And if McKenna couldn't have children, would the people blame her – or Radine - for bringing an alien to their world, expecting things to remain as they might have been had he chosen one of their own for wife? Through her learning, she had found out that Radine's family had held rule of the planet, and the people's love, for over ten generations. Their average lifespan here was well over a hundred years, close to one hundred fifty. How could she expect him to jeopardize that? He had been a beloved king for the last ten years, and would continue to be so, as long as he kept the faith of his people.

Words were powerful when in the right hands. If only Espis considered her a whore, McKenna could deal with it. But if Espis began to influence others, especially ones in power, would they turn against Radine? The fact that they had not been able to find Espis meant that she was either in deep hiding, licking her wounds at his rejection, or whispering lies and innuendos to anyone who would listen about the puny Earth woman the king had brought back to Taburon and intended to make queen. Most likely both, rubbing salt into those wounds to make them more inflamed.

Plus, the women here were so beautiful, much more so than she believed of herself, and so much more equal to this man sitting next to her. Tall, muscular in a feminine way, their hair golden wheat and their eyes sparkling with golden color. Radine had lived with them all of his life, grew up with them, had sex with them. McKenna admitted to a certain amount of jealousy, wishing she were taller, maybe thinner by that ten pounds she'd always wanted to lose, able to flow with the grace that seemed natural to these women while she was convinced she clunked across the floor. Oh, Radine had given her pretty dresses and her servant could put her hair into whimsical and fantastic dos, but that was all window dressing. She was still McKenna, the woman from Earth when she woke in the morning.

And while she loved Radine with all her heart, a fact that had nearly brought her to her knees when she realized it four days ago, she couldn't jeopardize his position, his rule - his life. It was entirely possible the people could revolt and Radine would be in grave danger. McKenna wanted to spare Radine any strife, wanted to do what was best for him, but her heart wouldn't allow her to give him up, not yet, and her struggle with what to do was heavy.

She couldn't help the pain that showed in her gaze, and the return expression of hurt that crossed his. Cupping his cheek, she forced a wavering smile. "I love you, so very much. But am I really what your people need in a queen?"

"What do you mean?"

"I'm not from Taburon, nor Taburon. How can I ever possibly hope to take the place of a Taburon?" Her hand dropped. "The people love you, Radine. What if that changes, because of me?"

"If the people love me, then they should love whom I choose for a wife."

"It's not that simple. You have obligations to them, you have to think of them in whatever decisions you make. If one person is unhappy, he is easy to placate. But what if a whole group of them, the whole planet, becomes unhappy? How will you fix that? What if I'm the reason they're unhappy?"

"I would give up the throne in that case."

"Would you be happy with that decision? In the long run, isn't there a chance you might come to resent me, because you thought you had to choose between the two?" Her head tilted. "I couldn't ask you to abdicate. Your family has ruled for so long, it's as much a part of you as the blood that flows through your veins."

Sitting back against the carriage, he felt his world start to unravel before him. "Are you saying you wish to return to Earth?"

McKenna's eyes moistened and she turned away from him. "I don't know what to do. I'm trying to look far into the future, to imagine what might happen if things don't turn out the way we are trying to envision them. All I know is that I care too much to hurt you, and it's tearing me apart." She wiped her tears from her cheeks. "Maybe I was fooling myself to reality before Espis came into our bath, not thinking with my head, but feeling with my heart."

"That bitch Espis did this to you," he growled.

"Maybe she just said something that was a wake-up call. And since she hasn't been found, who knows what kind of damage she might be doing trying to hurt you."

"We will find her," he said vehemently.

"I know, I trust you in that. But I don't trust her. She was very angry, Radine, and a very angry woman is not someone you want to tangle with." She caught his rueful glance to his lap. "That was just a knee-jerk response," she clarified. "True anger is internal, it festers and grows, until it explodes in a most horrific way. That is what you need to be afraid of. That is what a woman like Espis is capable of. And that is what scares me like you wouldn't believe."

Gathering her close, he pulled her into his lap, wrapping his arms around her waist. "Then we need to fight her together, McKenna. If you give into your fears, she wins. If you leave, she wins. Even if those things were to happen, if you left me, I would never take her for my wife, and she would never be queen. Yet she still wins, for she has made you leave me and broken my heart. I will never be hers, there was never a chance of that, even before I met you. She was what you called a fuck, nothing more."

"But she doesn't believe that."

"That is why I have Jaima doing everything he can to find her. At first I wasn't going to confront her, but she needs to hear it from me, to be made to realize just what she has done before I banish her from the city for the rest of her life." He kissed her lightly. "And I need you by my side when it happens. I need you to have faith in what we have, to be strong in front of her, for me, for yourself, for us."

"It still doesn't answer the problem about you taking someone not Taburon as a wife and queen."

Raising a fist, Radine pounded on the top of the carriage. The vehicle slowed to pull to a stop. "Why don't you let the people make that decision?" He slid her from his lap as he reached around her to open the carriage door.

They had stopped in the middle of the city, in a combination shop/housing district, the streets crowded with people going about their daily business, pausing in their pursuits especially upon seeing the king's carriage traveling the road through the town. The troop of soldiers, the king's guards, riding the horse-like *crufas*, surrounded the carriage, the hooves of the animals clopping on the pavement, ready to protect their ruler.

Radine stepped down from the carriage, surveying the area, bowing his head to the gathering crowd, reaching a hand back to help McKenna exit the vehicle. A groom raced from the back of the carriage, too late, to help his king, but holding the door open, his head bowed.

The faces of the people broke into wide smiles upon seeing their king. It was a rare treat when he stopped in the city and dismounted his *crufa* or disembarked his carriage. Usually he was on his way to some important meeting, passing through the city, acknowledging the people with a wave, but little more. Perhaps twice a year he would come into the town to visit with the people and see how they were doing in their lives. Word had spread that he had found a woman to be his wife and queen, but that she was from some planet called Earth. They were anxious to meet her, and he had brought her down to them.

McKenna blushed when a round of applause rose from the crowd, smiles all around, the people crowding closer to the royal couple. Radine raised a hand asking for silence, keeping McKenna next to his side. "Thank you for your welcome. I wish you to meet McKenna, your future queen and my wife to be. She fears you may not approve."

As one, the crowd bowed to her for a moment, then applauded again as they straightened, reaching out to touch the woman who would rule next to their king. There were no scowls or frowns on their faces, only pleasure and happiness for their king. He'd been a long time without a wife, he needed to marry and have the joy it brought, along with a couple of children to fill the royal nursery.

From between the legs of the adults, a child of about seven or so pushed her way through, a bouquet of flowers in her hand. The girl had long, curly blonde hair and wore a blue tunic over a pair of brown pants. She curtsied prettily, shyly, her eyes down, shoving the flowers forward. "For you, Your Highness," she said in sweet voice.

McKenna's heart melted. Drawing the flowers to her breast, she bent down to the child, raising her face with a finger under the child's chin. "Thank you," she replied as she smoothed a hand along the girls scalp. "What is your name?"

"I am Lasa, Your Highness."

McKenna buried her nose into the bouquet, taking a deep whiff. "These are *freemas*?"

"Yes, Your Highness."

"They are my favorite, Lasa. They have a scent like the cinnamon back on Earth, and I love cinnamon." Lasa's smile stretched from ear to ear as she curtsied again.

Radine stood back as she interacted with the crowd, every one of the people wishing to speak with McKenna, offering her gifts from their shops or what they might have had on their person when the king's carriage stopped. Mostly, they offered their well wishes and congratulations on landing such a fine man as the king, and their assurances that she was welcomed and would be a great queen.

Seeing one shopkeeper with whom he was familiar, Radine waved the man over and whispered in his ear for several moments. The man nodded and moved back through the crowd to disappear into his store.

By the time he returned, McKenna's arms were laden with gifts, items that the groomsman began plucking from her to make room for more, placing them in the carriage for safekeeping. The king opened the package the man passed to him, nodding in approval at the item inside, then fishing in a pocket for coin. The man waved payment away, it was his gift for the new queen. With a handshake and a word of thanks, Radine stepped back to the carriage door.

He thanked the people for their warm welcome, saying they had to leave. Helping McKenna back into the carriage, he stepped in after her, taking the seat next to her as the groomsman shut the door. The carriage shimmied slightly as the groomsman climbed back on, the driver flicked the reins and they began to move off to the cheers of the people. The guards once more surrounded the carriage, keeping pace.

"So?" Radine asked.

"They are wonderful," McKenna answered, her face buried in the bouquet again. There was a light in her eyes that he hadn't seen in days.

"Do you still doubt you will not be accepted?"

"No, not anymore. I still don't trust Espis, and I won't feel comfortable until she is caught."

"Nor will I, little one."

"You didn't tell me where we are going."

"There is a cottage on the outskirts of the city. It is in a park, you call it a botanical garden. We will stay there overnight."

"But I didn't bring a change of clothes."

"You won't need them. We'll have total privacy. As soon as we get there, I expect you to remove your dress. You won't need it until we're ready to return."

"What about your injury?" He shot a glance to his crotch, her eyes following. The obvious bulge showed that he had most likely recovered from her unfortunate knee-jerk reaction, the outline proof that he no longer wore the protective cup. McKenna's eyes widened, her lips pursed in a small moue. "Oh," she murmured.

Having pulled one of her hands onto his thigh, one finger traced the lines on the inside of her hand, the touch so soft it was barely a touch, but Radine concentrated hard on the swirls his finger was making. His eyes slid towards her, his head turning just enough to see her face. He nodded in agreement. "Oh, indeed," he confirmed. "I intend to make up for lost time, little one," he promised.

Chapter Seventeen

As Radine thanked the carriage driver and groomsman and directed the guards to scatter, but not too far, McKenna walked around the cottage.

It was a cottage only by the strictest of standards, the entire place more than twice the size of her entire apartment on Earth. They entered into a large sitting area, plush furniture scattered around, throw rugs covering the floor. A large fireplace graced one wall, firewood set and waiting for a match to light it. Beyond the sitting area, two hallways split the building, one short, the other longer. The shorter one led to a kitchen area. Opening a cooling unit, she found it stocked with enough food for twenty. A dish was warming in the oven, the table for two already laid with utensils and glasses. He'd planned this well in advance.

The longer hall ended in a bedroom. A single, wide bed sat against a back wall, night tables on either side. The bed was decorated in thick blankets and at least a half dozen pillows. There was a large wardrobe opposite the bed, empty for now, but she could see it filled with their clothes if they made visiting the cottage a habit. To the right of the bed and through a doorway was another large bath, the tub big enough for four. Above the tub was a free flowing waterfall, the calming splash of the water a white noise meant to soothe. She passed her hand under the waterfall, surprised to find it warm enough to stand under. Off to the side on a shelf was a collection of soaps, oils and shampoos, waiting. McKenna twisted the cap from one of the bottles and sniffed – *freema*. She had been honest saying she loved the scent of the flower and soaps, creams, powders and perfumes were being created for her use.

From the outer room, she heard the door close with a definitive click followed by the tread of Radine's boots on the floor as he went in search of his woman. A shiver raced down her spine, her pussy swelled and flooded and she rubbed her thighs together to contain the excitement that filled her breast. Hurriedly closing the bottle, she left the bath area only to encounter him as he entered the room.

One of Radine's eyebrows rose expectantly. "McKenna," he simply said. He'd checked out his 'equipment' the day before and everything worked fine with no discomfort. He was going to make full use of his endowments.

She blushed furiously but reached for the fastenings to her dress. The top opened at the back of her neck, the sides splitting to fall forward.

At her shoulders, she pulled the garment forward slowly, teasing him as she lowered it to reveal her breasts. Arching her back, she pushed them forward, never taking her eyes from his, pleased as they darkened, the pupils widening.

The bodice fell as she hooked her fingers at her waist, pushing it further along her body, wiggling her hips back and forth. Bending at the waist, her breasts dangled, jiggling enticingly until she had lowered the dress far enough for it to finish falling by itself. McKenna made sure she shook her shoulder enough to make her breasts swing, to tease him, her nipples hard peaks that pointed to the floor. Straightening, she stretched, her arms rising above her head, her heart beating faster when he groaned in response. Her pussy was totally bare, the hair removed permanently by the cream he had told her about days ago. Delighted at the results, she had used it on her legs and underarms as well. She let her eyes close slowly then open just as slowly, her gaze settling on the placket of his trousers. He had engorged at least a third more because of her striptease.

Radine's blood pulsed through him as she completed her little striptease, shaking her breasts in his face to tease him unfairly. He'd waited so long for this day, his frustration growing daily until he believed he would explode for wanting her, wanting to bury himself deep inside her and feel her sheath encompass him tightly, wetly, and warmly. The waiting was over.

He rushed her, grabbing a fistful of her hair, tilting her head back as he pulled her closer by her waist. She groaned, partly in rising passion and partly in dismay at the loosening of the ribbons that her hairdresser had spent the better part of two hours tying into her curls. Ribbons and pins drifted to their feet. "You are mine," he growled before punishing her with a crushing kiss. His lips were hard, grating, demanding, his mouth sliding over hers until he'd forced her to open. With his tongue, he darted into her mouth, coaxing, dancing with her tongue, sweeping around to taste every part of the warm, moist interior. He sucked her tongue into his own mouth, nipping the end of it with his teeth.

Her lips were swollen and well kissed when he released her. "No more doubts, McKenna. I love you, I will always love you. I am stronger with you, and we will make sure the people see that what we have is so much more important than anything else. They will weep with wanting to have what we have." Holding her by her arse, he lifted her and pressed her tightly against his crotch. As he rubbed his cock against her pussy, she realized for sure that he no longer wore the device. There was a stain of pre-cum on the front of his pants when he set her back on her feet. "On the bed, legs spread," he ordered. "Now!" he added, emphasizing the command with a swat to her butt. McKenna yelped and ran.

Radine stalked her into the bedroom as she hopped onto the bed and stretched out on her back, spreading her legs until they reached almost to the edges. Her pussy was wet, weeping profusely, her thighs covered in moisture. Propping herself up by the elbows, she watched him. He toed off his boots as he tore at the fastenings of his pants, already having discarded the belt with the weapons in the sitting area. Once he had the trousers opened, he went to work on the shirt, ripping the buttons off in his haste to get rid of the garment, heedless of the ones that scattered across the floor, the shirt joining them. The trousers quickly followed, his cock springing forward, fully engorged, the end weeping more drops of pre-come.

He couldn't wait. Climbing between her legs, he let his cock find its way home, shoving into her in one move until he was balls deep in her sheath. He needed to do it now, his need so great that he knew he would have never lasted if he'd spent time rousing her further. She screamed softly with the invasion of his cock, falling back against the bed, arching her back, her breaths fast. Holding himself above her, his arms locked, he pounded her pussy mercilessly, his hips bucking like lightning, grunting with every thrust.

When he felt his balls tighten, his limbs quivering with an impending orgasm, he shifted slightly to rub against that one spot in her sheath that would drive her over the edge with him, still pistoning into her with unyielding force.

His body started to quake and he threw his head back, the tendons in his neck tight, to yell out as his cock pulsed, his balls tightening, slamming her with every spurt of come that shot from the end of his cock. He'd not totally lost his mind, reaching between their bodies to seek out and furiously strum over her clit until she screamed at reaching her own peak and falling over. The spasms of her sheath dragged everything he had from his cock until there was no come left in him to bath the opening to her womb.

Radine's head hung down, his hair, having loosened from its tie, falling over his shoulders. His back heaved with his breathing, a drop of sweat dripped from his chin. Radine drew in a deep breath of air, slowly pulled his softening yet still sensitive cock free from her body and collapsed next to her.

"I am sorry, McKenna. I knew I would not last long."

Rolling towards him, she slipped an arm over his waist, her hand resting on his chest. McKenna lightly scraped over his nipples. "I enjoyed every second of it," she teased.

He growled playfully. "Give me some time and I promise that I will take a lot more than a few seconds. Even more than a few minutes. Perhaps several hours," he mused.

McKenna giggled. "Are you sure the guards are far enough away?" she asked. "I can get kind of loud."

"They would never dare to interrupt their king," he promised. "Only with a matter of life or death." Flexing his arms, he indicated that he wanted her to move. "Straddle me." She slid a glance down his body. He was already hardening again, each heartbeat pulse lifting his cock higher above his body.

McKenna lifted herself to settle over his groin, scooting up when he gave a tug on her knees. His hands immediately went to her breasts, wrapping over them to squeeze. "You have beautiful breasts, your nipples are so sweet, so responsive." And taking the little nubs between his thumb and middle finger, he pinched them, rolling his fingers and her nipples until she moaned. Tugging, he lowered her to his mouth, his lips sucking on her left nipple, nipping until she winced, then soothing with a swipe of his tongue. Her right nipple received the same attention.

Pairing them, he managed to catch both nipples at the same time in his mouth, his tongue flipping them together, her breasts squeezed tightly. "Before we are through," he promised, "I will thrust my cock between your breasts until I come, your tongue will taste the end of my cock and you will drink every drop." Radine sucked around her breasts, lifting enough skin to nip it then soothe with a lick. "I will teach you how to suck my cock, take it down your throat and swallow. It creates the most delicious feeling, so tight as I plug you."

Her heart beat faster, her blood began to boil and her pussy flooded, coating his stomach with warm wetness, making it easier for her to slide across his skin. Behind her, his cock had fully risen, pulsing with blood, punching into the small of her back. When she slid forward, it touched on her anus. His hips lifted every time he felt his cock tap at the small, wrinkled flower. "I will teach you to take me into your arse. It'll pinch at first, but there are so many nerves inside to excite. With a dildo in your pussy, you will be so tight. Then I'll switch it and put a dildo in your arse and we will share nadryl. You will feel so full, like there are two men inside you." He landed a particularly hard bite to a nipple, satisfied to hear her utter a soft squeal. "But it will be me," he growled, "only me."

Radine pulled her down by the shoulders until her breasts touched his chest. With his hands at her hips, he lifted her, his cock seeking out its home, finding it without error and slipping inside. Helping her by directing her by her hips, he set a steady rhythm of entering her pussy and then withdrawing to the tip of his plummed head before shoving back in completely.

When he began to feel her sheath flutter in impending orgasm, Radine stilled, buried deep inside her body until her body calmed. He didn't want to end this too soon. After a few minutes, he shifted her, placing her on her hands and knees, coming at her from behind. Penetration was deep and satisfying, the tip of his cock touching against the entrance to her womb. Every time he thrust in, the head of his cock kissed against her cervix, her breath coming out in a gasp with every deep stroke.

Again, when she started to come, when her sheath fluttered, he buried himself totally within her and stilled, waiting. McKenna groaned in frustration, the second time Radine denied her her release, so close yet so far away and desperate to peak and find ecstasy. Finally, he stretched out on the bed, laid her next to him, her back to his front, lifting her top leg and sliding home. In this position, he played with her breasts until he could feel her approaching climax when his fingers delved through the folds of her pussy and found her clit. He pinched it – hard.

She screamed as she climaxed hard and fast, her entire body shaking with orgasm, milking his cock to his release within her pussy.

Growling stomachs woke them from the doze they both fell into, curled around each other, his cock still held within her pussy until he rolled and disengaged. Putting a meal together became a test of endurance – which one could hold out the longest against the 'accidental' spills on fingers, chest, breast, nipples, or cock. Finally exhausted from trying to prepare something to eat, they grabbed whatever they could find and raced back to the bed to enjoy a repast of food and sex. Sated, sexually and with food, wrapped in each other's embrace, they slept.

Chapter Eighteen

McKenna woke with a start, disoriented for a moment until the warmth from the naked body behind her brought back the memories of a night spent in passion. Radine was a considerate lover, making sure she was more than ready to take him in her sheath before plunging inside. Not counting the first time when he had no control over his need to have her.

Their stop in the city and the warm reception she'd received did wonders to boosting her confidence in her being accepted as Radine's wife and the future queen of Taburon. His hard, fast, and then gentle loving proved how much he wanted her, how much he was willing to give up for her, no matter her feelings on the matter. She was still totally convinced that she wouldn't allow him to give up the throne, but how she would deal with the problem, if it ever became one, was still up in the air. She only knew she loved him beyond all reason. He was her heart and soul and everything in between.

Lifting his arm carefully, she slipped out from under it and off the side of the bed. The floor was cold on her feet, the air chilled against her skin. Grabbing his shirt, she pulled it on, leaving it unbuttoned. There weren't many buttons to bother with any more anyway, most of them scattered across the floor. Her mouth felt dry. Taking care of business in the bathroom, she padded barefoot into the kitchen for a drink.

Glass in hand, lost in the glowing aftermath of his lovemaking, she was not aware of the six men coming out of the shadows of the sitting area until they stood less than two feet from her, blocking her in the small area. Each man was dressed, head to toe in black, their faces covered so only their eyes showed. Their eyes were feral. One man held rope in his hands, another had several pieces of material dangling from his fist. A third had strapped Radine's weapons belt around his waist.

The glass fell from her hand to shatter on the floor. "Who are you?" she asked, crossing her hands over her body, deeply aware that all she wore was Radine's shirt and it dangled open, her breasts on display with the slightest movement.

"Get her," she heard one man say, his voice muffled by the mask.

As one, they all advanced on McKenna, rushing her until she backed into a corner. McKenna screamed, fighting her attackers with

191

blows that landed with little effect. Kicking at them was useless as she wore no shoes on her feet and only hurt her toes in the process.

A gag was stuffed into her mouth and tied, her hands were brought together. With a sudden burst of strength, she shoved through her attackers and started to run for the bedroom and Radine, until one of the men grabbed her by the hair. She screamed again as he backhanded her across the face and she fell to the floor. Once again, her hands were grabbed and rope was wrapped around her wrists several times and secured.

"Let her go!" Radine bellowed, having been awakened by McKenna's scream. He'd not bothered to dress, racing from the bedroom to find, horrified, six men attempting to abduct his woman. He instantly felt regret for being careless enough by leaving his weapons in the other room and well out of his reach. His heart lurched as he saw one of the men with his belt and weapons around his waist. "I am your king, I order you to release her!"

One of the attackers laughed. "And what do you plan on using for a weapon, *your lordship*, your cock?" he goaded. Laughter filled the small area as the rest of the men chuckled loudly.

Three of the men broke away from their continued fight to tie McKenna, her feet proving a problem as she kicked out and struggled. A second smack across the head caused her to see stars and stunned, she stopped struggling long enough for her feet to be tied together.

The three men surrounded Radine as he crouched into a fighting stance, his eyes trying to follow each man. Feinting, one man drew his attention as another stepped into his space and punched him in the side. Radine twisted in that direction, another blow landed in his stomach from the opposite side, driving the breath out of him. A third punch to his back had him nearly seeing stars. Once she'd been secured, two of the remaining three men joined their compatriots in attacking the king, now outnumbered five to one. As he hunched over, down on one knee, trying to catch his breath, they fell on him as one, landing blow after blow on his torso until they'd beaten him to the floor. McKenna, held tightly against the last man, watched, tears falling from her eyes at the sight of Radine falling beneath his attackers.

The man with the sword raised the pommel and slammed it into Radine's head. The king grunted, falling further. His hand raised, the attacker pommeled Radine once more, felling the king completely, his body still under the assault. Once more the attacker's hand lifted. This would be the killing blow.

"Do not kill him!" came the order from the side near the door to the cottage. McKenna felt her heart fall as Espis moved into the cottage and closer to the group. The attacker's hand paused, then fell to his side as he straightened. "He is your king, and I want him alive to suffer." Espis knelt down to make sure the king was still breathing, then stood. Radine moaned, trying to lift his head, but couldn't, bordering as he was on the edge of darkness.

Her glance slid over the captive woman, disgust written all over it. The amount of malevolence McKenna saw frightened her to her very soul and she knew she could not expect to live much longer.

Espis's lips lifted in a snarl as she turned away. "Bring her," she ordered. Grabbing the struggling woman, not caring exactly how or how much they may hurt her, McKenna was hefted, then tossed over the shoulders of one of the attackers. She began to weep when they passed by Radine, the puddle of blood under his head slowly spreading across the floor. The door slammed shut on the grisly scene.

Chapter Nineteen

Jaima pounded on the door to the cottage again. "Radine!" he yelled for the third time. The guards sent with the king had not reported in for the last two hours, which had had Jaima jumping onto his *crufa* and racing out the palace gates, a troop of men on his heels. He'd not even waited for the animals to stop before hitting the ground and stalking to the door, his laser weapon drawn. When there was no answer, he turned slightly and slammed at the door with his shoulder, then slammed it again when the first time was ineffective. The door burst open and he nearly fell in, catching himself on the jambs before he stumbled. Behind him, guards crowded the doorway. Jaima paused to scan the room.

"Gods' rods," he uttered softly going to one knee next to the still body of Radine. He was afraid to touch the man, terrified that the king was dead, but a single rise and fall of his chest allied his fears. Jaima placed a hand on the king's shoulder. "Radine?"

The king groaned, stirring, attempting to rise, moaning with pain. He fell back to the floor. Jaima swiveled on his heels. "Send for the king's physician!" he ordered to the men who gathered around. Without waiting to see, he knew one bowed and fled to mount his *crufa* and race back to the palace.

"McKenna?" Radine mumbled, his voice soft, his head pounding, his body beyond sore.

"Search the cottage," Jaima ordered. "Lay still, Radine," he said to the king, pushing on his shoulder. "I've had your physician sent for."

Radine struggled to rise again. "Have to find McKenna," he growled. "They took her."

"Who? Who took her?"

"Men dressed in black. They tied her, hit her."

The guards returned, shaking their heads. There was no sign of the woman. "There's a broken glass in the kitchen," one reported, "and some blood on the floor."

"They took her," Radine repeated, trying once more to rise and falling back to finally give in to the pain and weakness.

"Get something to cover the king," Jaima said. "Radine, you shouldn't move. You're bleeding from your head." A blanket was

196

draped over the king's nude body, someone else handed a towel to Jaima to press against the wound. Radine hissed in pain, but remained still. Jaima sat on the floor, crossing his legs as they waited for the physician.

"It was Espis," Radine said softly, remembering. "I heard her voice after they beat me."

"We'll find her, Radine. I promise."

His voice faded. "Couldn't find Espis," he whispered. "Should have found…"

Jaima kept a hand on his king and friend. "No, we didn't, and I am so sorry," he apologized to the unconscious man.

When next Radine regained consciousness, he had been moved to the bed, his head was turned to the left side and someone was tugging on his hair. Only his hips had been covered with a sheet so Pologa could examine the rest of his body for broken bones and injuries. "Ow!" he cried out vehemently, trying to move from the torture.

A heavy hand clamped down on his head, holding him still. "If you move again," Pologa said in a calm but authoritative voice, "I will sedate you. You have a nice sized gash in your head and I need to clean it before I can stitch it. It's too wide for the healing ray." Radine felt the coolness of water at the back of his head. "Good thing you have a hard head," the physician mumbled.

Radine ceased, letting the man tend to his wound. "McKenna. Has there been any word on her?"

Jaima stepped into his line of vision. Funny, Radine thought, one Jaima was bad enough. Now there were two. "No, Sire, we've had no word. No one has seen anything. At least no one we have been able to find yet."

Radine winced. "I want every single troop out looking. If they're off duty, pull them back on. There has to be some clue, somewhere. Where are the guards who were stationed around the cottage?"

"Dead, Your Majesty. Their throats slit."

Radine's eyes closed briefly in regret. They were good men, all of them, most he knew by name, and now they were dead. Espis had a lot to answer for. "Promote all of them," he ordered, "and make sure those with families are taken care of. They did not have to die." He swore softly. "Leave off, physician. I am in enough pain already." Pologa glowered, ignored the king and continued tending to the injury. The man could be such a child at times.

"I'll have word sent back to the palace. Their bodies are being returned there."

"Every one of them has earned a funeral with honors. See it is done."

Jaima bowed. "I will, Sire."

"And Jaima, have a warrant for execution drawn up."

Jaima stiffened. "Radine, you cannot. She has royal blood."

"I can and I will," Radine ground out. "She assaulted her king, and kidnapped my woman and queen. When Espis is found, whether or not McKenna lives, she dies." Pologa dabbed a numbing cream over the now cleaned wound, preparing his needle and thread for stitching while he waited for it to take effect. "Make seven of them, one each for the six men who helped her. They die as well." Radine lifted his head slightly, dropping it back down when dizziness overwhelmed him, and with a groan, he breathed deeply. He was still nude he discovered, though someone had tossed a sheet over his hips. He caught sight of bruising at his ribs, and his body hurt from trying to rise. The bedcovers were still tossed back the way he'd thrown them when McKenna's scream had awakened him. "What time is it?"

"Near dawn. The guards were killed about three hours ago."

"How did you know?"

"After Espis's first break through security at the palace, I had the guards set so they would report to each other every half hour, then one they designated as team commander would report to me every hour. When they didn't report the first time, I waited a half hour. When there was no report the second time, I raced out to see what was going on. I found you on the floor, bleeding, starting to come to from being hit on the head several times."

"Several?"

"At least twice, Your Majesty," Pologa confirmed. "The second one ripped a chunk of your scalp loose. Another strike, and your skull would have been broken. You probably have a concussion as it is." The physician leaned close and began to sew.

"The rest of me?"

"Bruised, all over your chest and back, and you'll be sore for a few days, but nothing broken. Which surprises me. There's a boot print in one of those bruises." He concentrated on his stitching. "Had to cut some of your hair, but it'll grow back." He pulled a thread through the skin. "You'll have to keep this dry."

"Yes, yes," Radine agreed impatiently. He'd been through it before. A king who was a fighter at times did not go through life without a few scrapes and scratches that needed stitching. He scowled at Jaima. "Why are you still here?" He waved his hand. "Go, find my McKenna." Jaima shot a glance to the physician, questioning, getting a nod in response. The king would be all right in time, there was no need for him to stay and stand guard.

"Stay with the king," he instructed to the guard by the doorway to the bedroom before leaving.

Radine sighed heavily, resigned to waiting for others to do what he was desperate to do himself. Life wouldn't be the same without his McKenna, he wouldn't know what to do with himself if he had lost her.

No one would be able to take her place. He would die a single man, the kingdom turning over into the hands of others, and he would not care a whit. Let them have it. He felt broken already, his heart ached.

He lay quietly as the physician finished stitching and bandaged the wound, all silent in the bedroom save for the physician's sound of satisfaction and the king's steady breathing, punctuated on occasion by an curse when his wound pained. Gathering his tools, the doctor set them aside. With a small vial from his medical kit, he filled a glass with water and dropped ten drops from the vial into the glass, swirling it around.

"Here, Your Majesty, drink this," he instructed, sliding a hand under the king's head and lifting.

A wave of dizziness washed over the injured man. "I'm going to be sick," he warned. Pologa shoved a pail under his face right before he threw up, emptying the contents of his stomach, his head swimming with dizziness that forced him to close his eyes. Still the room tilted. Radine heaved forcefully, his stomach emptying of its contents, though not much remained so long after he'd eaten. His stomach burned and twisted, his mouth tasted soiled. When he'd heaved everything he had, feeling as though he'd been cut in half, his body shaking from the effort, he laid back, slinging his arm over his eyes.

"Let's try that again," Pologa offered, lifting the king's head again more slowly. He tipped the glass gently, letting the king sip.

"Gods' rods, that's vile!" Radine groused, but finished the potion filled glass at Pologa's insistence.

"It'll ease the pain and help you rest." The king fought to rise instead, but was easily pushed back. "You need to rest for now. You've been badly injured. If you go off gallivanting around now, you'll only make things worse."

"I have to find McKenna," the king insisted, his voice slurred as the drugs took effect. Within a minute he was sleeping, his breathing slow and even. The physician covered the man, shaking his head. He hoped the woman was certainly worth it, he thought as he pulled up a chair next to the bed.

Chapter Twenty

McKenna was totally sore, from her head to her feet. Tossed over the back of a *crufa*, the group rode for what seemed like hours, at first galloping like the devil himself was nipping at their heels. As the darkness lifted, she could see fog blanketing the ground, swirling around her hair which hung below her, slung over the animal as she was.

When she began to slide towards the body of the man who held her, she grimaced, his clothing scratchy and rough against her skin. They were riding onto higher ground, the animals listing to the rear. She bounced and banged on the creature, the hand of the rider who steered the animal gripped around a swath of her shirt, holding her in her spot, but not very well. She was afraid that at any second she was going to fall from the *crufa*, her head hitting the ground first, her modesty not far behind.

The back of the shirt was pulled up. She knew her pussy was on show for anyone who bothered to look and once when they slowed down to navigate a treacherous stream, the rider's hand had strayed to finger her ruthlessly, laughing at finding her unresponsive. He slapped her ass hard, catching both cheeks where they met the tops of her thighs, gaining a muffled squeal of pain and revulsion from their helpless captive. Once or twice another rider would bring his *crufa* close to slide his hand along her slit or play with her pussy, delving between the lips to find her treasures, to touch what the king had deemed his. Her buttocks would be red by the time they reached their destination with all of the swats it was dealt.

They were going to rape her, she was sure of that. She could survive. Any torture Espis was planning to throw at her, she could survive. But she also knew that when they were done playing, when Espis had felt she had sucked enough pain and humiliation from her victim, she would be killed, horrendously put to death in order to cause Radine the most suffering as possible. The thought of that was enough to bring tears to her eyes, tears that dropped to the ground and stained the rocks as they rode.

By the time she was ready to give anything to Espis might she have wanted as long as she spared Radine, they slowed in their flight. Lifting her head, McKenna glanced around the leg of the rider and saw a large house – a castle of stone – at the end of the road. As the gates opened, they clopped through, bringing their *crufas* to a halt in a courtyard.

McKenna was dragged across the saddle of the *crufa* and made to stand on the hard, stone ground, held up as her legs folded under her, then lifted to be slung over another of the men's shoulders. "Take her to the dungeon," Espis ordered. "You may play with her, but no nadryl until I say so," she reminded.

"Yes, milady," came the reply and she was bounced around as the man followed orders, his footsteps heavy, deliberately making her wince in pain as his shoulder cut into her belly. Three of the kidnappers followed, chuckling in glee. During the whole trip through the castle, her captor kept one hand to hold her by the thighs while the other fingered her pussy, searching out and finding her clit, making short forays into her body though she was dry and it hurt.

Down a set of steps, into frigid temperatures, they carried McKenna, through a heavy wooden door where they stood her on her feet. As lights were turned on, she looked around the room, dismay filling her as she made out the devices and instruments of torture scattered around the room. The walls were stone, there were no windows or other avenues of escape except for the door through which they'd just entered.

A large wooden cross took up one wall, straps hanging from the corners, whips on pegs nearby. Against another wall was a triangular stand, the point at the top, shackles waiting near the floor. Various benches and other furniture filled in the rest of the space. Chains hung from the ceiling and all around the room, ending in shackles. A dark satin covered many of the implements and she would have been quaking furiously had she known positively that it was dried blood.

Hefted by the waist, she was placed in front of the cross, her back against the wood. A hook above her head kept her hands anchored and controlled. As one man held her feet tightly, the ropes around her ankles were freed, shackles were wrapped around each ankle and her legs were spread wide, each ankle tied to bolts in the floor. The stretch on her tendons was fierce, and her pussy was totally opened to whatever devious plans were in store for her.

Following the example of her feet with her arms, they were stretched out along the crossbeam and shackled. Her neck was secured with another rope, forcing her to tilt her head back, her breasts outthrust, quivering. Her nipples had tightened in fear and cold, plucked to firmer hardness by the man directly in front of her, an evil grin on his face. They left the gag in her mouth. McKenna feared they were going to cut her when, revealing a knife, the man who'd pinched her nipples sliced through the material of her shirt, shredding it and pulling the tatters from her body to toss aside into a corner.

Two of the men took a breast each, the third dropping to his haunches at her feet to spread her pussy lips further apart. McKenna shook her body viciously, trying to shake them off, but she was tied so well that all it did was shake her breasts, making the men laugh. The one on the right lifted his hand and slapped her breast hard.

"Stay still, *skala*, we won't hurt you, much. We'll leave enough for Espis to have her turn."

McKenna screamed as he grabbed her breast with both hands and squeezed it, making the nipple stand out. His partner followed. Latching on with his mouth, he bit the nipple, hard, until she screamed louder, sawing his teeth back and forth. She feared he was going to chew her nipple from her body, but he took care to only cause her unbelievable pain that radiated throughout her tender breast tissue.

Between her legs, the third man found her clit and sucked it, hard, until it hurt, grabbing the tender nubbin with his teeth and holding on as he worked her with his tongue. She tried to close her legs, but she was tied tightly and wide open. His fingers pistoned in and out of her body, her channel dry, his fingers like sandpaper against her inner sheath.

McKenna screamed until her voice failed, hanging listlessly on the cross as they continued to torment her, biting, pinching, spearing rough fingers into her body, her tears falling endlessly. The pain was overwhelming. Her round ass globes were separated and a dry finger was shoved into her rear opening, drawing a screech from their helpless victim. She tried as long as she could until finally she began to block it out, to let her body fall into a state of apathy until even the strongest of bites no longer had any effect on her and garnered no response. They slapped her, they swatted her arse, squeezing the rounded flesh until they left nail marks. They pinched her nipples and clit until the nubs reddened, and she showed no response. Losing interest for a toy that would not fight back, or scream or show any indication that it felt anything, the three men, disgusted, left her alone, adding one last slap to her face to punish her for her lack of involvement. McKenna's head fell forward, her body quivering, pained from head to toe, praying for a quick end.

McKenna remembered the night with Radine, the loving, the laughter, the gentle cuddling and quiet talk after hard and fast nadryl. The feeling of him deep inside her body, his mouth on her breast, suckling like a babe, and the dream she harbored that someday there would be a real baby to hold at her breast to nurse. Radine would be a great father, caring and supportive. He knew how to laugh, and even though it was adult games for now, he knew how to play. McKenna wanted that for him, she wanted to give it to him, to comfort him when he was sad and be his sounding board when he was frustrated with the role he held on Taburon. She wanted to know more of his people, to go back to little Lasa and give her a bouquet of flowers, invite her to the palace and share sweets and tea with the child.

McKenna had been honest when she'd said she trusted Radine, but not Espis, but she realized with finality that it did her no good now to think 'I told you so' because of it. She was going to die. There was going to be so much she would miss, that she wanted with all of her heart. She remembered being told as a child that every cloud had a silver lining and knew that if there was an afterlife, she would finally be able to see her parents and brother again. McKenna took small comfort in that, and would spend whatever time she had left preparing for that time. She'd never been religious, but she prayed that whatever god might exist that he would forgive her for whatever bad thing she'd done. After long consideration she knew her slate was clear, there would be no holding her back when the time came.

Vowing to not give Espis any satisfaction in whatever form of torture she had planned, McKenna steeled herself to endure whatever pain came her way. Perhaps she would cry out, that was inevitable, but she would never beg, if begging was Espis's goal.

How long she hanged there she couldn't even try to guess – long enough for the cold of the room to penetrate deep into her bones. She shivered uncontrollably, the cold seeping deeply inside. McKenna would never be warm again. Cold torture, cold death, cold burial – that was her future. Radine would avenge her, of that she was sure, but there was no warmth for McKenna.

The door swung open, grating on its hinges. McKenna's head lifted enough to see who had come in to torment her now, acceptance filling her when it was Espis that entered the room. The Taburon was so haughty, too haughty for her own good, too stupid perhaps to realize that nothing would ever entice Radine to take her for a wife now. She walked with the bearing of someone who believed they were above the law. McKenna wondered if they had an equivalent to the old saw about the bigger they are the harder they fall, Espis was heading to a monumental nose dive.

Espis sauntered to the Earth woman, grabbing her by the hair and slamming her head against the back of the cross so she could look the Taburon in the eye. McKenna cried out, her chest heaving.

"*Skala*," Espis hissed. "Miserable, puny Earth woman. You are not fit to clean the mud from my shoes, nor his shoes, yet you think yourself high enough to become the wife of a king and his queen? Pah!" Espis went to one of the walls, perusing the whips there. Lovingly, affectionately, she caressed each one, sliding the strands through her fingers, rubbing the leather against her cheek. "Does he have to go easy on you during nadryl, denying himself his full pleasure because he is afraid of hurting you? Or do you enjoy the pain of his cock fully embedded in your pussy, his thrusts as he penetrates you time and time again? He is a big man, it cannot be pleasant for you, but you tolerate it because you see a crown in your future." Her hand gripped the handle of one particularly vicious looking whip, pulling it form the hook. She strolled back to McKenna, caressing the handle like a lover, sliding it down her cheek and across her mouth. "Do you think he will mourn you when you are gone? Hah! He will find that only a Taburon woman can make him happy. Only a Taburon woman should sit by his side on the throne, not some weakling alien animal." Snapping the whip, it made a satisfying cracking sound. It would sting unbearably, but it had not been designed to cut.

Taking a step to the middle of the room, Espis swung the whip, snapping it sharply, and the fire that burned in the side of her right breast had McKenna standing on the tips of her toes, screeching. Espis swung it again and the sting of a thousand bees exploded in McKenna's left breast. She screeched again, dancing like she was suffering an epileptic fit, the whole cross shaking. Again and again, the whip tore into her flesh, until she was a single mass of burning, molten fire from her breasts to her thighs. Stripes of bright red crisscrossed over her fair skin, none of them bleeding – yet. Eventually, Espis would get to the whip that cut flesh and tore to bone.

Her arm tired, angered by it, she stomped to the door and yanked it open. Two of her men entered. "Take her and string her up," Espis ordered, flexing her arm to work out the strain. She wanted to punish the woman, punish the parts of her the Radine had paid the most attention to. The parts that all men lusted after, panting like *cursads*, mounting a woman to spend themselves, then loping off to stick their cocks in the next willing female. Before she was done she would whip the woman's pussy into a mass of devastated flesh. Then, only then, would she permit her men to have her any way they wanted, as long as she continued to feel pain and suffered. Until then she had time to play with her victim, to cause her agony like she'd never felt in her miserable life, to teach her that reaching above her station always had consequences.

McKenna fell forward as soon as her hands were released. She hadn't the strength to hold herself up. Dragged across the floor after her feet were untied, her hands were placed in manacles from the chains hanging from the ceiling. Pulling them up by a winch on the wall, McKenna was forced to rise until she stood at her full height, her arms above her head. Taking an ankle each, her legs were spread and shackled to the floor, pulled impossibly wide. The winch was turned again. She was lifted until she was standing on her toes, barely touching the floor, her joints protesting in fiery pain as they seemed to pull free.

She heard the swish of the whip before she felt the bite of the lash on her buttocks. Fire ripped through her. Her body bent forward away from the agony, but the lash followed, again and again and again. Like the front of her, her back was now a series of lash marks crisscrossing from her neck to her thighs, again none of them breaking the skin but burning like the fires of hell. McKenna screeched until she could screech no more, her voice gone completely, her throat dry.

Espis drew her hand over the whip marks, her fingers unleashing a new agony as she touched them, every one. All of the fight had gone out of the Earth woman, justifying Espis's opinion that she had no business being on Taburon and definitely no place next to a Taburon king. Once more she grabbed McKenna's hair, lifting her head. Studying the woman's face, she saw defeat and resignation. The *skala* had accepted her fate. Espis sighed heavily. That was going to take some of the fun out of the next hours, or days if she lived that long. "Take her down," she spat, tossing the whip aside and leaving the room.

Leaving her feet and hands tied, McKenna was dropped to the floor, screaming in agony as her abused body flooded with pain. Pulling her legs up to her chest, she huddled on the floor in misery, her thoughts on Radine, only Radine, and lastly on Radine. Mercifully, blackness closed in.

Chapter Twenty-One

The squeeze of a hand on his woke Radine. His head throbbed and his mouth was dry, but he managed to turn his gaze towards the person who'd held his hand, joy filling him for a heartbeat, thinking McKenna, his beautiful McKenna, had been found. His sigh was audible upon finding his mother seated next to the bed, her brow creased with worry.

"Mother," he croaked through the parched feeling. "Has McKenna been found? How long have you been here?"

Inoa shook her head in sadness. "No, no word yet, Radine. I am so sorry, son. I came as soon as the messenger arrived at the palace to tell us you'd been injured and needed Pologa."

"May I have some water?" he rasped.

"Of course." Inoa poured from a pitcher set next to the bed then started to help him to rise enough to drink. "Slowly," she cautioned, "Drink slowly. Your stomach might still be queasy."

He drank until he pulled away, nausea threatening if he drank more. "How long was I sleeping?"

"Just over six hours. Pologa dosed you heavily. I brought a change of clothes for you."

"Thank you. I shall need them when word comes."

"You can't possibly think to get out of bed before Pologa says."

"I need to find McKenna. Espis has her, and she will kill her. After she tortures her."

"Why would Espis have taken McKenna?"

"You were not told?" he asked with surprise. For a woman who'd admitted just days ago that she knew nearly everything about his sex life, that she was in the dark over this startled him. Inoa shook her head. "Espis intruded on me and McKenna that first day. We were in the bath." Radine took a shuddering breath, remembering. "She thought I would be willing to share nadryl with her again and was willing to let McKenna join us."

"How did she get into the palace, and especially into your chambers?"

"She released a *salor* into the palace and when the guards went to investigate a scream, she snuck in. She called McKenna a *skala,* an animal, and warned that we had not heard the last of her after I ordered her to leave my chambers."

"Is that why McKenna has been so downhearted of late?"

"Yes. She began to worry that an Earth woman would never be accepted by the Taburon people, especially if she couldn't give me an heir. She thought I might tire of her and find solace in another woman, a Taburon woman. As well as an heir. I proved her wrong when we stopped in the town and the people loved her. They readily accepted her, gave her presents. We were happy again, except for the fact that Espis had disappeared and no one could find her. Instead, Espis found us and took McKenna.

"She will kill her, Mother. McKenna understood her like only another woman could, and she knew – she knew – that Espis was waiting. I didn't listen well enough. I thought I could protect McKenna, yet even though I had guards around the cottage, they killed them and came in and took McKenna." His eyes filled with moisture and he flung his arm over them to hide his show of emotion. He was a man, a king, a warrior, he should not be so emotional, able to control his feelings. But this cut, hard and deep, and he'd never felt like this before in his entire life. He never wanted to feel this way ever again.

"You really love this girl."

"Enough that if it came to it, I would give up the throne to be with her."

"How could it have happened so fast? You've barely known her."

"It is hard to describe, except that I felt it in my soul when I first saw her, touched her, kissed her. I knew then. She is the other part of my soul and my happiness."

Inoa's expression was knowing. "I felt the same way when I first met your father. But to experience it with an alien…I must trust in your feelings, Radine."

"You must trust with me, Mother. If you have any doubts, if you ever falter in your faith, others will see it. She is my match, she will be a great queen, and wife."

"And what if you can't have children?"

"Then the throne will go to whomever I designate. I care not. I care about McKenna. I can't lose her, Mother. And that's why when word comes, I will go to her. I will do everything I can to see that she comes through this. But if it comes down to it, if I can do no more than hold her if she is found, dying, I want the last voice she hears to be one of love, the last touch she feels to be one of gentleness and to come from me. I owe her that much."

"She'll be found before that."

Radine's face hardened. "Either way, Espis has been condemned."

Inoa's reaction was the same as Jaima's – shock, her hand rising to her chest to hover over her heart, her eyes widening. "You cannot! She has royal blood, her parents will protest. She is their only child."

Now Radine seethed, he could feel his heart thud in his chest, his blood begin to boil in anger. "Let them, if they dare to go against their king. I knew Espis was a slut when I slept with her, she is still a slut. If they do not know this already, they need to learn it soon and accept it. I have already instructed Jaima to draw up the warrants."

The burden of this new knowledge drew Inoa's shoulders down. She had known Espis's parents for many years. She had watched the girl grow up – and recognized the signs of a child overindulged, spoiled, and so self-centered that her circle of friends was very small, including only a few like-minded girls. The rumors had reached even Inoa's ears about her sexual exploits. And like so many, she had believed that someday, somehow, the girl would settle down once she matured, married, and became a mother. The queen had just never conceived that her son would fall prey to the machinations of the young woman and into her clutches. And now they were paying the price, perhaps with a young woman's life.

"Your Majesty," A young guard called from the door. "Lord Jaima returns."

"Help me to get up," Radine asked his mother. She supported him as he raised himself, piling pillows behind him. By the time he was sitting, Jaima entered the room, puffing as he fought to catch his breath, his sword rattling at his side. He looked like he'd ridden hard, his hair windblown, his face haggard. He didn't bother with a bow – this was not just subject to king, but brother to brother.

"Radine, we think we may have located her."

"Where?"

"There is rumored a castle, thirty miles to the east, high on a mountain. A group of riders was seen heading that way several hours ago, cloaked in black, one of them had something slung across his *crufa's* back."

Radine struggled to fully rise, tossing aside the covers only far enough to swing his legs over the edge of the bed but keeping his groin covered. A wave of dizziness swept through him and he hung his head a moment, gripping the edge of the bed tightly, taking deep breaths until it passed, then straightened. "My clothes," he ordered. "Jaima, they took my sword. Is there another? And a laser weapon. And get Pologa ready."

Inoa placed his new clothes next to her son and turned her back to him so he could dress in some semblance of privacy as Jaima knelt to aid his king. She feared for him, running off so soon after being injured, he could complicate his wounds such that he would end up in bed for weeks instead of the days that Pologa preferred, if he even survived the upcoming fight. And a fight there would be. Espis, if she indeed had done what Radine believed, would not give up easily. Nor would any of the men she may have convinced to help her, especially knowing the price they would be paying for their treachery.

She winced every time he grunted as he dressed, turning around as she heard the closings on the trousers snap shut. Jaima stood from helping the king to don his boots. Unbuckling his own weapons, he reached around and set the belt over the king's waist and tightened it closed. Radine pulled the belt higher slightly and then it settle comfortably.

"My *crufa?*" Radine asked.

"Outside with the others. I knew you would want to go once we had some word." Jaima made for the doorway.

Radine started to follow only to be stopped by his mother's hand grabbing his arm. "Radine, I wish you all the best, but please, have a care. You love her, but I love you."

Taking her by the arms, the king placed a kiss on his mother's cheek. "I love you too, Mother. Go back to the palace. We'll come there once I have her back."

Chapter Twenty-Two

Cold hard stone pressed into McKenna's shoulder and hip, adding to the deep bone chilling ache she already felt, waking her with a start. Disoriented at first, she glanced around and nearly started to cry when she remembered where she was, and why. She discovered her hands, though still tied, were in front of her face, and preferring doing something to help herself instead of wallow in self-pity, she worked the gag free, spitting the old, salty, spit moistened rag from her mouth, coughing. Holding her hands in front of her, using her teeth, she worked at the ties at her wrists until the knot loosened. Her hands free, she freed her feet, then curled up into a tight ball, her arms wrapped around her legs to conserve warmth.

She knew she had to find the strength to rise, to stand and walk, to move, to run until she could find the way out and back to Radine. Her chances were slim, she was buried deep in the bowels of the castle and there would be such a long road to walk, yet she had to try when she could to get free and away from Espis. But she hurt, so much. She was so cold. Her skin stung from the whip marks, only the cold of the stone beneath her kept the fire of the lash marks at bay. As soon as she warmed, she knew it would return with a vengeance.

Her hands shivered as she cupped them in front of her face to blow warmth into them, her fingers stiff and difficult to move. Rubbing furiously, she tried to get the blood in her arms moving again, then reached to her legs to rub as well. She still shivered, but felt some tingling in her muscles, tiny pinprick spasms that proved she still lived. And as long as she lived, she decided now, she would fight to stay alive. Radine would expect nothing less. Like him, his queen had to have some backbone, had to be able to stand for herself, to become a warrior fitting to sit next to him and rule. Earlier, she was ready to die, if it would save Radine. But her death wouldn't save him, only make him more vulnerable to the cruel and insane Espis. Espis was determined to torture her, take her apart piece by piece until she died, but with newfound determination, McKenna wanted to live even more. Espis was not going to win, for even if McKenna did die, she would do it fighting to the bitter end, and she would make sure Radine knew who had caused her death. She had just found her heart's desire, and she was not anxious to give it up, not now. She was not going to give up like her mother, but follow her father and brothers' examples. They had died fighting. They would be disappointed in her if they met in an afterlife and found out she had given up.

Her legs barely held her as she stood, tottering unsteadily, hunched over to hold in what little warmth she'd rubbed up, to keep her stomach from heaving when there was nothing inside for her to vomit, looking around the room. The crosses and other furniture were too large and bulky for her to make use of, and she had no idea or experience in the use of a whip. The chains presented possibilities, but they were too high up and bolted to their roots. She needed a way to defend herself.

McKenna's eyes settled on the straps around the benches. Each one ended with a huge, heavy buckle. If she could only get one or two loose, she could use the buckle end to swing at an attacker, hopefully before he – or she – saw it coming.

And while she could not wield a whip, she could take several of them and braid the lashes together to use the handles – heavily, carved wood – for another weapon.

McKenna tugged for all she was worth, pulling the nails from the straps until each one fell from the benches. She hung the straps around her neck. Gathering the whips, she sat gingerly on the floor since her stripes had begun to ache, holding the handles of the whips between her feet so she could braid the lashes. Each one of these she also draped around her neck. Armed with four belts and three braided lash weapons, one dangling from her hand, she waited for the next time someone should enter the dungeon.

She had no idea how much time passed as she waited, only that it was enough for the cold to begin to set in again, stiffening abused limbs and battered muscles, making her wonder if she could wield her weapons if her body was frozen. Just as she had begun to think she'd been forgotten, the door handle rattled, turned, and the door opened. Positioned against the wall where the door opening would hide her for a moment, perhaps giving her single moment of good fortune, McKenna waited, her lash/whip weapon swinging silently back and forth.

Espis, standing just inside the doorway, searched for her victim, not surprised to see the gag and ties laying on the floor. She had hoped the Earth woman would try to escape. All the more reason to inflict more punishment on her puny, weakling body. Her screams earlier had been quite satisfying. She was anxious to hear more, to bring the *skala* to her knees, to hear her beg for mercy, of which there would be none. This time Espis planned on cutting the *skala's* skin, short shallow cuts that would bleed and sting more than the whip, open for the burning cream she would rub into each one to increase the agony. If the *skala* had thought her skin on fire under the lash, she would know that that had been a mere flicker to what she could do. Then the real torture would begin.

Espis knelt to pick up the gag, disgusted by the saliva that soaked it. She never saw McKenna step from against the wall, the weapon swinging. Aiming for the head, a chance move prevented her from catching her intended target, instead hitting Espis on the shoulder. But it was a hard blow, knocking the larger woman to her hands and knees on the floor.

"Gods' rods!" Espis cried, holding her hurt shoulder. She rose and spun on her heel. Shock that her victim was now the aggressor stunned her for a moment, a moment that McKenna took to swing again. Espis ducked and semi-rolled out of the way. She moved out of range, rubbing her shoulder, keeping her eyes on her opponent. "*Tritio*," she hissed. "You know what that is?"

"Prick, on my world. I'd call you a bitch, but you don't qualify." McKenna's smile was vicious. "I'm sure there are *skalas* on Taburon with more class than you."

"You still think he'll marry you? Make you his queen? When the people stand against him, he'll drop you faster than a shooting star." Espis circled around, McKenna keeping pace with her. "You're a convenient pussy until he finds a real woman to fulfill his needs. And he has a large appetite, my Radine. That weekend we spent together, he could barely keep his cock out of my pussy. I let him have me any way he wanted, in my pussy, my mouth, my arsehole, as often as he could take me. I could barely move when he was done. It took me days to recover. But oh, it was so good," she taunted, rubbing her hand down the front of her body as she spoke, squeezing her breasts and ending at the junction of her legs where she pushed against her pussy through her clothes. With a malevolent look, she grinned. "You'd never survive."

McKenna swore she would not let the bitch's words get to her. Espis had no hold over her emotions, whatever she said may have been true once, but was all in the past now. Besides, she'd had Radine's cock

225

in her mouth and pussy, and he was a hungry man when it came to sex. But she could be as hungry as he, especially since they had found each other and she'd discovered that sex with the right person was far better than anything anyone could describe. And she could keep up.

Espis would never allow another chance for McKenna to swing her lash weapon at her head again. This was a weakling *skala*, so far below her that it was unthinkable that she, a member of royalty, could possibly be at the mercy of losing this fight. When the human's pitiful body was found, it would end all chances of them ever coming to Taburon to take the places of true Taburon peoples. Radine would thank her once he realized how terrible his decision to bring her to Taburon had been.

McKenna had to find another way to get at Espis, to get her helpless, perhaps knocked out or tied up so she could escape somehow. And even if she did somehow manage that, there was still the problem of the men she had to sneak by. But if she had the bitch secured, her chances improved.

Hoping for a lot of luck, a good swing, and unsure that it would work, faking the Taburon out by swinging the weapon at Espis's head, she quickly changed direction, swinging her lash at Espis's legs while the woman concentrated on ducking, praying they would tangle around her feet. She grinned as the weapon did exactly as she'd hoped, quickly reaching up to grab a second lash/whip as soon as she released the first. As Espis bent down to untangle her feet, McKenna hastily snapped the last one from around her neck. This one she swung at the Taburon's head, clipping her against the skull.

Espis fell with a thud, not unconscious, but now madder than hell that the puny Earth woman had dealt her such a blow. With a cry, she heaved to her feet, revealing a dagger that had been hidden in the top of her boot.

Fearing that Espis would pick up the one lash/whip, McKenna went on the offensive, swinging her weapons, giving them up as Espis grabbed each one until she could no longer hold the ones she had. A lucky shot knocked the dagger from the Taburon woman's hand to clatter on the floor, sliding across to come to a standstill a foot or so by McKenna's feet.

McKenna saw that Espis was losing control, infuriated that the woman she considered no better than a germ was holding her own. Giving into anger meant mistakes would be made, and Espis made her first by tossing the lash/whip weapon she had pulled from McKenna's hand to the ground. Her eyes blazed and sparkled.

McKenna kept her calm. She'd learned long ago that calm gave her an advantage to either escape or fight reasonably. She'd kept calm when her brothers had teased her without mercy, hoping to get a rise out of their baby sister. She'd kept calm when the system had coughed her out to fend for herself. She'd been calm walking out of her job and away from her overly touchy-feely boss. And when she'd kneed Radine on

227

his ship, she'd been calm then, too. She would wait, watch and try to take advantage of whatever opportunity Espis gave her.

It wasn't long in coming. With a growl of pure hatred, Espis launched herself at the Earth woman, hands outstretched, fingers clawed, intending to rip into her flesh with her bare hands. Forget the torture, she wanted her dead – now.

The body blow of a full grown Taburon nearly crushed McKenna, but she was fast enough to reach to the side and grab the knife, holding it perpendicular to her body, the handle braced against her own body. Espis fell directly onto it, her eyes going wide in surprise. She glanced down to the spreading blood, then to her opponent. The thought that she would lose, to this – this thing – had never crossed her mind. And now she was fatally wounded, and she knew it. She raised her hands to try to grab at McKenna, but the Earth woman shoved the knife deeper, redirecting her attention, ignoring the Taburon's cry of dismay and disbelief. It had been a matter of kill or be killed, and McKenna, determined to win, would have no regrets.

McKenna's smile was as malevolent as Espis's had been. The blood flowing out of the fatally wounded Taburon was warming her body, and if this was the only way she could get that warmth she so desperately needed, she would take it. McKenna raised her head enough to make sure Espis saw and heard her. "Fuck you, bitch," she ground out with every ounce of hate she could muster. "And he is *my* Radine! Go to hell!" she finished and twisted the knife.

The light and life went out of Espis's eyes. Her head dropped down to McKenna's shoulder, a trickle of blood dripping from her mouth. McKenna laid her head back, attempting to take a deep breath and failing. She had a six foot four dead woman on her body pinning her down. But for the first time in hours, she was warm.

The horror of what she had done took over. McKenna started to laugh, a soft giggle that expanded and grew until she was gurgling hysterically. Soon after, her glee turned to tears and she found herself sobbing uncontrollably. She pushed ineffectually at the dead woman, giving in to the fact that she was too weakened, too distressed, and the woman too heavy to move.

With the immediate threat over, McKenna became aware of the sounds outside of the room, the clash and ringing clang of steel against steel punctuated with an occasional soft whine from laser weapons. Adding in the harsh sounds of men's grunts and cries, raised voices in defiance and command, McKenna knew that she was on the verge of rescue – or utter defeat. Depending on who was winning the battle.

But she had to free herself, for the others would soon possibly be coming looking for their mistress. Now that she had an actual weapon, McKenna needed to free herself instead of lie there to become a victim again. The strength she'd found to fight had fled in the face of her small victory. Besides, the handle of the knife was driving itself into her breastbone, and it hurt.

The door to the dungeon slammed open, thudding against the wall. McKenna's time was up. With her hands on Espis's torso, she heaved with all of the might she could muster, adrenaline flowing once more, fight or flight kicking in with a vengeance. She pushed the body to the side, screaming at the pain from her tortured muscles that really did not want to cooperate, grabbing the slickened handle of the knife. It made a squishing sound as it slid free of the body, but she held on, to the knife and the sickening surge of the contents of her stomach as she rolled to her knees. Swiping her hair away from her face, she faced her new opponents.

And collapsed back to the floor. Radine stood in the doorway, shock written all over his face. Behind him, Jaima crowded the doorway, blood on his shirt. Radine held a sword in his hand, blood dripping from the tip.

Chapter Twenty-Three

Radine dropped the sword and advanced on the woman he loved, falling to his knees. "McKenna," he whispered, caressing her cheek. "Are you hurt? You're covered in blood."

McKenna pointed to the body with the knife. "It's hers. I'm so sorry, Radine," she choked, sobs resurfacing. "I'm so sorry. I killed her."

Pulling her close, he embraced her tightly, falling completely to the floor as he enveloped her, ignoring the blood that coated his pants and legs. "It's all right," he soothed. His voice rumbling through his chest and against her ear was comforting, his hands petting her hair lovingly, tenderly. "It's all right. As long as you're not hurt."

"Your clothes," she wailed. "They're all bloody now."

"They're only clothes, little one. As long as I have you back."

"She gave me no choice. I didn't want to kill her, but I had no choice." She sobbed, his shirt getting wet, her hands clutching at him, her tears mixing with the blood stains.

"Shh," he repeated, "it's all right." He had to stop speaking until the fright that had choked him cleared, the tears of relief that had clogged his eyes falling unheeded and unchecked. With the breath stopped in his chest, he found it difficult to breathe, but he finally forced himself and his body shuddered with the effort. He gently smoothed his hand down her head, pressing his lips against her hair to place a kiss there. Her hair was matted, yet a single ribbon still remained, a determined token reminder of the time they'd spent just hours ago in each other's love. As other troops began to enter the room, Radine closed himself around her even tighter, not wishing to expose her to prying, curious eyes. He tucked her head under his chin then looked around. "Jaima," he said softly. The second in command whispered to one of the other troops and the man disappeared the way they'd come. Pologa edged his way around the rest of the men and stooped near, scrutinizing the young woman.

"McKenna," he soothed, "little one, it is okay. You're safe now. I'm going to take you home." He petted her gently. "It's all right. Come on, little one, stop now."

McKenna hiccupped and coughed, but struggled to stop crying, wiping her running nose with the back of her hand. Nodding, she gazed up at him, her eyes widening at the moisture on his face and cheeks. She reached out with a finger to trace the wet. This man, this warrior king, had cried for her. No one had ever cried for her in her entire life.

"Are you hurt anywhere?" Pologa asked.

The shake she gave was jerky. "She whipped me, but there are no cuts. She hadn't gotten to that yet."

"Were you violated?" Radine's voice was raspy, but he had to know. Though it wouldn't change how he felt about McKenna.

"Raped?" He nodded. "No. She was saving that for later." A bloody hand raised to almost touch his scalp, but she pulled it back before she soiled his hair. "Your head?"

"Is very hard, according to Pologa." He smiled while the physician snorted. "I'm a hard man to bring down."

Radine was pleased to see her mouth turn up in a small smile. "Not so hard," she mumbled. He chuckled, gathering her close, his touch soothing. She would need a lot of love to recover. She breathed in pants the way people do after a long cry, quivering physically, unable to control it just yet. A blanket draped around her shoulders helped, covering her body and providing the warmth she so badly needed. But her cold now was internal, a deep fatigue from all that had happened. Radine tried to lift her, but his battered and bruised body protested. Stepping in, Jaima picked her up, intending to pass her to his king once they reached the *crufas* waiting outside, understanding that Radine needed to hold her for the trip back to the palace, to know she was well and alive, to offer and receive comfort, knowing she was with him. Keeping her head against his chest, Jaima made sure she didn't see the carnage covering the floors and walls as they walked through the castle. Troops would remain to clean the mess and gather the bodies for burial. The men Espis had hired would share a common grave. Whatever Espis's parents decided to do with the body of their daughter was their business, as long as she wasn't interred within a day's ride of the palace. Radine did not want any reminder of the woman near.

With slow and deliberate movements Radine climbed onto his *crufa* and settled into the saddle. Jaima handed McKenna up for him to drape across his lap. A second blanket was draped over the shoulders of the king, since he was still suffering the effects of his beating, effectively cocooning the two people in a thick layer of warmth on the back of the animal. Quite a different position from the one that had brought her to this place. She was held in loving arms now, soothed by a soft voice, touched by gentle hands. Stressed beyond endurance, she fell asleep to the gentle rhythm of the *crufa* and the warmth emanating from Radine's body, rousing only long enough several hours later to realize they had arrived at the castle.

Passed once again to Jaima, this time the other carried her through the halls to reach the king's chambers. Radine had surrendered her readily. His face had paled and his body ached. He was fighting a headache. It had taken all he could muster to make the trip back to the palace, the jarring of the *crufa's* gait affirming, accentuating and increasing the pain of every bruise he'd suffered at the beating. By the time they reached the palace, he was barely holding on, sliding from his saddle into the arms of two of his men who helped him through the palace to his chambers, several of his other guards running ahead to clear the halls before him. His mother would scold him roundly. He didn't care. As long as McKenna was safe.

Summoned to care for their mistress, three servants escorted the Earth woman into the bath to clean her of the blood that covered her from head to thigh, Radine held at bay from watching as they tended to her, knowing she might feel embarrassed by how she might look in the light of a bath. They washed her and shampooed her hair, carefully combing the tresses free of the knots, then massaged a scented cream into her skin that would help in healing her injuries. Dressing her in a sheer nightgown, one that would not irritate her skin, they first started to steer her to her own chambers when Radine redirected them to his bed.

He'd nearly fallen to his knees at the crisscross hash marks on her body when he saw it bared for the fleeting few seconds he was given before being hustled out of the bath, her beautiful skin marred by the lash. But Pologa, after checking her further, assured him they were but skin deep and would fade in time. He burned with unresolved anger, wishing he could bring Espis back to life just so he could have the satisfaction of executing her for what she had done to his McKenna. His lovely woman was marked, striped as no one should be, as no one had been in over a thousand years on Taburon. Whipping was a forbidden punishment, its scars went deep both physically and emotionally. Civilization did not tolerate punishments that scarred a person for life when doled out for a single infraction. Taburons believed that once punished, the mistake was forgotten and the culprit started fresh. While McKenna's marks would heal and fade, Radine was afraid of what the emotional fallout might be.

Once she'd been settled on the bed with his mother fussing over her, Radine sank into a chair nearby, suddenly bone weary. Purnia had made the king shed his bloodied shirt and with warm water, washed his chest, arms and face before slipping a clean, soft shirt back over his shoulders. Once he'd sunk into the chair, Purnia tugged his boots from his feet and discarded the soiled socks. He would clean the boots while the king rested. The weapons belt was left by the door – Jaima would most likely wish to have his own weapons returned to him and they needed cleaning. Radine remembered that someone had retrieved his own sword from the man who'd stolen it, he would have to make sure it was returned and cleaned. For now though his headache had not abated and he felt as though every bone in his body had melted away. He waited for his turn for a little sympathy and tender loving care.

Inoa was the one who managed to get McKenna to drink the drugged tea Pologa provided, sitting next to her on the bed, keeping one arm draped over the younger's shoulders and gently combing through her hair until she fell into a deep sleep. And once that had been accomplished, she rounded on her son, and she was not feeling very charitable. All of her fears for both of these people, one whom she loved dearly and the other she was beginning to care for deeply, had kept her on edge until she'd heard the news that McKenna had been found alive and was returning with the king. Yet the exhaustion on her son's face tempered her emotions for the moment.

"You fool," she accused, "look at you." She held her hand out without looking, expecting Pologa to pass a second cup to her for Radine. "I swear, Radine," she vowed, giving him the cup, standing over him and tapping her foot until he'd drained it to the dregs. Inoa leaned down to place a kiss on the top of his head. A man he may be, but he was still her son. "I'm glad you found her and got her back. You love her very much, and she will make a fine wife."

The king stood on wobbly feet, the drug fast. "Thank you, Mother, but if you don't want to see how well your son has grown, then turn your back or leave," he warned, his hands at the fastenings to his trousers.

"As if I haven't seen it before," she huffed, crossing her arms over her chest, waiting.

Radine shrugged and dropped the garment, shucked off his shirt and naked, climbed between the covers next to his woman. Spooning the sleeping McKenna, he left himself to drift into sleep, content for now. "Arrogant child," Inoa snorted, yet pleased that her son had finally found his true mate. With a snap of her fingers, she indicated for Purnia

237

to remain near the sleeping couple and not let either of them out of his sight. Taking up the sword, she left the room to seek her own rest.

Chapter Twenty-Four

Violent shaking disturbed Radine from his drugged sleep, blinking blearily through the muted light. McKenna was dreaming, her body responding unconsciously to the inner demons that were tormenting her. Scooting closer to her, he turned her to face him, holding her close, gently rubbing up and down her arm, pressing soft kisses at her temple. "McKenna," he called softly, "wake up, little one. You're dreaming. Come on, little one, wake up." He gently brushed her hair along her temple. "McKenna."

She whimpered, curling up on herself, her breaths hitching, panting. She was quaking violently, but as she woke, she buried her head into his chest. "Are you awake now?" he asked softly. McKenna nodded. "Want to talk about it?"

He heard her sigh, her breath warm against his skin. "I can't stop shaking," she whispered desperately.

"It is reaction setting in. I have seen it often. After a battle, an untried soldier who has fought in his first battle will have the same reaction. It will pass."

"You've had it happen to you?"

"I did not just walk into the throne after my father died. There were other factions interested in ruling, and I had to fight to keep what was mine by birth. I was embarrassed as a soldier and an as yet uncrowned king that I vomited the first time I had to kill a man."

She lay silent, absorbing his nearness, his voice rumbling against her ear pressed to his chest. His hands soothed along her body, large hands that held the power of a planet in them. They could be so hard when necessary, yet so gentle. "I never thought I had it in me," she finally confessed.

"Had what?"

"The ability to kill."

"It was life or death, little one. You did what you had to in order to survive. I am proud of you."

"I killed that woman," she repeated with horror, as if he hadn't heard.

"She was dead the minute she took you. You only did what I would have had to do had she lived."

There was surprise in her voice. "You would have executed her?"

"I am normally a very patient and understanding man, but as a king I have learned to harden myself when I must. There are times when I must be as bloodthirsty as those who commit bloodthirsty crimes. She attacked her king with malice. She kidnapped my intended, fully seeking to do her harm, even kill her. It is an executionable offense. I ordered the warrants be drawn as soon as I regained consciousness."

Her voice quaked, her eyes moistened. "I have been nothing more than a burden to you ever since you met me."

"One I have gladly taken, and would take again, over and over. I love you, it is my right to protect you, to help you when you need it."

She glanced up at him, her eyes wide. "Even when it causes you pain?"

His smile was understanding. A hand caressed her cheek. "Even when you are the cause of that pain, little one. McKenna, you are my heart. Happiness, sorrow, laughter, pain – it is all part of life. I hope we have more of the good than the bad, but together we can face all of it and come out stronger because we did it together." Cupping her face, he tilted her head. "Better now?"

Her nod was jerky, the shaking having abated some, but not totally gone. Radine kissed her gently before he sat up, McKenna grabbing for the covers to keep her modesty. She'd shown enough of herself over the last day. "Purnia!" he yelled.

Radine's personal attendant entered from the spot he always took, close enough to answer the king's summons, but far enough to give him privacy. McKenna had discovered her attendant also hovered close when she was in her chambers, and it had at first unnerved her. She supposed it was another thing she would have to get used to as queen.

Purnia bowed. He'd been Radine's personal servant since before he was crowned king, had marched with him into battle, saw to his needs in grooming and dress, made sure he ate when the other forgot, and kept his opinions about the king's dalliances to himself unless specifically asked. But then he'd been honest to his king, a fact the other appreciated tremendously, especially when the servant had saved the king from some rather sticky situations.

This time, however, he fully approved of the young woman with the king and that approval came from knowing his master and his needs. The way Radine treated her, the way he looked at her, touched her, all told the servant that the king had finally fallen in love. This woman, though alien to their world, was no passing fancy. And if rumors held true, she was worthy of him, a fighter in her own right.

"Your Majesty?"

"Some wine, please. And maybe something to eat."

"Shall I have a light supper sent in?"

"That sounds great, yes, please."

Purnia returned within minutes, a tray in hand, a carafe and two glasses on it. Setting the tray near the bed, he poured one glass which he passed to McKenna, bypassing the king. As Radine waited expectantly, Purnia replied with a raised eyebrow, then shook his head no. He pointed to the head injury the king still sported, bowed and left to chase down a meal for his sovereigns.

Radine scowled, like a child denied his favorite toy and threw himself down onto his pillow, then winced, having forgotten the injury Purnia had just pointed to. While she may have still been shivering, McKenna still managed to laugh softly. "I swear I keep meaning to replace him," Radine mumbled.

"You may be the king, but we know who rules the roost."

"Enjoy your wine," he growled in jealousy. "It is Baccan, the finest on the planet."

Several sips later, the shaking stopped. McKenna placed the remainder in the glass on the table on her side of the bed, scooting down under the covers, pleasantly calm, squeaking in surprise when Radine crawled over her to grab the half full glass. He drained the vessel in one gulp, replacing it back on the table. She giggled.

"Never let Baccan wine go to waste," he explained.

"I was going to finish it, just not right now." McKenna wiggled herself deeper into the bed. Radine hovered over her, laying partially on her but holding his weight off her body.

"Comfortable?" he asked.

"Um," she purred in her throat.

Radine kissed her lightly. "We're a fine pair aren't we?" he asked, finger combing her hair. It was silk in his hands, long and soft, the color, even in the muted light of the bedroom a beautiful mixture of brown and red and gold.

She stared up at him with curiosity. "How so?"

"I would love nothing better than to make love to you right now, but I'm dead on my feet. I hurt like there is no tomorrow in places I didn't know could hurt. The mind is willing, but the body is saying don't even think about it. And I'm sure you're too tired yet as well. Again we are denied sharing nadryl."

A smile graced her lips, her hand smoothed down his chest. "One thing Espis said is true. You are a lusty man."

His head arched up. "I do remember that weekend as particularly lust filled. But it was only lust, McKenna, there were no other emotions involved in that time. I had never entertained the idea of marrying that woman. Rumor had it she was well experienced. I was curious."

"Didn't turn out so well, did it?"

"No, for which I will forever be sorry. I should have listened to Jaima when he warned me about her."

"Sometimes men are led around by things other than their good reason."

"I have no excuse. I was stupid and she was more convincing."

"She tried to hurt me by comparing her to me for your sexual needs. She said I could never satisfy you."

"Not true," he promised. "Before you, sex with other women was just that – sex. With you, there's a connection that goes deeper, feels stronger and is more fulfilling than having a convenient pussy in which to release my seed. I can't think of anything other than being with you when it comes to sharing nadryl, it feels as though every one of those women are but shades to what we share when we're together. I miss it terribly right now, not being inside you especially after what happened. I want to give you comfort, and take comfort, and reaffirm that we survived this nightmare. Sometimes the only way to do that is to share nadryl. But I also know that holding you as I have these last hours has been just as comforting and life affirming, feeling you next to me, listening to your soft breaths, feeling your warm skin. Though a little nadryl wouldn't hurt, I can wait until you're ready."

"Oh, you can turn a girl's head with words like that," she breathed. The wine was making her somnolent. "I look forward to when we can resume sharing nadryl, and soon I hope." With a glance down his body, McKenna winced. He was covered in bruises from the beating, black and blue marks peppering his chest and sides. He must have been in so much pain when he came to her rescue, but he came anyway. He must have been so sore as he held her while they returned to the palace, but he held her anyway. Words were wonderful, but actions always spoke louder and he could not have proven his love and devotion any better. Her hand slid along his skin, gently so as to not hurt him anymore, catching the few times he winced when she hit a particularly sensitive spot, but letting her explore, her fingers tracing the injuries from one to another until she reached towards his head. She gently placed her fingers over the bandaging on his head. "I'm so sorry, Radine. You lost some of your beautiful hair."

"It will grow back, McKenna, and it's not your fault." He moved to stretch out beside her, folding his arms behind his head. She twisted to roll towards him, laying her head on his chest where there were no bruises, a hand draped across his waist. "I'd tell you to go back to sleep, but then you'll miss dinner. And if I know Purnia, it will be well worth the wait."

"Then wake me if I fall to sleep," she murmured, rubbing his skin slightly with her cheek, content to hear the steady beat of his heart. If every day for the rest of her life could be like this, she would die a very happy old woman. He was strength, he was comfort, he was love, and she would never let anyone come between them ever again, not with words or actions.

"Your wish is my command, Your Highness."

"And don't you forget it."

Chapter Twenty-Five

Two groomsmen held the reins of their crufas as Radine dismounted then went to McKenna, his hands at her waist to aid her as she slid from the back of her crufa. The king thanked them, giving them leave to seek their pleasure as they may, reminding them to return in the morning at sunrise.

Their journey to the Lanzess Mountain had taken two days. A contingent of guards had accompanied them, Radine unwilling to take any more chances of someone interfering with them again. When they'd camped for the night, he'd kept her next to him and surrounded their tent with guards. They hadn't made love, just cuddled and slept, but it had been an uncomfortable sleep for McKenna those two nights, plagued with harsh dreams and waking at unusual sounds. Radine soothed McKenna until she slipped back into slumber, but then lay awake himself, hurting for her, praying she would soon be able to forget her ordeal. But they had to be here tonight, for the king to miss out on sky clad when he had pending nuptials would have shaken his people's faith in him.

When she asked why they used the crufas to go to the mountain instead of his shuttle or ship, he explained that though they had such modern transportation available, in order to keep the planet clean from mechanical emissions, they had forgone the dependence on such vehicles for everyday use and relied on the crufas almost exclusively on the surface of the planet. Besides, it gave them a chance to enjoy the scenery as they passed, and the king a chance to acknowledge the people who came out as the entourage passed. He was the people's king, and they loved him.

Tonight was sky clad, the night when the Gods gave their approval for the peoples' relationships. The king was not the only one arriving on the mountain – there were at least a hundred other couples looking for a spot to wait, spreading blankets on the ground, emptying baskets of food. For the night would be filled with the sounds of lovemaking and, should the Gods approve, joy for everyone. The king, however, didn't have to search for a place – it had already been chosen and laid out for him and McKenna.

They both wore cloaks over the few garments underneath, everything would be discarded for the ceremony. Sky clad meant nude, each person having to present themselves without hindrance. McKenna had balked at first, still uncomfortable in front of the servants, but learning to deal, having Radine as a fine example. He had no problem traipsing about his chambers in the nude in front of Purnia or Jaima or even Annatt if she were in the room helping her mistress for some reason. McKenna drew the line at being naked before Jaima, but not Purnia and Annatt, her personal attendant. She was learning that there were times when it was unavoidable and even downright necessary to have a personal servant who knew you almost as intimately as you did yourself. Now he was expecting her to stand nude in front of hundreds of Taburons, even share nadryl, and she was quaking in anxiety.

Draping an arm around her shoulders, he led her to the spot that had been picked out for him. Of course, the blanket had been placed over the grassiest spot, where the ground wouldn't be quite so hard or lumpy, though a thick padding had been added beneath for their comfort. There was a pile of pillows and blankets near, in case they needed any of them for their comfort through the night. A huge basket sat to the side, filled she was sure of the best wine and finer dishes the kitchen could prepare.

"The actual ceremony no longer really matters," he had been saying, explaining the ceremony to her, "but it has become tradition. There used to be formal prayers and offerings, music and dancing. In the ancient times, the people believed the Gods actually lived on Icide and Liva and the light from them was divine. Of course, we have since learned the truth, but the tradition still lives on, a time to celebrate being a citizen of Taburon."

250

McKenna glanced around as he led her onto the blanket. All around them, couples were disrobing, holding hands, indulging in a round of touching and kissing prior to the time when the moons of Taburon would rise. The sun had yet to totally set, so everything was still easily visible. "Don't worry," he continued, "the others will be so busy with their own love making that we will be ignored – for the most part."

Her eyes went wide. "For the most part?" she asked.

He grinned. "Well, I am the king, and this is the first, and only time, I will be participating. Of course, they are curious," he finished, nodding to a subject who'd recognized Radine by bowing to him. The fact that the man was totally nude made no difference to the man, his woman draped in only a very sheer tunic. Word spread quickly, heads turning in their direction to catch a glimpse of their king and soon they were being offered 'good sky clad, your majesty and your highness' as they settled on their blanket. Radine opened the basket, withdrawing the flask of wine and glasses. He poured, offering one to McKenna.

Her whip stripes had all but disappeared. He still wore the bandage in his hair and the bruises on his torso had turned a bright blue color, but he was well enough. He had to be for this time wouldn't happen again for another year. And while it wasn't necessary for them to forgo the wedding until then, participating as was tradition would only bring good relations to the new queen from the people as she settled into her role as a sovereign. For her to be here boded well in the eyes of the Taburon people.

When the two moons rose and aligned, the reflected light from the setting sun would shine bright on but several spots on the planet. Lanzess Mountain was the one place on this side of the planet. There were two others, but too far away for the king and McKenna to travel, considering that only three days ago, she had been rescued from the clutches of the maddened Espis.

Tonight would be a time for them to physically reconnect as well. They'd not shared nadryl since her rescue, and held back as they'd traveled to the mountain. Their first intercourse would be as once before, fast and furious. Then the slow and sweet would follow.

Searching through the basket, Radine began to pull out foodstuffs, spreading them near so she could pick what she wanted. Finding one particular closed dish, he removed the cover and sniffed deeply. The entitans were heavenly, perfectly prepared, a meat and fruit pastry spiced with herbs that had aphrodisiac properties. The palace chefs were making sure the king would have no problems with his duties this evening. He would make sure McKenna ate a healthy portion as well, since he had plans. Breaking a piece off, he popped it in his mouth, giving a similar sized piece to McKenna.

"This is delicious," she complimented. He groaned as he watched her jaw move while she chewed, and then the tip of her tongue swept out to lick at her lips. His cock swelled and his chest tightened.

252

He wouldn't last long once they got horizontal – he felt ready to burst now as it was. He was as randy as he'd been as a young man. He blamed her. She brought it out in him. Wasn't it wonderful?

"It is one of my favorites. It is called entitans."

"We'll have to have this more often."

"It is supposed to be an aphrodisiac."

McKenna swallowed with an accusatory look in her eyes. "You don't need anything to help you," she remarked, her glance pointed as she took in his engorged cock threatening to burst his trousers. It caused a responding reaction in her body, her breasts tightening, nipples puckering, her pussy moistening. Her eyes closed as she took a deep breath to calm.

"But they taste good anyway," he offered, aware of her body preparing itself for what was to come. He lengthened further, his balls tingling as they pulsed with seed. He would fill her up so much tonight that if she didn't become pregnant he'd be extremely surprised.

She laughed, a husky sound. "Yes, they do. More." She leaned towards him, opening her mouth, waiting.

He chuckled, breaking off another piece. She leaned closer since he decided to play, drawing her in, taking the piece with her mouth, showing a long view of her cleavage to his eyes, sucking on Radine's fingers, licking them clean as she slowly slid her lips free. "Tease," he groaned. McKenna giggled. Two could play games. Radine finished cleaning his hand, keeping an eye on the sun as it sank slowly behind the horizon. "Watch," he indicated, nodding to the sun.

The orb sank further, the color of the sky turning brilliant orange, then red, then the color of blood. As it completely disappeared, a single beam of light shot out, shooting into the sky to fade in the heavens. The beam thinned and shrank, and once it was gone, darkness fell on the mountain. Cheers were heard all around the mountain top. Radine lighted a small lantern before he scooted closer to McKenna, sitting behind her, resting her back against his chest. "Well?"

"It was the most beautiful sunset I've ever seen. Is that normal?"

"Only at certain times of the year and only from certain vantage points."

"How long until the moons rise?"

"Icide will come first. Only after Liva crosses its path will the light reflect back to Taburon. The stronger the light, the better the future for everyone here. At least, that is the tradition."

"We could use a little of that in our lives."

His hands untied her cloak, pulling it open and away from her body. She wore a simple tunic, so sheer that nothing was hidden from his gaze. As he nuzzled at her neck, he hefted her breasts, his thumbs swiping over the nipples until they were hard, tight nubs. Two fingers pinched and rolled the delicate flesh, squeezing the way he'd learned she enjoyed, her back arching to present her breasts for his enjoyment – and hers.

His cock expanded and lengthened even more, pressing against his trousers until he feared the material would rip. Freeing one hand from her delicious breasts, he opened his trousers to give himself more room. They would be taken off soon enough.

Going back to paying attention to her body, he slipped a hand to her pussy, delving through her moist swollen folds to find her clit, strumming a finger across the organ as she squirmed against his lap, his cock poking her in her back. Radine was sure he wouldn't last long, she needed to be needy when he thrust himself into her. Sliding deeper along her slit, he found her soaked, her thighs wet with her feminine fluids. She roused quickly, it pleased him to no end. They could find time between his infernal, never-ending meetings for a quick nadryl any time of the day. He would return to his meetings with a stupid smile on his face, and calmer.

"Radine," she stuttered. "Shouldn't we wait?"

"Yes," he whispered against her ear, "but when the time comes, I'll have no willpower. As I'm sure many around us will be. I will take you without spending time to prepare you, so I do it now while I must wait." He sunk three fingers into her, her passage tight, hot and wet. "Are you ready for me, little one?"

McKenna closed her thighs to trap his hand exactly where she wanted him, loving the small movements he made against her flesh, turning his hand so that he rubbed at her G-spot. She undulated her body, grabbing at his thighs that rested along her legs, panting. "Radine, I'm going to come."

"Come for me, McKenna, let me feel you wrap around my fingers and pulse as you peak. Imagine it is my cock, which will fill you soon. Come for me, love."

She arched farther, a soft keening sound rising from her throat. Turning her head, Radine pressed his mouth over hers to muffle her, though all around them, her vocalization wasn't the only one on the mountain. There were grunts and groans, moans and small cries echoing in the darkness. McKenna shuddered violently, losing control as she tipped over the edge, her sheath a vice around his fingers, hindering movement. "So sweet," he murmured for her. "You come so sweetly. I am bursting my trousers wanting to be deep in you. I have so much seed saved up, you are going to drown in it." Discovering she'd relaxed slightly, he flicked over her clit, she shivered as the orgasm revived with short electric zings along her arms and legs, coalescing in her pussy. Radine pulled his fingers free, coated in wetness. Bringing them to his mouth, he licked them clean, humming at the sweetness of the taste of her fluids. McKenna felt her face flush at such a blatant display of sexual pleasure, especially in front of so many people. Who, she discovered as she glanced around, were not paying them any attention.

"Look," he pointed out, "Icide is rising."

When she could think again, she faced the direction he indicated. The silvery curve of a moon was breaking above the horizon, steadily rising.

McKenna reached back to fondle his cock. "Should I relieve some of the pressure for you?"

"You will, when I fill you with my cock. I am anxious, but not desperate." He divested himself of his own cloak, letting it fall behind him. Gathering the hem of her short tunic, he pulled it over her head to bare her body to the sky and everyone else. "Moonlight becomes you," he decided, nuzzling at her neck again. "The gardens at the palace are beautiful at night, and private if I so order. We shall have to share nadryl in the moonlight as often as possible."

She faced him, working the ties to his boots, pulling each one off. "Your hair is more golden," she offered in response. "And your eyes glow," she continued, pushing him back by the shoulders until he lay flat. "I have loved your eyes from the moment we met." His cock stood tall and proud through the opening in his pants. Stripping him of the garment, she soon had him as naked as she, her hand wrapping around his shaft possessively. "Mine," she claimed.

"Only yours," he agreed.

Her hand pumped up and down several times, his body tensed, his hands clutching the blanket to stave off impending orgasm. He wanted to give her everything he had this night, not spew it onto the ground and waste it. As she held him tightly, he reached under her hand and pulled at his testicles, finding that spot that put a damper on his rising passion. His voice trembled as his head turned to check the moons. "Liva comes."

Rising in front of Icide, a second silvery orb began its ascent, drawing in front of the larger moon from the left. As the two crested the horizon, they started to align. Couples stood, all of them now naked, some next to each other, others holding their partner from the back. Silence descended on the mountain top as everyone waited with baited breath for the final moment, hoping for when the light would be returned to Taburon to bless the people.

Radine calmed himself with a deep breath, tamping his desire for just a few more moments, then rose. His cock was so engorged that it pointed straight out, rising slightly towards his stomach. He wasn't the only man in such a condition, there were dozens of male shafts all over the mountaintop making their presence pointedly obvious. Standing, he reached down to offer McKenna a hand. With hers in his, he pulled her to her feet, placing her in front of him, enclosing her in an embrace. His hands crossed across her waist, his chin rested on her shoulder. "Watch now," he instructed. "Soon they will be as one, he covering her, and together they will brighten the skies with their passion. If their love is true, they will share it with us and we will be blessed." He swayed with her slightly. "I love you, McKenna."

"I love you, Radine."

He backed away from her, to stand next to her, holding her hand, facing the moons as they were fully revealed, rising as one, the smaller encompassed totally by the larger. The light from the two brightened to a blinding white, a halo formed and spread, rays reaching in all directions, a single one landing on the mountain until the whole top was coated in light. Cheers rose from the crowd, clapping broke the silence, and couples fell into each other's arms, dropping to the ground to indulge in passion. The Gods had given their approval. Now they needed to consummate their love while in the light.

Radine was gentle as he laid her down, but all bets were off after that. Spreading her legs, he waited only long enough to make sure she was still wet, three of his fingers sinking deep into her pussy, spreading her folds, then he speared into her body with his cock in one punishing thrust, fully embedding himself. McKenna cried out at the penetration, but quickly adjusted, throwing her legs over his waist to tilt her hips. Bracing himself with his hands at her sides, he pounded her pussy relentlessly, sinking in deeply with every inbound thrust, kissing the entrance to her womb, before withdrawing nearly completely. McKenna grabbed his arse cheeks in her hands, gripping so tightly she would discover later that she'd left small half-moons in his flesh from her nails.

He'd been right, he didn't last long. A handful of thrusts had him tensing, tightening, his balls pulled tight against his groin, his cock pulsing as he erupted inside her, his warm seed bathing her cervix.

While he still pulsed, delivering on his promise to flood her pussy, he reached down to rub her clit furiously. Her sheath tightened almost painfully around his cock as she came, clamping down on him, her pussy flooding with her own fluids to mix with what he'd given. She screamed his name as she came, her voice one of many heard through the darkness.

Radine collapsed, his body damp, his face buried in the curve of her neck and throat as he panted heavily. Her pussy still fluttered around his cock, shocking him, making him shudder in response. "Stop," he begged. "It's too much."

Her arms slid around his shoulders. "I'm not doing it deliberately. But if you want…" She tightened the muscles of her pussy, nipping the end of his cock, dragging a loud groan from the man still sunk deep inside her body. His embrace tightened as she worked through the exquisite sensation.

"McKenna," he warned quietly, his cock softening finally and slipping free. Radine dropped to his stomach by her side. "If nadryl were the only measurement, we are going to be very happy." He reached out to paw through the basket again, retrieving more food and drink, pulling out a second flask that was not wine. He sat up, crossing his legs in front of himself, pairing out what he'd gathered. McKenna lazed wantonly on her back, her eyes closed, absorbing the night. "You're naked you know," he pointed out.

She was feeling very lax, boneless, satisfied for the moment. "I am," she agreed.

"Not concerned about what others might think?"

"Are you? You're the king."

"Any man who sees you might want you."

"As might any woman want you. Do you plan on sharing?" She rose to an elbow to take the drink he passed to her. His cock had begun to harden again as he perused her body, lingering on her breasts.

She could see the thought pass through his mind. He was so open at times. But in the same moment, he dismissed it. McKenna was his exclusively and he would never share her with anyone, ever! "Absolutely not."

"Neither do I. Let them look, maybe they'll learn something. Of course, turnabout is fair play. I can look all I want, if I want."

"Do not dare," he growled. "I am a large man, but perhaps not the largest. I would not have you making comparisons."

She scoffed. "Only men have penis envy."

"And only women have a desire for a large penis," he corrected.

"It's not the equipment, but how it's used," she clarified.

His head tilted as an eyebrow rose. "And how is my technique?"

She drew a finger nail down his chest. "You'll do," she teased.

"You should be spanked," he considered.

"Don't even think about it," she replied warningly. "I don't get angry," she reminded him, "I get even." Her grin was meaningful.

Radine immediately covered his cock, then grinned at her. He trusted that she would never resort to such tactics again, and if she did, it would probably have been well-earned. Turning serious, he stretched out beside her, a plateful of tidbits near. They had all night to share nadryl. And from the sounds rolling across the mountain, they would need little inspiration. "We will be married within the week."

McKenna nearly choked on the food in her mouth. "That soon?"

"And the coronation will immediately follow."

"Radine…"

"I want to marry you, McKenna, as soon as possible. That is the shortest amount of time my mother is willing to give." He ate heartily. "Your dressmaker will meet with you when we return in two days to get started on your dresses."

"Dresses?"

"One for the wedding and coronation, and one for the reception after." He fed her a piece of fruit. "I would like you to let your people know what has happened to you. Perhaps in a year or two, we can return to Earth to show what has happened to you, and answer questions about Taburon."

McKenna was silent, thinking. "One of the biggest problems we've had on Earth is no one has come back to tell about their experiences with otherworld people. It's made women hesitant to go to other worlds."

"I would welcome more of the people from Earth on Taburon. It is good to meet different people and have them live among you. You may be our first ambassador."

"I would be honored to represent Taburon, Radine." She swatted at him, missing. "Don't change the subject. What will I have to know for the wedding and coronation?"

He leaned close and kissed her, passion on his lips, the taste of the food in his mouth as he swept his tongue inside her mouth. "You only have to say yes, little one." Moving the food plate away, he covered her with his body, ready to resume sharing nadryl. "Say yes, McKenna," he coaxed, undulating with his hips, his cock fully engorged once more. "Say yes," he whispered, his lips hovering close to hers.

Staring into his eyes, she melted. He loved her so much, he could never get enough of loving her, nor she of him. She was going to be his wife, and queen, something she had never dreamed about, even as a child. Her childhood games had never involved the little girl princess kind, life had been too harsh even then. She had dreamed about

263

being a business person, or rising in government, fighting for the causes of women. But now, she realized, she could do just that, even better, with the power of the throne of Taburon behind her. Radine would deny her little, his love and faith in her was complete.

She hoped she could give back to him equally – as a helpmate, a lover, and the mother of his children. She hadn't considered having children in the past, but now that the future had opened it up to her, she wanted it, very much. She wanted it for herself, but mostly she wanted it for him. For wasn't that what love was about – giving your partner a chance to have their dreams?

But children didn't grow on trees. She spread her legs wide open, his hips falling between them as if they knew no other home. His cock nudged at the entrance to her pussy, coating itself with her abundant juices before gliding slowly in without hindrance. "Yes," she whispered in return.

Chapter Twenty-Six

The temperature in the king's chambers was quite comfortable, the warmth of the mid-day sun shining into the room cooled by a soft breeze that blew through the opened floor to ceiling windows. Stirring the gauzy drapes, the small wind swept through the room, rippling the bed linens and Radine's trouser legs as it passed.

Radine sat at a table, papers scattered across its surface, one held in his hand that he was reading intently. As usual, several days away from the palace and work piled up that needed to be dispensed before the wedding.

They had returned to the palace after sunset yesterday, exhausted and hungry with only enough energy to drop into bed and sleep until she had awakened with her nightmare. After comforting her, they settled down to a small repast before falling back into bed, curling around each other as they fell to sleep. McKenna had been both pleased

- and perhaps a small amount of perturbed - that Radine had not initiated sex, his attitude towards her as platonic on the return trip as it had been going to the Lanzess Mountain for Sky Clad. He had told her as unconsciousness took her mind that he wanted to give her more time to recover from her kidnapping, that the sex during Sky Clad had been unavoidable because of the situation. As an adult, no one had ever treated her with such concern before and she smiled into the darkness to sleep peacefully.

Until morning. Still unaccustomed to having personal servants, having Purnia awaken them just after sunrise, catching McKenna, naked, half-draped over an equally naked Radine drew a squeal from her as she hid under the bedclothes. Radine had burst into laughter as he waved Purnia from the room for as long as it took for her to don clothing, her face flushing beet red when he returned with more servants laden with more trays of food.

Radine explained again that personal servants never batted an eye at their 'masters' state of dress – or undress in this case – it was not their place to comment, though Purnia did sometimes inject his opinion into Radine's life, a long - time relationship giving him familiarity that Annatt would develop with McKenna over the course of her service. McKenna quipped that it would most likely take her the rest of her life to reach that level of comfort. Radine had chuckled while reaching over the table to take her hand in comfort, promising her that she would adjust.

She left soon after to dress and join his mother to continue her lessons on Taburon and begin the fittings for her wedding finery. After bathing, Radine had Purnia bring the work he had missed while away, sighing at the pile set before him. Quick reads separated the importance of each paper into piles and he was going through the most important now.

There was a soft knock on the door to his chambers. Purnia hurried from wherever it was that he waited, available to answer the king's needs, opening the door enough to peer around it. Radine continued reading though he had turned an ear towards the doorway to listen to the hushed conversation. He still held the sheet he was perusing when the door softly hissed as Purnia pushed it slightly closed. He came to stand next to his king, waiting.

"What is it, Purnia?" Radine asked quietly.

The servant bowed, something he so rarely did when they were alone that Radine glanced up. The expression on the other's face was one of wariness. "Your Majesty, Lord Quorol wishes an audience with you, and he has brought several other members of the Council with him."

Radine set the paper aside and rose, going to a small table upon which sat a carafe of tea and plate of snacks. He poured tea into a cup, taking his time in doing so, then added sweetener, stirring slowly. "Any thoughts on why they are here, Purnia?" Servants were the life blood of any palace, going about their business unobtrusively, unnoticed, and picking up information others spoke thinking they were having a private conversation. A good servant usually kept this knowledge to himself, unless he was asked directly.

"Only rumor, my Lord."

"And what is the rumor, Purnia?"

"That you are wrong in marrying her highness, Princess McKenna. She is not Taburon, my Lord."

Radine took his tea back to his seat, setting the cup down. "Anything else?"

"That is the heart of the complaint, Your Majesty."

"And everything else stems from there," Radine finished knowingly as he seated himself. He was surprised they had waited this long to voice their dislike with his choice of queen and wife. No matter. Even open rebellion would not deter him or change his plans. Radine set the paper he'd been reading aside. "Show them in, Purnia," he ordered, sitting back in his chair. The servant made to go to the door, but swerved instead to snag the crown from the bedpost where Radine had placed it last night. He handed it to his king, nodded once, then went to the door. Radine placed the crown on his head. Purnia opened the door fully, bowing as the group of men entered the chambers.

Lord Quorol was a squat Taburon, barely reaching six foot five, overweight from a life of indulgence and privilege. He wore heavy clothing in shades of gray and blue, his shirt's high collar concealing the double chin that grew below his jaw. His hair was cropped short and tight to his scalp. He had dark golden eyes that darted around the room upon entering, making obvious note of the furnishings and décor before landing heavily on the king in front of him. Tucking his hands in the belt around his expanded waist, he sauntered close to stand less than two feet in front of the king's table.

He had always been the one advisor Radine could trust to see the opposite of anything Radine proposed, argumentative at times, dismissive usually, at odds always even when his observations were valid points. Radine knew it stemmed from the fact that when, many, many generations ago the decision had to be made who would assume the throne, it had been Radine's family given the crown and not his. Were it not for that, Quorol would be king now and Radine simply a lord somewhere.

Behind him, four other men lined up to his sides, two on each side, their looks determined yet obviously subordinate to the Lord Quorol.

Radine gave each man a perusal, slow and thorough before settling his gaze on Quorol. He waited.

Each man flushed, especially Quorol before bowing to their king. "Your Majesty," Quorol murmured.

"My Lord," Radine responded, equally as soft, yet firm to remind each that no matter their issue, he was still their king and that alone demanded the respect he was owed.

"Your Majesty," Quorol began again, "we've come to discuss what we feel is a very important matter concerning your throne and position as king."

One of Radine's eyebrows rose. "Indeed?" he asked. "And what would that be, My Lord?"

"Your choice of wife and queen, Your Majesty."

"I should think that after ten years as king, you would be delighted to see me take a wife, Lord Quorol, since you've been one of my loudest advisors in taking one."

Quorol shuffled slightly. "It's not that you're finally taking a wife, Your Majesty. It's who you have chosen for that honor."

"Is she too old, or ugly?"

"No, Sire. But she's not Taburon."

"No, she's not. She's from Earth."

"That is the point, Sire. She's not Taburon," he repeated. "Was there not a woman qualified to be queen from among our own people?"

"If there was, I might have married sooner. Lord Quorol, you, my mother, and a number of other members of the advisory council have paraded any number of women before me in hopes of one of them being suitable as my wife and queen. I disagreed, for a varied number of reasons."

"I can think of a dozen or so that were eminently qualified for you, Majesty."

"For dynastic reasons, trade agreements, family relations, providing heirs, that sort of thing?" Radine's voice dripped with sarcasm.

"Of course, Your Majesty. Why else does a king or queen marry except to improve the position of their people?"

"What about love, Lord Quorol?"

He scoffed. "Royals do not marry for love, sire. You should already be aware of that."

"Maybe generations ago, but not with this royal. Every women passed by me was interested in the crown and the position, not me or what we might share as husband and wife. I wanted more than a pretty face that brought profits and was content to become a royal brood mare. I wanted someone to love, to love me, to appreciate what I could give her as my wife and not expect it as a queen." Radine circled the rim of his cup with a finger. "I want someone to love me for the rest of my life, as I will love her."

"And what about children, Sire? Can this woman give you heirs?" He took a deep breath. "Your future and the throne is not totally secure until you have an heir."

"Could you guarantee that any Taburon woman I may have married would be able to give me heirs? Would you vet every woman as to her fertility before marriage?" He sat forward. "We are sexually compatible, we've already proven that. Whether or not we have children, only the future will tell. But that is a concern for the future, and completely my concern."

Quorol shook his head. "No, Sire, it concerns all of Taburon. Your family has ruled for generations. What might happen if someone not of your family becomes king after your demise? We have trade agreements with planets throughout our system. They could be broken the moment someone else takes the throne."

"Just as they could be broken when my son becomes king, simply because he's not me. There are no guarantees in anything, Lord Quorol. My children will be raised to respect our current policies, but if they believe there is something better that can be done for our people, they will do it, with or without your approval. The future is not written, my Lords."

"The future unfolds based upon what is done today, Sire. What if the people do not accept this half-breed child as their king?"

"Are you suggesting the possibility of rebellion, My Lord?"

"No, Sire. But the people must be your first concern, even above a wife you can love. They are your people. She is not."

"She," he replied forcefully, "has spent every day since her arrival learning about Taburon. She has shown a love for Taburon that I've not seen in anyone from any other planet who has visited Taburon. She has met many of the people and been readily accepted by them. She participated in Sky Clad, willingly and totally, and the people there that night approved." He lifted a hand. "And, My Lord, if you ever refer to any child we might have as a half-breed, I shall certainly see to it that you regret it. They will be of my royal blood, princes and princesses all, and due all respect."

Quorol flushed. "We are only concerned for your rule, Your Majesty, and the future of our planet and people."

"And you have expressed your concern, Lord Quorol, as you should. But my decision stands. McKenna brings nothing to this marriage except her love for me, and the love that is growing within her for our people. She is an intelligent woman who can rule by my side with compassion, foresight, and acuity. If it turns out there will be no children, I will make sure my successor is one the people can accept and who may rule as you have been accustomed."

"We have your word on that?"

"Yes, you have my word. I would insist that you get to know McKenna before you pass judgment on her. There is much she needs to

273

learn, but she has made remarkable progress in the little time she has been here. And after what she has been through, I think you owe her that at the least."

Quorol looked to his side, at each man that accompanied him, receiving the slightest of nods from each man. He faced the king again. "What will you offer if she does not – cannot - uphold her part as queen? If the people disapprove, if she finds it too much of a burden, if there are no children?"

Radine was silent for a moment, his fingers toying with the cup that by now had grown cold and he would not drink once the men were gone. Did he love McKenna enough to make the ultimate sacrifice, to give up his throne and home and life as it had been for the last thirty-four years, privileged and honored and revered by his people? Could he make his mother make that drastic change in her life, since if he left, she would most likely be expected to leave as well?

Of course, there were rights he had even should he abdicate. He would still retain his other titles and any home he owned because of them outside of the palaces. There was a lot he would have to give up, but he wouldn't be destitute by any means. And life, on a strictly social status level, would still be better for McKenna than what it had been for her on her home planet. That he could give her, indeed, she might prefer it to becoming a queen, a daunting position if nothing else. One that she'd already expressed doubts about holding. Though she was giving it an honest try and he believed in her.

As time passed, she would become more and more confident in her role on Taburon. As more and more of the people came to understand her, and she them, they would find a mutual respect for each other. Acceptance was easy once everyone understood each other.

Yes, he would do anything to keep her. They loved each other. Of that he had no doubt whatsoever. Eight days had passed since she'd been kidnapped and she'd not said a word about returning to Earth. Radine had been waiting for her to ask, relieved beyond measure when she agreed to Sky Clad and participated joyfully. She was enthusiastic about the wedding, of that he was positive. And he loved her with everything he believed and held dear.

The king glanced at the expectant faces watching him as he went through his thoughts, and the royal sighed. "If you will accept, I will abdicate the throne, if – only if – she fails. As long as McKenna tries, and keeps trying, you must give her the benefit of the doubt. If, and only if, the majority of the people disapprove will I abdicate, but only after she has been given time to prove herself to them."

"You would give up the throne, for a woman? An alien woman?"

Radine saw red, but kept his calm. "For someone I love, yes."

"You can't," McKenna cried from the adjoining door to their suites. "Radine, you can't give up the throne if it's because of me." Radine stood to meet her halfway into the room, taking her hands into his and pulling her further inside.

275

"I can, and I would. I love you."

"But the people need you. You are Taburon."

Bringing her to his chair, he gave the men on the other side of the table a meaningful look. Each man bowed, if not completely, at least his head dipped. "Your Highness," each man greeted.

There was still distress in her eyes as she nodded in return. "My Lords," she replied, facing Radine again. "Radine, what's going on?"

"You haven't had much of a chance to meet members of the advisory council. This is Lord Kenet, Lord Coret, Lord Quorol, Minister Spiva, and Lord Redmay." Each man bowed again as they were introduced. "They were concerned about our relationship, and I was just reassuring them that they have no real reason to be concerned. Is that not true, gentlemen?"

"Yes, Sire, of course."

Radine smiled. "And I think her Highness has just proven that she is perfect for the role as queen, since she places the good of Taburon above her own happiness."

Quorol placed a hand on his chest over his heart. "May it always be so, Your Majesty."

Radine bowed in return. This conversation was over as far as he was concerned. "The wedding is in four days. I'm sure you will be in attendance. If that is all?"

Once more each man bowed, but the expression on Quorol's face was not pleased, not pleased at all. Yet they all left without a word, pulling the doors closed behind them. From the side, Purnia appeared and grabbed the now cold tea, taking it to the tray. Placing the cup on the tray, he picked up the entire loaded tray and disappeared to refresh the drink. Radine sat, pulling McKenna across his lap.

"Now, do you want to tell me the truth?" she asked.

He encircled her waist. "I told them you were intelligent," he observed, attempting to change the subject.

"Radine," she scolded warningly.

He sighed. "They had the same concerns you had the day we headed out to the cottage." He could feel her stiffen slightly, but he hugged her tighter until he felt her relax. His hand rubbed along her back. "It's their job to advise, to question, and then be reassured."

"But you said you'd abdicate."

"I choose love over rule, McKenna. As long as you love me, I have more than I've ever hoped to have. The crown means little if I have to give you up to keep it. Never doubt that, my McKenna."

With a finger, she traced along his jaw. "I am very honored to have you in my life. I will love you until the day I die. And even after, I suspect I will still love you."

"And I," he said as he pulled her closer, "am certainly the luckiest man in the universe." He sealed it with a kiss – long and full of promise, sweeping across her lips with his mouth until she opened to let him in. He indulged himself, exploring until he began to feel the usual response he got whenever they indulged in each other.

There were papers to get through yet, work that needed to be cleared before the wedding. That would never get done if he continued to kiss her and gave in to the emotions racing through his body, the need that grew with each passing day and every time he was near her. Later, he promised himself, he would have Jaima join him on the practice field for some well-earned exercise, to exorcise these incredible feelings until after they were married. Only one more night.

He took a deep breath, coming up for air. "So, tell me how the fittings went," he invited, keeping her on his lap.

Chapter Twenty-Seven

Annatt approached McKenna as she shook her nightgown down around her ankles in preparation for bed. She would sleep alone tonight, her last night as a single woman. Tomorrow she would marry Radine and become wife and queen all in one day. A daunting future without a doubt, but one she was willing to undertake wholeheartedly.

She pulled the fall of her hair free of the collar of the gown, giving her head a shake to let it fall in waves against her back. Her fingers rose to button the neckline of the gown.

Annatt curtsied. "Your Highness."

McKenna slid her glance to the young woman, a smile crossing her lips. The girl was enthusiastically learning her tasks as a maid of honor and teaching McKenna at the same time how life as a royal might unfold. They had found a pleasant comfort zone with each other, though McKenna still balked slightly at the amount of intimacy she was expected to endure. Never having someone bath and dress her was still too new.

"I really like this gown, Annatt. You made a fine choice for me. Thank you."

"Your Highness, Lord Quorol is outside your chambers and wishes to speak with you."

"At this time of night?" McKenna questioned. "I wonder what he wants." She finished buttoning the gown. "He does realize that I'm getting married tomorrow?"

"Yes, my Lady. He says it is urgent and must speak with you."

McKenna reached for the robe draped over the end of the bed and shoved her hands through the sleeves. "All right, I guess you'd best let him in."

Annatt curtsied again. "Yes, Your Highness." McKenna pulled the sides of the robe closed and turned on her heel to face the entrance as the young woman went to the doors to permit the lord to enter. She bobbed another curtsy as the man brushed past her, his face intent.

Quorol walked directly up to McKenna and stood, two feet away. He nodded his head in a poor imitation of a bow, pulling a piece of paper from a pocket. "I think you should read this before you make a grave mistake tomorrow," he said without preamble, shoving the paper into her hand.

McKenna's face blanched, all color leaching from her as she scanned the writing, her knees going slack. Grabbing the edge of the mattress, she carefully lowered herself to it as if she would break. Her breath caught in her throat and her hand started to shake, her chin wobbling in effort to keep from breaking down completely in front of this man. "When…" she whispered in disbelief. "when did he write this?"

"Before he left for this so-called bachelor party. He asked I give it to you after the Queen had left for the night."

Her whole body shaking now, McKenna felt the tears well in her eyes as a vice gripped her heart, squeezing until it could no longer pump the blood she needed to any part of her body. She was numb, to everything, her breathing, her heartbeat, the bed beneath her body, the floor under her feet. Yet she was freezing. Her muscles contracted until if she could, she would have folded in on herself until she'd disappeared completely. The world was heavy on her shoulders, its weight pressing down on her through and through. She couldn't stand if her life depended on it right now, and she didn't know what to do.

Her hand reached out blindly as she sank to the floor. "I can't…" she wheezed, "I can't breathe." Annatt rushed over to help, wrapping an arm about her shoulders as she shot a scathing glance to Quorol.

"Try, My Lady," she encouraged quietly. "You can breathe if you try."

With a wail of despair, McKenna folded in on herself, hugged by the young woman, watched impassively by the lord, who then shook his head with undisguised disdain. "You cannot stay, woman. I have a transport ready for you to take you back to your planet."

"My Lord?" Annatt asked, shocked, her face pale.

"The king has changed his mind and has canceled the wedding. It would be best if the human were not here when he returns. I offer to return her to her own world. But you must hurry and get her things together. The transport will not wait forever."

"She should talk to the king first, My Lord," Annatt protested, hovering over the distraught woman. She'd not made a sound, not begun to cry, just fought to take that all important breath that had escaped her when she'd read that letter.

"You forget your place, girl," Quorol warned harshly. "The king will need these rooms for his intended in the near future. Your only concern is to help this woman get herself out of them."

McKenna looked up, her eyes teary, but not dripping. She would not allow herself to break down here and now. There would be time enough for that later, once she was alone back on Earth. When she would let herself fall apart, break into a million pieces that would never be whole again, no matter how much glue was used. "He's chosen someone already?" she whispered with surprise.

"He will soon. The Council has decreed he must marry in the next six months or lose the crown. There must be an heir, or the promise of one within the year."

McKenna nodded with understanding. "And since I might never conceive…"

"The reason for his decision to dissolve his promise to you," Quorol confirmed.

Finally able to take a deep breath, McKenna nodded again and rose on quaking legs, pulling her dignity around her as best she could as a shield. "If you'll wait outside, Lord Quorol, so I might change, I'll join you in a few minutes."

"It is the best for all." He spared Annatt a glance that said in no uncertain terms to do as she was told and not argue. He started to bow again then changed his mind and turned, not stopping until he'd pulled the door closed behind him.

McKenna began to strip, holding the nausea that threatened to spill over until she was safe away from Taburon. "Annatt, would you get a small bag for me please?" she asked softly.

"Your Highness, you should wait until the king returns, talk to him. I can't believe he would be so cruel."

"He said it all in this letter," McKenna said, crumpling the piece of paper she still held. "He doesn't want me, I was just someone to pass the time with, an easy fuck, until the Council put their collective foot down. Now he needs me to go home, like he promised when we first met."

"Your Highness…"

McKenna rounded on the girl. "I am not your highness," she growled, "not anymore. Just plain old McKenna," she corrected. "McKenna, the naïve, stupid girl," she whispered to herself, staring ahead at nothing. Giving herself a shake, she finished taking off the beautiful robe she wore. Annatt's eyes filled with tears but she went to the wardrobe and opening it, pulled a small valise from the bottom.

"I won't need much, just enough to get me back to Earth, then I'll get my own clothes once I'm home. A shirt or two, maybe a pair of trousers. That's all I'll take."

Sobbing vocally, Annatt nodded. "Yes, My Lady," she answered as she dragged several pieces of clothing from the wardrobe, folding them carefully before placing them in the valise.

Reaching over the servant's shoulder, McKenna grabbed several pieces of clothing, taking them back to the bed. Drawing the nightgown over her head, she dropped it onto the mattress and began to dress, her fingers doing the work without her thinking about it, her body still numbed from shock. She'd think about what was happening another time once she was far away.

Standing, Annatt started for the bathing room, but McKenna called her back. "I won't need anything from there, Annatt. Just leave it." The girl curtsied, bringing the valise to her former mistress. McKenna checked the contents and added a brush, then snapped the bag closed.

She didn't look back as she went to the chamber doors, valise in hand, stopping as the sobbing of the girl followed her to the entrance. With a final deep breath, she pulled open the doors and stepped through, Quorol turning to face her as she met him on the other side. Before the doors could shut, Quorol stuck his head inside and told Annatt to go back to her parents immediately, her services were no longer needed. McKenna felt a fresh wave of pain. The girl was sweet and innocent – she didn't deserve such inhumane treatment. But then, Taburons weren't human. She had no doubts now that aliens were so far different from her world and what she knew that they would never be able to cohabitate in peace and harmony.

The thump of the doors closing was loud in her mind, but she pushed it away with determination, her chin lifting. Quorol reached to take the bag, but she held it firmly, her lifeline to her sanity until she could fall apart in peace.

For the two and a half days it took to reach Earth she didn't eat once and barely took in anything to drink. When she left her quarters, which wasn't often, she wandered the halls of the ship in a daze, a pale, silent wraith avoided by all of the crewmen when they saw her coming. She didn't speak, she didn't emote, her mind shut down to everything and everyone around her. She lay on the bed in the quarters provided, but didn't sleep, too afraid of what she might dream while she slept. All she knew was she needed to get home as soon as possible, to curl up in her misery alone and let loose and vent her anguish in private where no one could know or see or hear.

She wasn't even sure if she had a home anymore. After all, she'd been gone for three weeks now. Her landlord would have certainly claimed her apartment for lack of rent, and her personal belongings confiscated or sold. She didn't know what she would do then, where she would go, how she would support herself. She was constantly nauseous now, her stress levels off the charts, and that she wasn't eating made her feel as though a belt were tightening around her waist more and more every hour.

She read the letter he'd written every day, three times daily now, the words still haunting her in their bluntness and finality. Brutal words, he'd praised her ability in bed. Not too highly, since his experience was far greater and while she'd been delightful enough, having to constantly instruct her had become boring after a time. Her next lover might be more pleased by what he'd taught her. She been an adequate pupil and he thanked her for letting him teach her.

The kidnapping by Espis and discussion he'd had with his Council and advisors had finally made him see that he really did need to take a Taburon woman as wife and queen, or face outright rebellion from his people, and his people would always come first. He was their king, and he had obligations to them before himself. He needed the assurance that he would be able to pass his crown to his heir, and she could not assure him that he would have an heir with her.

She would not be held responsible for killing Espis. It was in self-defense after all. In payment for her services, she could take anything she wished for her return to Earth, all of the clothes and most of the jewels, but not the crowns or crown jewels. He thanked her for her time.

She read and reread the letter before tucking it carefully back in the valise, pushing it deep into the side where it could not be seen but where she could easily grab it when she wanted to continue punishing herself and remembering that all men, even alien ones, were bastards at heart.

No words of love, no regrets, no remorse for leading her on and using her poorly. Nothing to show he may have had some thoughts about what he'd done other than getting a convenient place to put his cock. No apologies for the lies he told her the whole time they were together, the falsehoods spoken to get her to spread her legs, to let him into her body and heart, to share nadryl – no - to fuck – in front of all of those people at Sky Clad.

Her head wished she'd truly unmanned him. Her heart could not conceive of such a punishment.

287

He'd fucked her – her heart, mind and body. She should have stayed behind and let Raymond have her. It would have been more merciful.

Rain was pouring when they reached Earth, falling in sheets beyond the windows of the shuttle that took her back to the building she'd once called home. The pilot landed on the roof, as Radine had, opening the hatch, waiting patiently as she climbed out into the deluge. He handed her her valise, a moment of sympathy taking over when he asked if there was anything he could get her. Her softly spoken reply of some way to forget was not heard as she turned, her shoulders hunched, and headed for the roof top door, soaked by the time she reached the knob. The shuttle hatch closed and the vehicle lifted off as the roof top door shut with a hollow thud. She was shivering violently, her wet clothes cold in the darkness of the hallway.

Her apartment door was closed but not locked when she made it to the fourth floor. She pushed it open hesitantly, peering around the edge to make sure the apartment was empty of squatters.

It was also empty of most of her furniture, the sofa the only piece in the living room. With a soft cry, she dropped the valise by the door and walked through the place, taking inventory. The bed was gone, as were all of her linens, clothes, kitchen items and food. A lone unopened bottle of beer sat forlornly in the refrigerator, probably one of the ones she'd rejected three weeks ago as too spoiled to drink then.

She pulled it free and popped the top, draining the liquid inside into the sink, the smell creating a stirring nausea in her stomach. McKenna choked and dropped the bottle into the sink, running for the bathroom where she vomited, her stomach heaving violently though there was nothing inside to expel.

That was all it took. Curling on her side on the floor of the bathroom, she burst into tears, her whole body shaking with palsy as she let the hurt, the pain, the deceit flood over her and rattle her like a terrier a rat. She cried, she vented, she squashed the sobs that wracked her so she wouldn't be heard in the apartments surrounding her when she only wanted to scream, to beat her hands against his chest and hurt him as much as he'd hurt her. To dig through muscle and sinew to see if he had a heart and then wrench it from him, watch it beat until it died and matched the dead heart she held enclosed in her breast.

When she was through, she promised herself, she would harden herself against everything. No love, no warmth, no expression of feelings. She find a job somewhere, do her work each day then go home each night, close herself in, and ignore the rest of the world for the rest of her life.

But now she had to let it all out, to purge herself of the evil that had gnawed at her for days, the stiff upper lip no longer stiff, but quivering and spit slobbered as everything she'd kept inside erupted in heaps and bounds over the floor of the bathroom and into the toilet.

She cried herself into unconsciousness, waking hours later to peer at herself in the dull mirror. Her eyes were swollen, her nose red and dripping. Her lips were parched and her skin sallow. She knew she needed to rest as she splashed water on her face. Swiping her skin dry with a sleeve, she made her way back to the kitchen and finished emptying the beer bottle, clinging to the edge of the sink to keep herself from collapsing. Rinsing it out, she filled the bottle with water and carried it over to the sofa, where she sank down heavily. She didn't remember falling to sleep, the bottle dropping to the floor to spill water.

Radine was pleasantly buzzed, leaning on Jaima's shoulder as they both walked precariously to his chambers. The gathering of his close friends at the public house and drinking to his health as well as his nights in bed with a delightful woman, had been fun. They told ribald jokes, made many of the waitresses blush scarlet, stolen a few kisses and been generally amusing to the staff as they watched their king get snockered. He was getting married in the morning. It was understandable that he spent one final night as a bachelor with his friends doing things he wouldn't do once saddled with a wife, no matter how pleasant the woman.

They'd broken up well before the mid night hour. The king wanted to be clear headed for his wedding, reception, and especially the wedding night, not hung over or suffering a headache once he and McKenna were left alone. They wouldn't take a 'honeymoon,' as she called it. He'd been away from the palace too long lately to leave it again quite so soon. In several months, they would go away for a few days to honeymoon.

The servants still up at this hour smiled indulgently as the two men wandered through the hallways, giggling at some unspoken joke, then laughing uproariously at their giggling. Turning a corner, they were but steps from his chambers, pulling up short at the sight of Lord Quorol waiting at his doors.

Radine straightened. "What does he want?" he murmured sotto voce, pulling at his shirt to straighten it, rolling his shoulders.

"A good long visit in the dungeon," Jaima replied equally softly, also pulling himself taller and sobering a little. Once they dealt with Quorol, they could resume their jovial camaraderie without interference.

Quorol bowed deeply to his king. "Your Majesty," he greeted.

"Quorol," Radine replied.

The older man pulled a letter from a pocket and passed it over. "You have my apologies, My Lord."

"For what, Lord Quorol?" Radine asked as he took the letter and began to unfold it. The color drained from his face and his eyes darkened as he scanned the contents, instantly becoming sober. His back straightened abruptly, his body going rigid, his brows drawing close.

"What is it?" Jaima asked, alarmed by his friend's reaction, his expression shooting daggers at Quorol for ruining their good mood.

"She can't have," Radine whispered hoarsely. "I don't believe it." He crumpled the paper in his hand and turned, taking off at a run. Down the corridor he ran, barely stopping as he reached the doors to McKenna's chambers, flinging them open. He stopped just inside the room, scanning around from side to side. Jaima braked to halt beside him. Quorol sauntered to the doorway and waited.

"Radine?" Jaima asked, frantic.

The king howled, pain and despair in his voice as he tossed the paper at Jaima. The Commander picked it from the floor, flattened it and read, his eyebrows drawing together in horror.

Radine growled in anger, stomping to the bed and grabbing the sheets, flinging them to the floor. Grabbing the mattress, he tossed it, heaving it away from him with a painful cry. He attacked the table where they shared a morning snack and upended it with a roar, picking up the chair where she sat and flinging it across the room. It shattered as it hit the wall. Striding to the wardrobe, he yanked open the doors and tossed hangar after hangar of dresses to the floor, saving the wedding dress for last. This one he viciously pulled from its hangar and held it a moment, staring at the garment as though it would speak to him, then rent it in two with his bare hands as he snarled. At her dressing table, he swept every article on top to the floor, smashing bottles and scattering items across the floor. His shoulders shook with grief.

"Radine!" Jaima cried, "stop. You must stop!" He grabbed at the king's hands, holding tightly despite the other's struggle to be freed, leaning into him until the king sank to the floor.

"Why?" he asked forlornly. "I thought she loved me." He hanged his head. "I thought she wanted to be my wife and queen."

"I don't know, my brother. Maybe the kidnapping was too much for her. Maybe she was too scared to become queen. Maybe things were just too different here."

"She could have come to me, talked with me. We would have worked through it together, as we should have." He turned tear filled eyes towards his friend and brother. "I told her I would have given up the crown to be with her, she was everything."

"I guess she didn't believe you."

"I feel as though my chest has been crushed, Jaima. There is so much pain, how can anyone live through this?"

"You will live through it."

"She can't have been gone too long. Maybe if I get my ship and follow…"

"She didn't want you to. She said so in her letter."

Radine, who'd begun to rise, sank back down to the floor, defeated far more than he'd ever been in his life. "She played me, Jaima. I was a fool."

"No more so than any man who is turned by a pretty face and delightful figure, my king."

"Never again," Radine vowed. "If I marry, it will be for dynastic reasons. Love is a fool's game." He made to stand. "I hope she got what she wanted," he said derisively. Stalking to the dressing table, he opened the drawers he knew contained jewels and other gems he'd placed in her care, fully expecting them to be gone, taken by a woman out for a few weeks of fun and some sort of payment for her time. He was surprised then to find all of the jewels in place, each in its space securely and undisturbed, even those he'd given to her as hers. "Well, she left the jewels." He slammed the drawer closed and sighed. Spinning on his heel, he saw that Quorol watched from the doorway, his hands folded across his waist.

Radine shook his head, disgusted by his display of temper, his head throbbing in pain. He shook his head slightly, regretting it instantly as the throb increased exponentially. Radine rubbed a hand across his forehead, closing his eyes and seeing spots of light. "I am going to bed, Jaima. I will deal with this in the morning." Jaima rose as the king stumbled out the door, heading to his own chambers. Jaima's heart was breaking for his friend and brother.

"When did you get this letter?" Jaima asked the lord, anger tingeing his voice.

"Soon after you left for your gathering."

"Why did you not bring to the king then?"

"She asked for it to not be given to him until he'd returned."

Jaima scooped the letter up and folded it carefully, putting it in a pocket. "You have done the king a great disservice this night, Lord Quorol. You should have brought that letter to him immediately. They would have talked."

"He will forget her in time He will find a woman here on Taburon who knows her duty and they will marry. She will not treat him as some plaything to romp with and forsake when she tires of it."

Jaima listened, but his mind was on something more profound as he heard Quorol's words. He knew Radine better than any man on Taburon. The king was a man of honor and astute. He would not have been deceived by McKenna's charade, no matter how skillful an actor she might have been. He would not have denied himself her body if that was all she'd wanted. He would have shared himself and gladly, knowing there was nothing more to it than some simple pleasure for a short period of time.

If he hadn't believed she cared, he never would have told her his true identity and then asked her again to become his wife and his queen. Letting her believe he was little more than a soldier would have set them both free after their time together, both satisfied. He could have taken her to the cottage or any one of a number of places where his identity would have been kept secret for the time they were together.

Radine had been frantic when Espis had kidnapped McKenna. He'd cried when he'd found her, something the king rarely did. Even at his own father's funeral did he keep his composure and not slip once. He was vested in this relationship, body and soul. He had been happy, happier than Jaima had seen him in years. Two days ago, he and Radine had spent an afternoon talking about how changed his life was going to be and how much it pleased him. How frightened it made him to think that the relationship the two of them shared was going to change once he became a married man. He didn't want to jeopardize that. Jaima assured him that they would still be close, but he would have to put McKenna first, though there would still be things that only men would understand. And Jaima was always available for those discussions.

"I shall handle canceling the plans for the morning," Lord Quorol was saying, bringing Jaima's attention back to the present.

Jaima looked at the room, the disaster it had become. Tomorrow he would have someone set it to rights, return the dresses to the dress maker, and send the jewels back to the vault where they'd been kept until McKenna had come into their lives. For now, his concern was for his king and his emotional state. Jaima nodded once to Quorol's suggestion. The palace and local hostels were already filled with guests who would have be told there was to be no wedding now and go home. Let the lesser lord handle the mundane details. Radine would need the support of his close friends and family – his mother – to get him through this desperate time.

He waited for Quorol to leave, then followed, pulling the doors closed firmly.

Chapter Twenty-Eight

The morning dawned as beautifully as any morning on Taburon, the weather uncaring of the indescribable hurt in the chambers of the king. Radine hadn't bothered undressing, merely falling onto the bed as was and into a drink and pain induced stupor. Birds in the trees outside his window chirruped merrily and the normal sounds of the palace inhabitant going about their daily lives intruded through the open windows and along the outside hallways.

Purnia, having been informed of the debacle of last night, brought a tray laden with hot tea, sweet fruits and a comfit of medicine for a hangover headache. Radine groaned as he started to stir, the clinking of cups and utensils drawing him closer to wakefulness.

Radine groaned again. "Leave be, Purnia," he moaned. "Go away for the day."

"Your Majesty, it is time to rise. I have medicine here to help your head."

"Save it for later. I am not rising today. I have no reason to get up."

"Your Majesty, Lord Jaima told me what has happened. You have my heartfelt sympathy. But I have found that the best way to ease the pain is to do something, like your daily routine. The guests have all been told and are leaving the palace even as we speak. There are still petitions to be heard and Lord Jaima, who has gone to refresh himself and change, has asked that you prepare to join him on the practice field this morning."

Radine rolled onto his back and tossed an arm across his eyes. "Jaima can go play with *belkas*," he whined. "I'm not getting up."

"Aye, you are," Jaima corrected, entering the room, dressed for training, sword at his side. "I will not let you lay abed, commiserating."

"You forget who is king here," Radine growled.

"No, I do not, Sire, but she is gone and there is nothing you can do about it now. Come," he insisted, pulling at one of Radine's arms, making him rise to a sitting position, "have some tea and something for your head, work off some of that drink, and then you can start hearing petitions."

"Gods' rods, Jaima, can you not give me some time? The woman I was going to marry, today if you recall, has left me. She lied to me, said she loved me, yet when it came down to it, she only saw me as a good time, a chance to visit another planet, to be able to say she had sex with a king and then went on her way."

"I know, Radine, and I empathize with you. But you cannot wallow in sorrow. You are the king. You must be above this maudlin attitude."

Radine jumped from the bed, his arms waving wildly, his face reddened with anger. "Fuck you, Jaima!" he yelled. "It is a crude word the Earthers use, but now I understand why. Fuck you, fuck McKenna and fuck Taburon!" he added, stomping into the bathing room and slamming the door. A moment later, the shower turned on.

"He is hurting, My Lord," Purnia said softly.

"I know, more than he's ever hurt before," Jaima replied gently. "She didn't try to talk it out with him, she didn't wait to say goodbye. He didn't have a chance to make things right, he was left with having to just accept her decision without any input. Something Radine's never really had to do before because he is the king."

"I thought she loved him."

"As did I. I was convinced she was the one person in all of the galaxy who could make him happy and give him his heart's desire." Jaima sighed deeply. "Now we must deal with the aftermath," he

300

murmured, his eyes turning away from the closed door to the loyal servant. "See that someone is sent to clean the rooms she used. The king had a bit of a temper last night when he found out. Pack the clothes and get rid of them, strip the bed. Whatever you're not sure about put in a container and set it aside. I'll look at it later and decide what to do with it." He nodded towards the king's bed. "Did she sleep in those sheets?"

"Yes, My Lord."

"Change them, get rid of anything in here that can remind him of her. I'll try to keep him occupied as much as possible, keep his mind off of her. You might want to include some sort of calming tea at night so he can sleep."

"I shall, My Lord."

"Once he is dressed, send him out to the practice yard. I have a few guards that need to hone their skills." Hand on sword, Jaima spun on his heel and headed out.

For the next three days, Radine's routine was the same – rise early, train, attend to his duties as king, train again and drop into bed too exhausted for anything. He did sleep, though restlessly, angered that someone was always close in case he needed. The fourth morning, Radine was already up and dressed, eating a light breakfast when Jaima entered, pleasing the commander that the king finally seemed in control, having put her treachery behind him.

And Radine had learned to control, burying his emotions deep inside, keeping a tight rein on them. The few times they threatened to bubble up, he would stop whatever he was doing and fight to tamp them down, sending them back to that place inside where he would learn to never let them loose again.

He became a hard man in three days. He never smiled anymore, there was no joy he could find in anything. His decrees were harsh, he tolerated no stupidity on the field or in the throne room, handing out penalties and decisions with little or no remorse.

He flirted with the women who watched the training from a balcony, saluting them with his sword, but his eyes were hard and unfeeling. It was all for show, a tease that he had no intention of following. Women had become objects in Radine's opinion, to be used and discarded. Someday, he agreed, he would take a wife and get children off her simply because he did not want to lose the crown to an outsider, but his heart would not be in the process. His body would function as needed, that he promised himself, but it would be only enough for what he needed to fulfill destiny.

Jaima bowed after entering the chambers. "Good morning, Sire."

"Jaima." Radine was pulling on a pair of gloves.

"Are we going riding?"

"I thought a hard ride would feel good this morning, get away from the palace for a few hours."

"I'll go get my gloves then," Jaima offered.

"No, here," Radine contradicted, opening a drawer in his wardrobe and pulling out a second pair of gloves. He tossed them to Jaima. "After, we can have a mid-day meal before court, then hit the field for some training before evening meal." Radine settled his sword belt on his waist, buckling the leather tightly. "They are predicting rain for tomorrow. Hunting will be good the day after. We'll take the day."

"We've not been on a good hunt for months. I will enjoy it, Sire."

"Good. When we get back, while I am in court, gather together a few people who would be adequate company and invite them along."

"There are several who come to mind. I'll seek them out this afternoon."

Radine gave himself a quick perusal in a mirror before heading for the door. He stopped, waiting for Jaima to join him, his eye caught by a container on the floor under a table against a wall. Going to the container, he knelt down. "What is this?"

Jamia peered over his shoulder, his breath hitching slightly. "Forgive me, Sire. I had ordered that stuff to be brought to me, not you."

Radine pulled the container free, taking the lid off. His eyes closed, the pain flooding up and engulfing him for a moment before he ruthlessly tamped it down, taking several deep breaths. "These are McKenna's things."

"Yes, Sire. Again, I'm sorry. You should not have been given them."

"No matter," Radine dismissed, reaching in to pluck out an item. The plant she'd felt necessary to bring to Taburon had wilted while being kept in a closed container, but it was still alive. Radine placed it on top of the table. "Someone has to water this thing," he commented, reaching for a second item. "Strange," he said, puzzled, revealing the picture of her family, "she didn't take this with her. Her family meant a lot to her." He glanced up over his shoulder at Jaima. "You would think if she was going back to Earth that she would want this, if anything at all. She said it was the only picture she had left of all of them."

"She was in a hurry?" Jaima suggested.

"She had enough time to pack a few things. No, I don't believe she would have left this behind."

A discreet knock on the chamber doors had Jaima stepping to them and opening one side. Queen Inoa waited there, dressed to ride, her gloves matching her outfit, her hair tied back to keep it from being disheveled during the ride. "Morning, Jaima," she greeted with a smile.

Inoa had been distraught upon finding out about McKenna's perfidy. She had begun to think of the girl as a daughter, and her leaving cut to the quick. She had so been looking forward to the children her handsome son and beautiful daughter were going to be giving her.

But she was more worried about her son and how he was taking the loss, knowing he'd banked on McKenna for so much he had been missing from his life and believed to have found with the human. She ached for him as she watched him grow into a hard man, wanting to talk to him, but held back by Jaima, who knew it was reaction to his hurt and time would heal. When he'd suggested joining him and Jaima for a ride, she'd jumped at the chance to get him away from the palace. Perhaps help him find some peace in the quiet of an afternoon away from the palace.

Jaima bowed. "Your Majesty," he answered, stepping aside for her to enter.

"It looks like it's going to be a wonderful day for a ride," she noted entering, glancing around to find her son stooped in front of a container. "Radine, what is that?"

"Things McKenna forgot to take with her." He held the picture up for his mother to see.

Inoa's eyebrow lifted. "Her family portrait? She left that?"

"It would appear so."

Inoa took the framed picture and held it. "She missed her family a great deal. I wonder why she left this."

"As were we," Radine agreed.

"Have you ever considered that she didn't leave of her own free will?" Jaima asked into the silence that ensued while they kept to their own thoughts.

Radine rose. "What do you mean?"

Jaima waited a moment, getting his thoughts together. "Well, who delivered the news and the letter that she'd left? And who was the one person advising you to find a Taburon for a wife and keep McKenna as a convenient skala? Where is Annatt? She's not been seen since the night McKenna left."

"Do you still have that letter?" Inoa asked.

Taking a glove off, Jaima pulled the paper from a pocket, passing it to the queen.

"You've kept it?" Radine asked with surprise.

"Yes." Inoa was reading the paper, her eyes growing wider with every line.

"McKenna didn't write this," she announced.

"What?" Radine was stunned.

"This isn't her handwriting. I know. She'd been keeping notebooks of everything she was learning. I still have them. I know what her handwriting looks like and this isn't it."

The stunned look on Radine's face deepened. "Quorol," he whispered.

"Quorol," Jaima confirmed.

Inoa went directly to the doors and opened one of them. The guard outside twisted and bowed slightly. "I want Lord Quorol brought to the throne room as soon as possible," she ordered. "And find Annatt, the lady's maid who served the Princess McKenna. Bring her as well."

The guard bowed. "Right away, Your Majesty." With a signal to his companion, both men moved away to carry out their orders.

Radine began to remove his gloves. "Mother, you should get one of those notebooks to prove the note wasn't written by McKenna. Jaima, I want a list of all ships that left Taburon the night McKenna left, when they left and where they were headed. If any of the captains are on Taburon, I want to see them in the throne room within the hour."

"Right away, Sire." His step was a little lighter as he left.

Once alone, Radine looked at his mother, an expression of curiosity crossing his features. "Could Quorol have really done this? Destroy my happiness because of his xenophobia?"

"Espis nearly did," she reminded him.

"When she returns, will we have to fight this every day of our lives?"

"You're going after her?"

"I have to. She left without knowing we were both set up. She has to know the truth. I have to bring her back home, here."

"You never stopped loving her."

"I will for the rest of my life." He dropped into a chair. "Even if we'd never found out about this traitorous act, even if I'd married a Taburon woman sometime in the future, I would never have stopped loving McKenna."

Inoa stood behind Radine, leaning over to place her hands on his shoulders. He was so tense, his muscles knotted and tight. As she massaged, easing the tension, he sighed deeply. He'd never realized how very tense he'd been, holding in all of the emotion had been harder work than he'd ever wanted to indulge in ever again.

Just a little longer and he would have her back where she belonged, in his arms, in his bed, by his side, with him every day. Laughter and joy would come back into his life. Life would be worth living again. As soon as he found her.

Quorol would pay dearly for his treachery, as would any other person involved in this charade. Once they admitted to their part, Radine would demand they tell him what they could about where she was. He was sure she was on Earth, but where would they have left her – at her old apartment, or somewhere totally different?

He felt fear now. Fear for her because she had no money, no job, no way to support herself that he knew of since she'd quit her job the day they'd met. Her boss from then wouldn't give her employment, but if she appealed to him, he would take her in to turn her into his whore. Would she be desperate enough to seek him out and take him up on his offer? Radine hoped not. Raymond would use her, abuse her, wear her out, then discard her when she couldn't bring him, or any of his 'friends,' any satisfaction. She would be a shell of a woman, a husk without any life or desire for living, and his heart would break for her.

Radine felt tears well and his shoulders began to shake as the past days caught up with him and burst forth, his whole body quaking. Inoa wrapped her arms around him and held on, letting him cry, offering the comfort that only a mother could, letting him get the hurt out so he could move forward with what he had to do now to find her and get her back. "I'm so sorry, son. We'll get this sorted out, find McKenna, and bring her home where she belongs."

Leaning forward, Radine buried his face into his hands, letting it all out, giving in to the flood until there was nothing left to expend. He stood, giving his mother a hug before he went into the bathing room to wash his face and ready himself for the confrontation to come in the next few hours.

Chapter Twenty-Nine

McKenna curled up on the park bench, hugging her valise close to her chest, watching the people who hurried by to whatever plans they had for the night.

She'd managed to withdraw the little bit of savings she had in her bank account, so she'd been able to eat over the last two days, though all of the meals had been sparse in order to save her ready cash. She'd bought a light jacket – the weather was chilled for this time of year – and she was contemplating whether or not to find a shelter to see if they had room for the night.

She'd spent that first night and the next day in her old apartment, and would have settled in for as long as possible were it not for the fact that as evening fell the second night, noises from the front of the building had her peeking through the curtains to find the landlord pulling up front in a large truck. Gathering her valise, she raced out the door and down the stairs to the basement, hiding out until she was sure the man had entered the building and was somewhere in an apartment. Scurrying out, she ran down the street as far as she go.

That night she'd slept in an alley among piles of junk, curling up tightly and pulling the trash close to fend off the wind that howled down the narrow corridor. In the morning, she'd gone to the bank and been very grateful that they knew her by sight, for she had no identification to prove who she was. She cleaned out her account, fabricating a story about moving across the country for a new job and needing the cash for the trip. Tucking the thin wad into her pants next to her body, she hit the first restaurant she came to to eat for the first time in days.

As the day wore on, she wandered the streets, looking in windows, trying to keep from remembering how it was that she ended up back on Earth, and why. Her heart hurt every time she thought about it, and her breath caught in her throat, nearly bringing her to her knees every time it threatened to overwhelm her. Every time she vowed to stop thinking about it, and every hour remembrance crossed her mind.

But it was getting dark again and she'd not been able to find someplace to stay she could afford and still have money left over. So, she settled on a park bench and curled up on herself to look unthreatening and uninteresting, nibbling on a piece of corn bread she'd purchased for dinner.

So far she'd not been accosted by anyone. These days most of the people on park benches were not men, but women, displaced by circumstances, but more understanding and forgiving than men had been to others in days past. She felt safe enough on her own, though still wary and aware of her surroundings. So she slept, but with one eye open and clutching onto her valise for dear life.

She tried to wash as best she could at a local supermarket restroom before purchasing a small amount of food for breakfast, walking out of the store as she munched.

She'd only gone a block when her stomach rebelled. Ducking into an alley, she emptied the contents of her stomach into the trash piled there, swiping across her mouth with a sleeve as she sank to the ground, shaking. She felt tears pool in the corners of her eyes, one more problem to contend with, as if she didn't have enough already. She couldn't afford to be sick now, not when she had nothing and no one to help her, to look after her while she fought off a virus. She let herself give in for several minutes, letting the stress flow away from her, then rose and set out again to another day of wandering the streets, trying to look like she had purpose and wasn't homeless.

She was standing outside a bookstore as the day was drawing to an end, staring in at the books on display in the window, wishing she had just a few of the books she'd loved so much from her apartment, tears falling down her cheeks for her loss. She so missed her books, her small eclectic apartment, her life as it had been before her boss had turned into a son of a bitch. It wasn't much, but it had been hers and she missed it terribly now. Now, she was like the child staring into the window of a candy store with no money, wishing on a star that would never race across the night sky. Sniffing, she cleaned her cheeks of moisture with the back of her hand, taking a deep breath, her eyes closing for a moment while she brought her despair under control. She wondered how her life had fallen so far from even her mundane hopes and dreams.

When she opened her eyes, she first saw the books, but the fall of a shadow and the reflection of a tall man behind her in the glass had her twirl, her eyes going wide in surprise.

"What…" she stammered, her brow furrowed. "What are you doing here?"

Radine, dressed in his best uniform, crowned, his sword gleaming at his side, his hair bright in the setting sunlight even when pulled back into a short queue, held out a small package. "You forgot this when you left."

She took the package tentatively, looking in his eyes to see if there was any deception in them, not sure whether or not to trust him. Pulling the string around the package, checking to watch his face all the while, she cried out, her hand going to her chest when she saw the contents – her family portrait. It took all she had to keep herself from throwing her arms around his neck. She'd been so distraught that night that she'd forgotten the picture, remembering it only after the spaceship had entered the wormhole. Its loss had only added to her misery.

"I can't believe you came all this way to bring it to me. It's just a picture, but I can't thank you enough, Your Majesty."

Radine's expression softened. "Is there someplace we may talk, McKenna?"

She hugged the picture against her chest, her arms crossed over it. "I don't think we have anything to talk about, Sire."

He smoothed a finger along her cheek. "A week ago, it was Radine."

She tilted her head away from his touch. "Things were different then."

"It is important that you listen to what I have to say."

"Are you alone?"

Radine's head tilted to the right. "Jaima is near." She followed his indication and saw Jaima standing, trying to seem unobtrusive, keeping watch over his king and friend. She nodded to him and he returned the nod, his face impassive in light of the situation. McKenna heaved a sigh.

"There is a park nearby where we can go," McKenna offered, leading the way. There weren't many people on the street by then, most home already, the sky darkening more, yet they still garnered strange looks as they walked, Jaima two steps behind, keeping guard.

As they entered the park, McKenna was greeted by two women, asking if she was going to spend the night again, reminding her to pick her bench before it was claimed by someone else.

"You sleep here?" Radine asked, aghast.

"My apartment was cleaned out when I didn't pay the rent." She led him to a bench and sat, waiting for him to join her. Pulling his sword out of the way, Radine sat next to her, too close for her comfort, but she had no room to move over and had to suffer his thigh touching her. "Say what you need to say."

He reached into his shirt and took out the letter that had been given to him by Lord Quorol, passing it over to her. "I was given this the night before our wedding," he explained. "Go ahead, read it."

She looked at him, the letter in her hand, then at him again before unfolding the letter, tilting it towards the thinning light, and scanning the words. "I didn't write this," she murmured once she realized what it meant.

"I know, now. But I didn't then. I thought you had decided that you had had a good time with me, a little adventure with a king from another planet, but that time was over and were heading home. I was insulted and furious after reading it. I am sorry, but I ripped your wedding dress to pieces."

"How did you find out?"

"Mother. She read the letter and knew right away you'd not written it, that it wasn't your handwriting. Of course, that was several days after that night."

She dug into her valise and pulled out her letter. "I got this from you that night. A thank you, you were a great lay, but boring after a few weeks. Have a good life, but get out."

He snatched the paper and opened it. "This is not my handwriting," he announced.

"Lord Quorol," McKenna accused knowingly.

Radine nodded. "It was Lord Quorol. We confronted him as soon as we found out, he confessed eventually and will be imprisoned, his titles stripped for all time."

She started to shake. "Why?" she asked. "Why would he do this? Because I'm human?"

"Because he believed you would dilute the Taburon royal blood, make us weaker. Because you do not understand Taburon for you are not Taburon. His plans were made the day he asked me to reconsider marrying you. He knew I would be leaving the palace for a few hours, so he drafted those letters, arranged for a ship to take you back to Earth, and made his move after I left the palace."

McKenna pulled her legs up to wrap her arms around them, hiding behind her limbs, holding on for dear life as fresh emotion welled and flooded over her. She stared out over the park.

"McKenna," he said softly, "I am so sorry you had to go through this. It was beyond cruel and inhumane for him to interfere like this, for both of us, but for you more so, I think." He tucked a strand of her hair behind an ear. "I came as soon as I could after taking care of Quorol and searched for you. I am glad to have found you so quickly."

She started to rock, her life in turmoil, pulled in so many directions she had no idea where she would end up right now. "What do you want?"

"You. I love you, I meant every word I ever told you about how I feel about you."

"But it'll never end, Radine. Can't you see that? First Espis, then Quorol. Who next? When will it end? Will it ever end?"

"Marry me and prove them wrong then. Stand by my side and rule Taburon with me. Or let me stand by your side as you rise above all of those who believe you can't be one of us. We belong together, McKenna. If you do not want to be queen, I will give up the throne. If you want to live here on Earth, I will move here for you. I've given you my heart. Please don't give it back."

She sat, silent, contemplative, her heart crying out to take what he was offering, her head still remembering what had happened just days ago and fighting to keep her from further pain. Her breathing began to hitch, her stomach turning and with a sudden lurch, she folded forward, emptying the contents of her stomach onto the ground in front of them in violent spasms. Radine held her shoulders, pulling her hair away from her face, soothing with words and love until she stopped heaving, sitting up, quivering.

"You are ill," he worried.

"I haven't been eating quite so well," she admitted.

"For how long?"

"Since that night."

"Gods' rods, woman, you will kill yourself that way." He looked for Jaima. "Jaima, have Sistan join us."

McKenna shook her head. "I don't need…" Jaima called up to the ship, his voice soft.

"You will let Sistan take a look," he ordered firmly.

She shot him a withering look. "For someone who isn't even engaged to me, you're awfully bossy."

"I am not engaged to you only because you are the most stubborn woman I have ever met and will not do what you know is the right thing to do." He smiled in reassurance. "I promise I will do everything in my power to assure this never happens again, no one will ever try to separate us ever again. I will make it known that to do so is a crime against the crown and the people of Taburon. What would you have me do to assure you?"

"Make an example of Quorol."

"I cannot execute him, McKenna. His crime is severe, but not that severe."

"You were going to execute Espis."

"She attacked me and you, nearly killing me and would have killed you."

"Then exile him, send him as far away as you can. Put him on that planet where they don't have any technology. Where he can't contact anyone and try this again."

Radine smiled. "I can do that," he agreed. She was proving a just woman, as a queen should be – handing out justice with aforethought and compassion.

"Does he have a family?"

"A son."

"Does he feel as his father?"

"He is a child, six years of age I believe."

"No mother?"

"She died in childbirth."

"Poor child."

"I will have him fostered with a loyal family. He will not suffer, and when he comes of age, if he remains loyal, he will inherit his father's titles and estates." He touched her face again. "Marry me, McKenna."

Covering his hand with one of her own, she studied his face for a heartbeat, the truth in his eyes, the love shining from his expression, the longing in his touch and the breath of his desire. She nodded once, a smile playing at the edges of her lips. He returned her smile and started to pull her closer for a kiss, but she pushed him away, shaking her head. "I don't think you'll like the taste in my mouth right now. I don't like the taste in my mouth right now." She did accept his hug, falling into his embrace completely, relishing in the feel of his body against hers, the scent of his masculine musk strong, his arms tight across her back. She felt herself flush, her body responding to the memory of being loved by him, his hands on her body, rousing her, touching her, bringing her to heights of passion then soothing as she calmed.

He buried his face into her hair, nuzzling at her throat as he had so many times before, ignoring the scent of despair that permeated her, glad to have her back where she belonged for the rest of his life. He would die with her holding his hand to gentle him into that ever after where he would wait until the day that she joined him.

They would share joy and children, ruling Taburon together for the better of the planet and its people, leaving a legacy of trust among peoples of different worlds.

He was content, his life complete with her, and he release her at the clearing of a throat from in front of them. Glancing up, he found Sistan watching with amusement, Jaima impatient, a hand on his laser pistol, his eyes wary as it became darker and visibility lessened.

"McKenna is ill," Radine explained, rising. "She has not eaten well for the past days."

"How many days?"

"Four, five?"

"Foolish," Sistan commented. "It is getting too dark for a proper examination here. Will you come back to the ship?"

McKenna nodded, reaching out to take the hand that Radine offered, helping her to stand. With a squeal, he lifted her into his arms, determined to carry her the entire way back to the shuttle where they would return to the ship. "I assume this means you'll be getting married?" Sistan asked.

"The day we return home, if not earlier," Radine replied firmly. He would not brook any dissention from anyone on his decision either. "As soon as we can contact Taburon, I will have my mother make the arrangements for the day we arrive."

"My shuttle is near," Sistan said. "You and I can return to the ship with your lady. Lord Jaima and my pilot will take your shuttle."

"You will leave the king unprotected?" Jaima asked.

"He will come to no harm on the way to the ship, Lord Jaima. Who would shoot at the shuttle? Humans?" He scoffed. "Come with me, Your Majesty."

Chapter Thirty

On board the ship, Sistan had McKenna lay on an exam table, changed from her dirty old clothes into a clean tunic type dress that reached to her knees, a cover over her against the chill of the room. Radine hovered near despite her asking him for some space. He refused to leave her alone even for the physician to examine her.

Sistan had given her a protein drink, something to build back her reserves, insisting that if she ate a full meal at this time she would most likely vomit the entire meal since she'd not been eating. He suggested she eat small meals for a few days until she felt better able to tolerate full meals.

Taking blood, he ran a few tests, the readings off for a Taburon, but having studied what he could of humans, he was fairly confident that he could understand the results. A look of surprise crossed his features and he turned away from his patient to take a tube of long thin papers from a drawer. With a needle, he went back to his patient.

"Give me your hand," he requested. McKenna frowned, but held out the closest hand. With a needle, he pricked her finger, ignoring her squeak, then squeezed until a large drop of blood appeared. Touching one end of one of the papers to the blood, he let the liquid soak into the paper. Holding the paper where he could see it clearly, he waited, watching the paper intently.

The paper, which had been a purple in color, changed to a dark red as they waited. Sistan switched his glance from the paper to the king. "Well, Your Majesty, the question of whether or not you will have children with a human has been answered."

Radine moved closer, coming to stand next to McKenna. "She's pregnant?"

"Yes, Sire."

Wonder crossed his face, surprise and joy. He had won her back and now they were going to be parents. His life was finally unfolding as it should, as he'd planned from the day he'd become king and found the woman who would complete him.

McKenna was stunned. She'd never realized, never considered she might become pregnant from their time together, even though they hadn't denied themselves sex from the first day when they'd been able to indulge.

Even more important, she had endangered her baby by her actions since Quorol had interfered. Not eating put the child in danger. Not keeping healthy had endangered her child. Had she continued as she'd been, she surely would have lost the baby, and then her soul. She reached out blindly for his hand. "Radine," she whimpered. "Oh my god, Radine."

"What? McKenna, what is wrong?"

"He could have killed our baby. He might have killed our baby."

"Who?"

"Quorol. He told such lies, hurt us so badly. I couldn't cope. The baby may have died because of what he did, because of what I did because of him."

"But he didn't, and now that we know, our child is safe. You'll get your strength back and we'll have a strong healthy baby." He perched a hip on the edge of the exam table, lifting her into his embrace. "I love you, and I thank you for giving me a child. You make me complete, McKenna." He would never be able to thank her enough.

Once he released her, he looked over her shoulder to Sistan. "Can she leave now?"

"Yes, as long as she rests. I'll have some billa tea sent to your quarters for the nausea. Make sure she drinks some if she feels sick." He set his tools aside. "Once you get home, make sure your physician examines her. We have never had a mixed child before. You will have to be careful."

"How so?"

"No heavy lifting, keep the stress down. Eat right and drink plenty of fluids. For Taburon women, this is a delicate time. Until the pregnancy is stable, you need to be careful."

Radine promised. He scooped her up. "Have Jaima meet us in our quarters."

Married via subspace before reaching the planet, Radine and McKenna, now Queen McKenna, sat on matching thrones at the head of the court, both dressed royally, both crowned, waiting patiently for the prisoner to arrive, Radine holding her hand across the space between their thrones. Queen Mother Inoa sat in a chair near the couple, beaming. She was going to be a grandmother and was quite proud of it too.

The room was packed, Lords, Ladies, and Ministers filling every space, anxiously awaiting to see what was going to unfold in the next few minutes. In the front of the room, a young boy watched, confused and wary, his hand held by a woman, the two watched over by a man standing close.

From the back of the room, the doors opened and two guards entered, flanking a single man between them, the former Lord Quorol, hands tied in front of his body, disheveled and forlorn looking, gaunt and pale from his days in the dungeon. As one, the crowd turned to face the disgraced man as he strode forward, his chin lifting as he passed the people to whom he was once equal. The crowd parted, a hush falling over everyone.

The trio stopped at the front of the room, directly before the king and queen, Quorol's eyes going wide as he saw the woman sitting next to his king. McKenna kept her face passive as she clutched Radine's hand tighter.

"Papa," the child called, tugging at the hand of the woman who held him. The man with the two stepped between the child and his disgraced father, grabbing the boy by his shoulder and holding him back. "Papa."

"Sarva," Quorol responded, reaching out towards his son, held in check by the guards, struggling futilely, his face despondent. "Son," he murmured, submitting, turning pleading eyes to the king.

Radine released McKenna's hand and stood, coming down the two steps to confront Quorol. He kept his face deliberately neutral.

"What will you do with my son?" Quorol demanded.

"Lady and Lord Reval will raise him. If he remains loyal to the crown, he will inherit his titles when he reaches his majority. As for you…You are to be exiled to Taburon Prime for the rest of your life to make as good a life as you can there, no communication with the outside galaxy permitted, a single suitcase of personal items to go with you." Now Radine allowed his anger to surface. "And you can thank Queen McKenna for this small mercy, Quorol, for after finding out the full extent of your perfidy, I was quite tempted to order your execution."

"Nothing I did warrants execution."

"Your lies and schemes put my wife into a state where, had it continued could have caused her great bodily harm, which of and by itself might have been taken into consideration. However, had she lost *our child*, it would have been a case of murder, and for that I cannot consider anything less than you have received." He turned and stepped up two of the three steps, then reversed to face the older man. "And be grateful I am feeling generous today, for I am pleased I am going to be a father." He finished ascending the stairs and reseated himself. "Take the prisoner out and see that he is transported off planet by the end of the day."

Quorol was dragged out amid the buzz of the watchers who contained themselves until the doors had closed on the traitor. A general round of applause rose for the round-a-bout announcement the king made, well-wishers surrounding the royal couple as they rose from their thrones and joined their subjects on the floor, the atmosphere more than making up for the fear McKenna had held concerning not being accepted by the Taburon people.

Chapter Thirty-One

King Radine of Taburon stood by the retracted gangplank of his new shuttle, his arm around the waist of his beautiful wife, Queen McKenna, as they waited for the vehicle to power down and the gangplank to extend so they could disembark. In the queen's arms, fifteen month old Rakenn squirmed, anxious to get down. The boy was hardly ever still, always on the go, a constant whirlwind of energy and bane to his mother and nursemaids. So like his father.

Radine had kept his promise to his wife. Today they had landed on Earth, to greet the government officials and tell her story, to invite the people of Earth to come to Taburon to visit, to work, to remain and become citizens. To show the Earth that at least in some cases, going to another world wasn't as terrifying as some would believe.

And she was in the process of starting a clearing house of sorts on Taburon for the women of Earth who'd gone to friendly planets, to find out how they were fairing and send word back to Earth. It was a tedious process, locating to where each woman had gone and how she was on her new planet, then making contact, arranging meetings, and having discussions. Most were quite happy in their new homes, settled and prospering. There were a few she'd discovered, who were not being treated as well as they could have been and she was working with Radine to see if there was anything that could be done for them.

Behind the king and queen, Lord Jaima, honorary uncle to the young prince and in charge of the royal guard, was mustering the troops, inspecting them, making sure everyone was in tiptop shape, their uniforms neat and pressed, their weapons properly displayed – just in case. The troops would exit the shuttle first, providing a lined path for the king, queen, and prince. They were to be greeted by President Constantine of the United States, as well as other heads of state from around the world.

Radine was dressed in the formal uniform he'd worn for the sentencing of former Lord Quorol, sword at his one side, weapon on the other, his shirt white and medaled, the trousers pitch black with a golden stripe down the outside of each leg. The boots reached to his knees, polished and brilliantly shining. His crown sat regally on top of his dark honey golden hair, recently returned to him by the child, who found the circle of gold fascinating.

Wearing a smaller version of her husband's crown on her head, McKenna had opted for a dress she'd once intended to wear for the wedding reception that never occurred, a beautiful blue necklace of the vireck gem he'd given to her the day they'd returned to Taburon dangling between her breasts. After the two ceremonies on board the ship in which she was married and crowned, Radine had carried her off to rest, the crew chuckling that their king couldn't wait to bed his new wife, unaware that she was pregnant and sick with nausea. They had been allowed to celebrate without the couple.

Once word had gone out around the planet after Radine's announcement that the queen was expecting at Quorol's sentencing, the celebrating started among the populace and lasted an entire week. Taburon was giddy with joy for their king, and awaited with baited breaths as her time drew near, gathering in crowds at the palace when she went into labor. Once the birth had been announced – they had a prince! – the people rejoiced the world over. Rakenn was named for both his father and mother, taking letters from both of their names to make one, as they had come together as one in conceiving the child.

Once the child had arrived and been declared healthy, Radine had commissioned for a new shuttle to be built, large enough for a contingent of troops and his family to land on Earth. They still used the space ship *Veleda* he had first arrived on, but the first shuttle had had only space for two. And Radine would never take his family anywhere where he could not provide security for them. This shuttle held fifty people, not counting the pilot and co-pilot.

The gangplank extended, the troops marched smartly down and formed two lines on either side of the ground from the end of the gangplank, their swords held high in parade salute. Around the landing area, the perimeter was surrounded by military troops, their weapons at the ready if needed. A squadron of tanks was evenly spaced around the perimeter as well. Members of the news media battled with each other to get the best view and shots of the visiting royalty. Beyond the military presence, crowds of people stood, four and five deep, to watch and witness the arrival of the aliens. Radine leaned to his wife to whisper in her ear - did the Earthers really believe they could outgun Taburon weapons - she nodded in reply and the two began their descent. At the end of the gangplank, the President waited anxiously, somewhat fearfully, for this Taburon was at least a foot taller then he and built like a well hewn soldier, all muscle and brawn, his shoulders wide, his thighs thick and corded. His eyes were the strangest gold in color, and seemed to sparkle. President Constantine was willing to admit, the Taburon king frightened him a little more than a bit.

But he sucked in his stomach, suddenly self-conscious of his own physique, and stood straight to greet the couple. With him were the Prime Minister of England, the president of France, the Prime Minister of Canada and the wives of all of them. Others would join the aliens inside the White House.

The king and queen stopped at the bottom of the gangplank, Jaima behind them at attention but watchful, and the president relaxed somewhat. How could they be any threat when they had a child with them, and the queen looked suspiciously human. Two women stood behind the large warrior who stood behind the king. The President stepped forward, and bowed. "Your Majesties, welcome to Earth. On behalf of the people of the planet, we bid you greetings."

McKenna pulled her husband down to whisper in his ear, the correct way to address this man. "Thank you, Mr. President. We are pleased to be so warmly received. May I present my wife, Queen McKenna, formerly McKenna Primm, of your planet, and our son, Prince Rakenn."

"Your Majesty, welcome home." He held his hand out to invite the couple to move forward. "I am Edward Constantine. My fellow heads of state, Prime Minister of England, Mr. Elister; the President of France, President Berchaud; The Prime Minister of Canada, Mr. Greenwalt, and our wives." Each person bowed slightly or nodded acknowledgement. "If you will come with us, Your Majesties, we have cars waiting to take you to the White House."

Radine turned to Jaima. "Jaima, accompany us please. Commander Rydul," he continued facing the guard closest, "dismiss the troops with the caveats we spoke of and enjoy yourselves. But not too much," he added with a grin.

Rydul bowed his head smartly. "Of course, Your Majesty."

McKenna, Radine, Rakenn, the President, and his wife climbed into the passenger part of the same vehicle while Jaima took a seat in the front, scrunched with his knees nearly in his face much to his distaste. The official presidential flags attached to the front of the car flapped in the wind as they pulled away from the landing field, passing by hundreds of onlookers that had lined the area for a peek at the alien newcomers. Rakenn bounced on his father's leg, though he watched out the car windows with avid interest. A convoy of vehicles followed the first as their passengers boarded. Every car was flanked by an armed escort.

"How old is your son?" the president's wife, Veronica Constantine, asked.

"Fifteen months," McKenna replied.

"He is quite adorable."

"Thank you. We tend to agree."

"Where did you live before going to Taburon?" the President asked of McKenna.

"Outside Charlotte. I worked as a clerk in a drug company." She laid her hand on Radine's knee. "And while I truly appreciate your greeting, Mr. President, and thank you, my home is Taburon, not Earth."

"I am sorry if I offended."

"You did not, sir. I just wanted you to know. I've discovered that most of the women who've left Earth consider their new planet their home now."

"What is it like on Taburon?"

"You'd find many things Victorian age like, but very modern for the rest of it, in communications and technology, way ahead of Earth in space travel, obviously. We rarely use vehicles for transport, but rely on an animal called a *crufa*, like a horse, only bigger and faster. They're very environmentally conscience and keep the use of damaging fuels down to a bare minimum. Because of this, Taburon is an environmentally stable planet and quite beautiful."

"And you are king of part of the planet, Your Majesty?"

"The whole planet, Mr. President. My family has ruled for ten generations." He bounced the baby until the child chuckled. Radine was a doting father, spoiling the boy ruthlessly, much to McKenna's dismay, for she then had to undo all of the spoiling the king did to make sure their son did not grow up a spoiled royal brat. The two of them together were Radine's pride and joy, he'd found true happiness in being a husband and father. "And since it is an inherited title, we shall continue to rule through our children."

The President's head tilted to the side. "What caveats did you give your troops?"

"They may explore your city, keep out of trouble, and be back at the shuttle by evening meal."

"I hope that you don't mind that some of my soldiers will be with them?"

"Not at all. Soldiers are all alike, are they not? Give them leave and they are sure to find some mischief. I have made it clear that I do not want any of my men to be responsible for any unwarranted actions. They will obey me, I assure you."

"That's good to know. We, unfortunately, are a suspicious race, and some don't trust what they don't understand."

"Shoot first, ask questions later," McKenna explained.

A kingly eyebrow rose. "If you feel there is a danger, I can have them remain on the shuttle," Radine offered.

"Let's see what happens first. If a problem pops up, we can make changes then."

"As you wish, Mr. President."

"You called your vehicle a shuttle. Is it designed for space travel?"

"No, Mr. President, only for travel between the ship and a planet's surface. Our ship is in orbit around your planet."

"Is it large, Your Majesty?"

"It is designed to hold a thousand troops, Mr. President. It is quite large." He tilted his head slightly. "Both are well-armed," he added as a warning.

The president nodded, the warning heeded completely. If anything happened to the royals while on Earth, Earth would pay dearly. So he let the king know he understood with a nod, receiving a nod in return. The men would get along as long as they understood the lines over which they could not cross.

"We have prepared rooms for you in the White House, as per your request. Given time, if you wish to establish diplomatic relations with Earth, you may set up an embassy in the city so your people are more comfortable. There are a number of buildings you may rent or purchase. I will admit, it was hard finding furniture made to fit your size."

"And you would swim in the couches and beds we use," McKenna commented. "I know I do. But then again, there's plenty of room to stretch out."

"You, little one, would steal the entire bed, if let you," Radine murmured close to her ear. "For one so small, you take up a lot of room."

"The better to make sure you snuggle, my king."

The rolling eye look Radine shared with the President was universal. 'Women,' it said. Both men chuckled softly. Rakenn giggled with delight, throwing himself backwards. He'd have ended up in his mother's lap if Radine had not caught the child before he could fall over. The child giggled up at his father – this was a game they played often. "Da, da, da, da, da," he recited, having recently learned the word. Radine pressed a kiss to his soft hair.

"We have a state dinner scheduled for tonight. There will be about a hundred heads of state in attendance. Tomorrow, a tour of the city in the morning and then meetings with the heads of state. If the queen would prefer, we can set up something for her and your son that she might enjoy better than meetings."

"I think my queen would like to sit in on the meetings, Mr. President, since I have found her opinions and ideas quite sound. However, our son might enjoy your zoo and animals he's never seen. His nursemaids can go with him, as well as several of my guards."

"Or we can go together another day," McKenna suggested.

"Or we can go together another day," the king repeated with resignation. Obviously, McKenna was loathe to let Rakenn too far out of her sight, especially as young as he was and this being their first visit. The mood of their reception was yet to be determined. Who knew what hostilities any one of them might encounter during this initial visit? He had to agree, since the child was the heir. The spare had yet to be born. They were working on it. Which reminded him. "We have brought a tea with us that I would like to have made for my wife for the mornings. She finds it settles her stomach during this time."

"You are pregnant?" Mrs. Constantine asked with surprise.

McKenna nodded. "Three months. The tea is called *billa*, and it saves me a lot of misery. It tastes a great deal like mint but has added medicinal properties."

"Make sure it is given to the kitchen. They'll make it up for you."

"Thank you, sir."

"Do you know if you're having a boy or girl?"

"He does," McKenna admitted, pointing to her husband. "I didn't want to know."

"We'll need a lot of dresses," Radine whispered not so subtly. Everyone shared a short laugh as Radine brushed McKenna's temple with a quick kiss.

The cars began to pull to a halt in front of the White House, the presidential car stopping directly in front of the doors. The escorts parked next to the car, and hopped out of their vehicles, running to open the doors for the president and royals. Radine passed the child to McKenna while he navigated crawling out of the car, then reached back to take the boy so she could exit. Jaima stood by his sovereigns, watching intently in all directions for any danger, his hand on his laser weapon. The president's wife left the car, followed by the president.

It was as the foursome moved to enter the building that they heard a scream. Surprised, they glanced around, looking for the cause, and a series of shots broke the silence. Jaima pushed the king to the ground. Radine grabbed McKenna and hauled her underneath him, covering her and Rakenn with his body. Rakenn began to whimper in fright. The escorts pulled their weapons, but Jaima was faster, locating the offender and pointing his weapon at the man, fired, ignoring whatever it was that thudded twice into his side and left an intensely burning pain. With a whine and a stream of blue light shooting from the laser weapon, a hole appeared in the man's chest and the obscenities he was screaming about the pestilence of aliens and human whores that slept with them abruptly cut off as he fell to the ground.

Everything was deathly silent for just a heartbeat. Rakenn began to wail as Jaima faced his king. The burning wasn't easing, in fact it was growing stronger by the second, but he had a job to do. "Your Majesty, are you hurt?" He leaned against the hood of the presidential car, the flag bending under his elbow.

The king looked confused, but offered a smile. "We are fine, Jaima, thank you," he replied, turning his attention to his son and wife, cupping the child's head in a large hand.

The queen, however, was looking at Jaima closely and her eyes widened in horror. His face had paled and he was beginning to slump over, finally reacting to the fact that he had been injured somehow. Feeling a warm wetness soaking his shirt, he tried to hide it, but she was too smart. He started to take a step towards the queen and swayed. "Jaima?"

Radine followed the glance of his wife. His face paled in stunned surprise at the spreading stain of blood on the left side of Jaima's shirt. "Jaima!" he cried, twisting, grabbing his friend and brother as the lord collapsed, his legs folding under him. The laser weapon he'd been holding clattered to the ground. "Jaima."

Together they sank to the ground, Radine cradling the injured man. "As long as you're safe, Radine."

The queen screamed. "We need help!" she yelled. "Please, somebody help us!"

Jaima's side throbbed, he could feel the blood pumping from the wound, his body not answering to his commands. He didn't know what had happened, but whatever it had been, it was better that he took the injury than the king. Taburon needed Radine, he was beloved by the people, and he was good for them, a fair and just king. Jaima knew that someday he might have been called to make the ultimate sacrifice, he had just hoped it wouldn't have been so soon. He would have liked to have seen the young prince grow up to become a man, or least close to becoming a man. He would have liked to have had a son of his own to befriend the prince, as he had young Radine when they were children. A best friend was worth all of the armies in the galaxy.

Men were gathering around, peering over the shoulder of the king. One man was speaking into a device, giving orders, asking for emergency help. Radine looked so lost, glancing up at McKenna, then back to his friend.

"You will survive," he ordered softly. "I command it," he added, his voice tremulous. Radine placed his hand over the spot where Jaima was bleeding his life away and pressed – hard. Jaima grunted as the king's attempt to help only increased the pain.

"You have always been so tyrannical," Jaima replied, his voice a whisper.

"How else would I have gotten you into so much trouble if not?" Jaima blinked. He thought he saw the king's eyes fill with tears. Radine never cried, except for the time when he'd thought McKenna lost to him and when Rakenn had been born. He'd not cried when his own father had passed away, standing proud and stoic, the heir apparent, the soon to be king, leading the funeral procession. But he teared up now. "I need you with me to teach my son."

Jaima tried to laugh, but a cough came out instead. Fresh blood bubbled under Radine's hand. "He's in trouble then."

"He needs you. I need you."

Pain ripped through Jaima and he groaned. "Gods' rods, Radine, this is quite painful, like the Fire Pits of Koloda," he ground out, grabbing onto Radine's sleeve and holding on tightly. He was sorry he was bleeding over the king's uniform. Blood was so hard to remove. "More than getting stuck with a sword, I should say."

"You are not thinking straight."

No, his head was clear. "No, I know what I'm saying. I do not recommend you trying this, Radine. You let yourself get stabbed just to see how it felt. Do you remember?" The prince, fifteen and untried in battle, had believed that he should know what the men experienced when a sword went through them. He convinced the sword master to stab him, shallowly and not to kill or maim. Jaima, having gotten word of Radine's plans, had not arrived in time to stop it, seeing the prince run through the side with a blade. A flesh wound, but enough to bring the prince to his knees in agony. The king and queen had been furious, with both their son and his friend. The sword master spent a month in the dungeon.

"I do. Not one of my better ideas." Radine's hand, the one not covering the wound, clenched and unclenched at the material at Jaima's shoulder. Jaima could feel the king's body quake in helplessness, fear, despair.

"Your mother nearly took my head off when she found out I was involved and didn't stop it."

"She was rather put out with you."

"She sent me to the dungeon for a week." His voice was getting softer with every sentence.

"She was being lenient because she knew I had told you to leave be. You could have stepped in."

"I would have taken the blade and disobeyed my prince had I."

"Gods' rods," Radine prayed, his eyes slanting skyward for a second, "save me from stubborn friends. Please be still. You need your strength to fight, to live."

Jaima would try, but darkness was taking over his sight, squeezing in from the sides of his vision. "I shall do my best, Radine, my king." He really did not want to leave the king. Dying, here and now, would tear Radine apart. He would have rather been hurt someplace where if he was going to die, it would not be in the arms of his best friend while his wife and their child looked on. But he couldn't help himself, shock setting in, his blood still pumping from the wound around the pressure of Radine's hand. Unable to fight it anymore, he gave into the blackness and let it overwhelm him. His body went slack, draping over the arms of the king.

"No," Radine whispered. His head tilted skyward. "Gods be damned," he cursed. "Don't take him," he pleaded. His head fell to his chest, his heart breaking.

Chapter Thirty-Two

He stayed that way until several men arrived and forced him to surrender his injured friend into their hands. Laying him flat, they ripped his shirt open to reveal the wound. There were two holes in his left side, near his ribs, bleeding readily once Radine had lifted his hand. One of the medics slapped a patch over it as another began to insert an intravenous catheter into Jaima's wrist. Attaching leads to his chest, they took readings, a fluid bag was hung, the fluids dripping fast. Another vehicle arrived, an ambulance, a stretcher pulled from the back almost as soon as the vehicle stopped and brought over. After he was prepared for transportation, he was placed on the gurney and rolled away. Radine scooped up the weapon Jaima had dropped and hitched it to his belt.

"I will go with him," Radine stated firmly. "We will stay next to his side."

"Of course," the president agreed. Signaling to his driver, he opened the back door of the car at the same time. "Follow the ambulance, take the king to the hospital."

"Yes, sir." Jogging around the front of the car, he slid into the driver's seat as the king and queen settled. The ambulance pulled away, lights flashing, siren screaming and the president's car followed.

"I want a full investigation," the president ordered. "How the hell did he get that close? And with a gun? Send a contingent of police to guard the hospital and secure the king and queen. Make sure this doesn't happen again." He waited as his orders were carried out, then with a scowl, he went into the White House, his arm about the waist of his wife. He had a lot of people to contact, and a press release to make. The Taburons first visit to Earth, and one of their people had been shot. Not the best first impression. And he was furious.

Radine called his shuttle as they followed the ambulance. "Rydul," he hailed.

"Yes, Your Majesty?"

"Recall all of our people, have them board the shuttle and stay there. Lord Jaima has been shot and is in need of medical aid. Contact the ship, have Sistan brought down to see to Jaima. I do not know if or how well these people can help him. I do not know…" he started to add and choked. "I do not know if he will survive," he finished in a despondent voice.

"Do you wish to return to the ship, Your Majesty?"

"No, we will stay with Jaima. Have a squadron set and ready to meet us at their medical facility to guard Lord Jaima."

"Right away, Your Majesty."

"And make sure the nursemaids are sent to us as well. Contac this President Constantine to make the request. Rakenn will need them while we wait for word on Lord Jaima."

"It will be done."

"Thank you, Rydul." He signed off and sat back against the seat, huffing a breath.

"He'll be all right," McKenna murmured, her hand on his arm in comfort. She winced at the blood staining Radine's once pristine white shirt, remembering that it could have just easily been Radine in the ambulance fighting for his life right now. Or, Gods forbid, Rakenn.

"I hope so, little one. He is a brother to me."

"I know. And I'm sorry."

"Your people are not ready for outworlders yet."

"I agree. Once we get Jaima home, we won't return."

"Not for a long time. If ever." He sighed. "That man was screaming about you being a whore."

347

"Words, Radine. They mean nothing."

"Espis didn't think so," he reminded her. "She called you a whore as well."

"Words, just words. I've forgotten those already."

"They were backed with weapons and torture, McKenna." He watched out the window as the buildings flew by. The ambulance was three cars ahead, its lights flashing still, the siren making other cars move to the side. "I can't lose him."

"The doctors will do everything they can to save him. And when Sistan arrives, he'll direct them. He knows Jaima."

The sirens quieted, the vehicle stopping under a canopy at a large white building. Doors opened and a half dozen people emerged, some women and some men, all wearing white coats or green outfits. They helped the ambulance attendants to remove the stretcher. Radine was sick at heart to see more things stuck into Jaima, his body covered with a white sheet and strapped to the gurney. A clear mask was strapped to his face. His feet hung off the end of the rolling bed. Between his legs, machines beeped and blinked, connected to his friend. He looked so still. Radine thought he'd never seen anything so heartbreaking since finding McKenna, covered in blood, laying beneath the body of Espis, his first fear that she was dead.

As Jaima was rushed inside, Radine and McKenna followed, ushered into a waiting area away from Jaima as the gurney disappeared behind a set of doors. A nurse with a clipboard approached the couple, hesitantly, never having seen anyone so tall and imposing. "I'm Joanna Simon. May I get some information from you about your friend?" she asked. She was a few inches taller than McKenna, with long blonde hair that had been rolled into a bun at the back of her head. A pretty woman, she had a slim figure, breasts a little larger than average and narrow hips. Her white stocking clad legs ended in the usual nurse's white shoes.

McKenna nodded, passing Rakenn, who'd now quieted, to Radine to give her husband something to hold on to. "Yes."

"What is his name?"

"Jaima."

"Jaima what?"

"Lord Jaima of Taburon. They don't have last names."

"How old is he?"

She looked over her shoulder to Radine. "Thirty-five Taburon years," he murmured. He was absolutely miserable about his friend.

"Do you have blood types?"

"Yes, but I do not know his. Our physician is coming. He can answer your questions better."

Then nurse hugged her clipboard, her expression going from business like to sympathetic. "I'm sorry your friend was hurt."

"Just do everything you can to save him," McKenna responded.

"Our doctors are the best in the city," she assured. "May I get you anything? How about for the child?"

"His nursemaids are on their way. Thank you though."

They waited for hours for word. Sistan had arrived and been taken back immediately. A small contingent of Taburon guards set up camp near the waiting room, their mere presence discouraging anyone from entering, let alone the swords and weapons at their waists. With further discussion, Rydul had taken the rest of the guards back to the ship and returned to wait close by if needed to transport the royals and Jaima, the shuttle closely guarded by both Taburons and humans, keeping the curious far, far away. The hospital was on lockdown to everyone except for emergencies. With Rakenn in the hands of the nursemaids, McKenna spent her waiting time holding Radine's hands after cleaning them of the blood that coated them. His clothes remained stained with blood and he remained armed even while waiting, Jaima's sword and belt draped across his lap.

"Your Majesty?" Sistan called as he finally approached. Radine rose, anxiety written all over his face.

"How is he?"

"He has had a bad wound, and lost a lot of blood. We have taken blood from several of the guards here, but his is an unusual type, and he will have to do with what we got. He has slipped into unconsciousness. If he survives the next hours, he may live."

Radine felt despair, and anger, surge. "There is nothing you can do more positive?"

Sistan shook his head. "No, Sire. The projectiles were removed, the bleeding stopped, but it is all up to him now to either live or die. They have put him on what they call life support, they are monitoring his heart and breathing, replenishing fluids, giving him medication against infection."

Radine made an indelicate noise, shoving his fingers through his hair in frustration. "Your news is not reassuring, Sistan."

"I am sorry, Your Majesty."

"What do you recommend? What can we do?"

"Return the queen and the prince to the ship where they are out of danger. I will remain with Lord Jaima until we know more. You cannot help him, and I fear for your safety and that of every Taburon on this planet. The fewer of us, the fewer targets, the less reason to attack." He also expressed his frustration by shoving his hands in a white coat he had been loaned. It was very short and tight across his shoulders. "I do not wish to stay here longer than necessary. As soon as Lord Jaima can travel, we should take him home."

Radine paced a moment. He did not wish to leave his friend, he did not trust these human doctors to do the best for him. If Sistan remained, he could monitor their care and if he felt Jaima's life in danger from their treatment, or lack of it, they would take him to the ship anyway. But Sistan was right, he had to protect the queen, their unborn child, and Rakenn. Making a decision he regretted, he nodded. "Very well," he announced, "we shall return to the *Veleda*. If the President still wishes to conduct meetings, he can do it there."

"I shall keep you informed," Sistan promised.

Radine nodded acknowledgment, searching for one of the human guards who were keeping watch for human threats, yet casting wary looks at the Taburons. When he found one, he waved him over. "My family and I will be returning to our ship. We need transportation to our shuttle."

"The car is outside, Your Majesty."

Radine nodded again, turning back to Sistan. "Do whatever it takes to keep him alive," he ordered. "Please."

McKenna yawned as she stretched, glancing to her right to find Radine slept still. It had become her habit to wake before her husband, wash, check on Rakenn and order their breakfast before rousing him. Sometimes she let their son do the waking, dropping him on the bed and letting him crawl all over his father, giggling merrily. Radine would growl for the baby, the big bad ogre catching the helpless child to tickle him until he cried 'uncle' in his baby talk. Father and son would collapse helplessly into the bed, laughing. Life at those times was great.

She slipped from the bed without disturbing her husband and pulled one of Radine's shirts over her shoulders, buttoning the garment from the bottom to between her breasts. Making a stop in the bathroom, she finger combed her hair as she went to check any messages that may have come for either of them. One waited from Sistan. There had been no change in Jaima's condition overnight. He was still unconscious. McKenna sighed heavily.

She was about to call to the galley for their breakfast when the door buzzer to the cabin sounded. Not wanting it to wake Radine, she hurried over to permit whomever had arrived to enter. The crewman bowed and kept his voice lowered. "Your Majesty, this message just arrived for the king."

She took the folded note. "Thank you, Stasha." She opened the note and read it, her heart sinking at the news. McKenna refolded the note and went quickly to her husband.

She hated to wake him, he'd slept so poorly through the night, tossing and turning, reliving the shooting and once calling out for Jaima. Their ship had set into synchronized orbit over the capitol city so if needed they could easily transport straight down without having to fly any distance. So the ship's time had been set to match that of the city. Once they'd returned to the ship, McKenna had settled Rakenn down for a nap and convinced Radine to rest as well. They'd had dinner together later and she slipped him a soporific tea so he might, for a short time, forget. He'd slept, but his dreams invaded anyway.

Sitting on the side of the bed, she shook him. "Radine."

He woke instantly. "Jaima?" he asked, his voice softened from sleep.

She shook her head. "No change. No, we got a message from home." She passed the note over and waited for him to read it.

His face paled as he sat forward. "My mother?" he asked. "No other information?"

"Not that I know of. I'm sorry."

"I need to go home."

"I know."

"I can't leave Jaima here, but he's too ill yet to travel."

"I have a suggestion," she offered, "and you may not like it, but you have to seriously consider it."

Radine fell back against his pillow. "What?"

"You go home, take Rakenn with you. I stay here to be with Jaima…"

"No," he interrupted immediately.

"Listen to me, husband. Rakenn does not need me to feed him anymore. His nursemaids can take care of him and he'll be safe. I can mingle here, fit in. I know how these people think, at least I hope so. I can keep an eye on Jaima and help Sistan as well. You go, take care of your mother and come back as soon as possible. By then, Jaima should be well enough to travel and we can go home. You'll be gone what... no more than two weeks? It's a logical choice. You can't remain, you stand out like a sore thumb. So does Sistan and Jaima, if it comes right down to it, but one is flat on his back in a hospital bed and the other won't leave his side, so he's not outside the hospital very much. If there is one person who hates Taburons, there will be more. I'll be safe enough, as long as I stay out of the spotlight."

"I do not like the idea, McKenna, but I must return to make sure my mother is well taken care of. I want to leave a squadron of guards with you..."

"You can't. They'll be too conspicuous. Leave me a laser weapon, you've taught me how to use one."

He covered his eyes with an arm. The message had simply stated the Inoa had taken a bad fall from her *crufa* and had been seriously injured. He needed to be there for her. But Jaima was a brother to him, he could still die, and Radine couldn't stand the thought of not being at his side if it became true. And to leave McKenna, while she carried their second child...For a heartbeat, he wished he was not king, just an ordinary citizen, with no responsibilities other than maybe a deadly dull job and a family for when he came home at night. But he wasn't an ordinary citizen, he was the king, and he often needed to make decisions that his heart said were wrong while his mind knew they were right.

"Very well," he reluctantly agreed. "I do not like this at all."

"It's the best way to make sure Jaima is treated fairly. I'll need money. Unfortunately, things here are not free. And being queen means little here when it comes to having a place to spend the night and food to eat."

"Take some gold. I understand Earthers like gold."

"They do, a lot. Are my clothes from when we first met still here?" Everything had been transferred to the new shuttle when it had been launched.

"No, wife. They were not in the best of shape after I tore them from your body. If you remember."

"Okay, then I'll need to get clothes as well. And some for both Sistan and Jaima once he's out of the hospital if you've not gotten back."

"Take what you need, wife. Use it as you need." He held his hand to her. "I am not happy about this, but if I must go without you for even two weeks, then give me the next hour to say goodbye."

She smiled as she slid her hand into his and let herself be pulled onto the bed.

Author Biography

Karen Milstein lives in West Palm Beach with her husband and son, her own small pride of cats and several birds. She enjoys reading and watching SciFi, Romance, Sword and Sorcery and Fantasy. *Sky Clad – Radine* is the first of a series of adult erotica stories about the people of Taburon. Her first novel, *Fergus and the Princess*, is a young adult book inspired by a papier mache doll given to her by one of her daughters and is available through Amazon and Barnes and Noble. Fergus sits above her computer to provide her with encouragement with her writing.